BLACKWING

BLACKWING SAGA BOOK 1

STEPHEN DRAKE

Copyright (C) 2016 Stephen Drake

Layout design and Copyright (C) 2019 by Next Chapter

First published in the US 2017

Published 2019 by Beyond Time – A Next Chapter Imprint

Edited by Ashley Conner

Cover art by Cover Mint

This book is a work of fiction. Names, characters, places, and incidents are the product of the author's imagination or are used fictitiously. Any resemblance to actual events, locales, or persons, living or dead, is purely coincidental.

All rights reserved. No part of this book may be reproduced or transmitted in any form or by any means, electronic or mechanical, including photocopying, recording, or by any information storage and retrieval system, without the author's permission.

Dedicated to Linda and Susan, for without their help and support, this work would not have been possible.

A special thanks to K.J. Simmill and J.C. Stone, authors in their own right, for their friendship, suggestions, help, and for taking the time from their busy lives to read my work. Words fail to convey my deep appreciation for them.

1

GRIMSTAR AND DRAGON'S BREATH

The landlord of the inn, who was standing behind the heavy, rough-hewn counter polishing his plain pewter tankards, gave a cursory glance toward the stranger who had just entered. The other customers stopped talking and watched the stranger, suspiciously and surreptitiously, as he passed.

"Wipe yer boots! I run a clean establishment," the landlord yelled to be heard over the din.

When the stranger didn't respond, he realized the place was strangely quiet, the usual low buzz of conversations had fallen silent.

When the landlord looked up once more, he saw the stranger walking toward the counter, with his head slightly down, his thick-heeled boots making a distinct clopping sound on the wood-planked floor. The stranger towered over everyone present, wore black leather from head to toe, and walked with a plain oaken staff, taking two steps for every thud of the staff on the floor. The landlord noticed that no water dripped from the stranger's clothes, even though it had been raining all day, and his well-worn boots were spotless and highly polished, instead of being mud-caked. The brim of the stranger's fedora was perfectly parallel to the floor except for the front third, which had been turned downward, casting a shadow over his face and eyes. As the stranger walked to a table to the left of the counter, the landlord noticed the stranger looked straight ahead, never looking left, right, or at the other customers or tables.

Once he reached the table he wanted, the landlord saw him lean his staff against the wall, and then heard the distinctive sound of coins hit the table as he seated himself with his back against the wall.

"Welcome ta' the Dragon's Breath Inn," the landlord said, as he cheerfully approached the table, wiping his hands on his makeshift apron. "What's yer pleasure?"

The stranger looked up to the landlord, his features, previously shaded, now more apparent. A large, ugly scar marked the left side of his thin face, drawing a thick, jagged channel from beneath the fedora to the start of his neckline. The only visible break of the gruesome wound was the black, cloth eyepatch. Trying to force his eyes from the disfiguring injury, the landlord attempted to meet the stranger's gaze. The near-white shade of the pale blue iris looking back at him shocked him. The stranger's hair was black, streaked with gray, and though twisted and wrapped around his neck, the end was held by three rings — two gold and one silver.

"Nothing," the stranger whispered, in the innkeeper's own tongue. His deep, *basso profundo* voice promised thunder if riled. "I am meeting someone."

The innkeeper was shocked to hear this creature, which was definitely not a faerie, speak the Fair Tongue. The innkeeper frowned. He tried to be tolerant of others who lived in the Seven Known Planes of the Fae, but only faeries spoke the fair tongue.

"You have a name?" the landlord snapped, obviously insulted.

"Blackwing," the stranger replied, in a deep whisper. "And keep it to yourself." He smirked.

The innkeeper grasped at his heart as it pounded, and stepped back to regain his balance.

"N-not Phelonius Blackwing!" he gasped, quietly, his face betraying his terror. *My heart is beating so hard I know it's going to stop.*

"What do *you* know of Phelonius?" the stranger asked, his right eye narrowed to a slit.

The innkeeper whispered, "O-only that he was… is… a Dark Enforcer. A *Storm Bringer*, some would say, one of the *T'et Faqin Q'estirions.*"

Blackwing gave a nod toward the coins on the table and the innkeeper reached for a gold one. Then, thinking better of it, reached for a silver one. Before he could pick up the coin, Blackwing pinned his wrist to the tabletop. With his free hand, the stranger pushed up the sleeve of his duster and then passed his hand, fingers twitching, over his bared forearm. The innkeeper saw the stranger's tanned forearm transform— a red and gold tattoo of a gryphon appeared, sparkled briefly, faded and disappeared. Blackwing released him.

His bonafides! A true T'et Faqin, doing the Council's business in the Faewyld. "Y-yes, sir, I understand," the innkeeper said, as he backed away quickly, pocketing the table rental.

Once he was far enough away, he took a moment to compose himself before he hurried to resume his work.

The innkeeper tried to calm himself once he was behind the counter. It was difficult to will his hands to stop shaking and slow his hammering heart. *A Dark Enforcer! Here!*

His grandfather had told him of Phelonius Blackwing. How he had destroyed an entire village, for a perceived minor slight of some kind.

"*The T'et Faqin Q'estirions are more than wizards,*" he remembered his grandfather saying. "*They are the most brutal, merciless, tenacious group that ever walked the Faewyld, maybe even the entirety of the Seven Planes. They are ferocious and unyielding warriors.*"

He glanced over to Blackwing's table in time to see a highly engraved pewter tankard with what looked like a dragon handle with gems in the eyes, float to the table top. And once there, Blackwing tapped the handle three times and the tankard filled itself.

His grandfather's words echoed in his mind. *"If you ever see one of the Q'estirions, go the other way. Failing that, don't anger them and don't offend them. T'ain't healthy!"*

You could remove your hat, at least. It's only good manners, ain't it?

After taking a few sips of the noxious brew in his tankard, Blackwing motioned for the innkeeper.

"Y-yes sir?" the innkeeper asked.

"Give me your hand," Blackwing said.

He picked up a gold coin from the tabletop and put it into the innkeeper's proffered hand and held it there while he closed the landlord's fingers around the coin. With his other hand, Blackwing reached into a pocket and produced a red crystal globe that shone with an eerie internal light. The innkeeper's eyes were drawn toward the globe. As he stared at it, he saw an image of another green faerie.

"Pontifar Grimstar. Seen him? Before you answer, you have Wizard's Gold in your hand, so if you manage to lie, which I wouldn't recommend, it will disappear and return to me, after marking you. So answer carefully."

"H-he comes in sometimes," the innkeeper said, guardedly, after calming himself. "I have not seen him," his voice cracked, "in a phase cycle or so."

"He will be here. Do not warn him in any way." Blackwing released the innkeeper's hand. "And do not interfere, if you value your freedom."

The innkeeper gave a nervous smile, bowing quickly as he backed away.

Blackwing swallowed more of the concoction from his tankard. It seemed to help suppress the pain from his ruined eye and the facial scar. He was half-finished with his second tankard when his staff started bouncing, making a tapping sound. When he raised his eyes, he saw Grimstar entering the inn. He placed a hand on his staff and it calmed.

Grimstar was talking with the other customers, sometimes laughing raucously, as he made his way to the counter. Blackwing set his tankard down and picked up one of the gold coins. He stood it on its edge, holding the top with a finger of his left hand, and flicked it with a finger on his right hand, making the coin spin in place. While it spun, he murmured a summoning spell.

Grimstar, drawn to the spinning coin, made his way, haltingly, to Blackwing's table. Once there, mesmerized by the coin, he reached to take it, but once his palm touched it, the coin flattened into a band and fastened itself around Grimstar's wrist.

"Hey! What is this?" Grimstar raised his arm to inspect the band, and saw no seam.

It was tight enough that he couldn't pull his thick wrist out of it. When he tried to get a finger under the band to pry it off, he felt it tighten. The more he tried, the tighter it became.

"Who are you?" Grimstar yelled. "Get this thing off me! You have no right!"

He glanced around desperately in search of aid, but no one in the bar seemed to hear anything he said.

"No right?" Blackwing stood, grabbed his staff and hit the base of it on the wooden floor.

Boom!

He opened his duster and a huge jewel floated from one of the inside pockets. Everyone in the inn turned to look as they heard the snapping and cracking of wood. As Grimstar watched, he saw the top end of the staff changing and growing into the shape of a finely carved, arched dragon's head, reminiscent of a shepherd's crook. They saw the jewel, which was such a deep red it was close to black, float over to the staff and insert itself into the dragon's mouth before it closed, securing the gem in place.

There was no sound for quite some time.

Finally, the silence was broken by the landlord, who had come over to Blackwing's table.

"Um... excuse me, sir," the innkeeper said. "Is there a charge against Grimstar?"

Blackwing turned and slowly bent at the waist to fix the landlord with his right eye, and glowered.

"I don't mean to tell you your business," the landlord said, "but his family will want to know."

"I am not going anywhere with you," Grimstar yelled.

"I am transporting him and his accomplices to *Sha-Tor-Ads-Moor*, for prosecution. The charges so far are illegal use of an artifact and illegal transmutation for the purpose of swindle. There will undoubtedly be more by the time we get there. Why do you ask? You may accompany him if you wish." Blackwing picked up his coins and his tankard and stowed them for travel. "Where is his family located?"

The innkeeper quickly declined the invitation to accompany Grimstar and started explaining where Grimstar's family could be found. When everything was ready, Blackwing started for the door.

"Turn me loose," Grimstar shouted. "You... you—"

He fell silent. His mouth was moving, but no sound left him.

As Blackwing walked, Grimstar was being dragged, his resistance not hindering Blackwing's pace in the least.

Once outside the inn, Blackwing took two steps, and on his third the pair vanished.

Moments later, they reappeared in a forest clearing. Grimstar didn't recognize the area, but it was apparent that his captor did. As Blackwing stepped forward, toward the center of the clearing, Grimstar stumbled.

"The disorientation from the wizard-step will pass. Just ignore it," Blackwing said, in a voice so low Grimstar had to strain to hear him.

As Blackwing entered the center of the clearing, he raised his staff and muttered something. A small cottage shimmered into existence and Blackwing entered, with Grimstar in tow.

"Is this your house, or did you liberate it from some peasant?" Grimstar looked around the small one-room building and saw only a hearth, a table, and three chairs.

"No. It is a resting place for *T'et Faqin Q'estirions*. Only we know where it is and only we can make it appear. Get the fire going and look around for something to eat."

"I am not your slave! Do it yourself," Grimstar snarled.

In that quiet, menacing tone, Blackwing said, "I require nothing from you. The fire and food are for you. You do not want food or warmth then go without. Any complaints later will be silenced." Blackwing sat in a chair that faced the only door and took out his tankard and a few pieces of dried meat. He remained silent while he ate and drank.

Grimstar grumbled and thought for a few minutes, before starting the fire and rummaging around the cottage for something to eat. About the time he found something, the door opened and someone—another *Q'estirion*, by the look of him—entered and sat opposite Blackwing, and the pair began to converse. All Grimstar heard were hushed words with soft sounds—unlike the usual harder tones—and he understood none of it. Even though Blackwing was the first Dark Enforcer he had ever seen, comparing the two left him with the idea that Blackwing seemed unkempt and road-weary. The irritating part for Grimstar was that neither of them acknowledged him in any way.

"This cannot be good," he mumbled. *Very few ever see a Dark Enforcer these days, and here sit two of 'em!*

Blackwing knew who was entering the cottage before the person actually entered.

"Malthuvius," Blackwing said, at his entry.

"Socrates," the other *Q'estirion* said.

Malthuvius glanced at Grimstar with a questioning look.

"Prisoner," Blackwing said. "What brings you so far from *Q'estiria*?"

"You do." Malthuvius sat and pulled several pages of folded parchment from the inside of his duster. "How is the eye?"

"Bothersome." Blackwing touched the patch covering his left eye.

"Sorry to hear that. We did our best. From the General." Malthuvius pushed the papers toward Blackwing.

"Defeating dragon riders has its cost." Blackwing opened the papers and read the drawn runes.

When he finished, he re-folded the papers and pushed them back to Malthuvius.

"Tell my venerable grandfather that I am currently executing a contract." Blackwing glanced in Grimstar's direction.

He took a slow drink from his tankard, making a face that told of his displeasure in the taste.

"You read the orders," Malthuvius said. "They take priority over a simple retrieval." He reached inside his coat and took out a sapphire crystalline sphere and set it on the table.

"Per the tenants of the *T'et Faqin Q'estirions*, I can refuse an order if it conflicts with the completion of a prior commitment." Blackwing reached inside his own coat, pulled out a ruby, crystalline sphere and placed it close to Malthuvius's.

Both spheres glowed eerily as they synchronized their information.

"Are you really going to force me to insist?" Malthuvius asked. "After all we have been through?"

"What am I supposed to do with Grimstar? I see no reason why those orders cannot be delayed to allow me to complete my current contract." Blackwing took another sip.

"It took me the better part of a phase cycle to find you, so any nominal delay that could have been taken has long since lapsed. I will finish your contract and deliver Grimstar. That would free you to execute your new orders." Malthuvius pulled out his own tankard and dried meat. "If you were less stubborn, you would not have been demoted and I would be taking orders from you." He started to eat and drink.

Blackwing glanced to the wide gold band holding Malthuvius's braided hair.

He chuckled mirthlessly. "You know that is not true. I was demoted because I am… inconvenient to have around. That would be more accurate."

"Being perpetually intoxicated does not help matters, either." Malthuvius took a drink.

"It helps with the pain."

The two spheres stopped glowing and they both picked up their own and secured them.

"Have you been taking the medication?" Malthuvius leaned back in his chair a little as he retrieved his own sphere.

Blackwing raised his tankard and shook it a little. "The ale helps to cut the taste to an almost tolerable level."

Malthuvius chuckled. "It does have a hideous taste, but you know it is the only thing that will help. Is the eye functioning?" He indicated the patch.

"It functions. It gives plenty of needed information, when it can, about half the time. When it cannot, I wish for my own eye, ruined or not. When you return, you can inform my grandfather that his legend is secure. The people still remember his tantrum."

Malthuvius nodded. "And what of him?" He shifted to the fair tongue and raised his volume.

The change in language and volume startled Grimstar.

Blackwing also shifted language. "He is to be returned to *Sha-Tor-Ads-Moor*, after I collect his family and cohorts."

Malthuvius motioned for Grimstar to come toward the table. "If released, will you run? You do know you can be summoned, no matter how far away you manage to get," he said, once Grimstar was close to the table.

He hadn't spoken loudly, but the words seemed to strike menacingly at Grimstar.

"How can I run?" Grimstar asked, dejected. "I am tethered somehow to *him*," he held up his wrist, showing the gold band, "and I do not know where I am or which way to go. I have been dragged out into the Faewyld, against my will and in a manner intended to confuse." *It will do me no good to plead with them. They are merciless. Better to save my strength for later.*

Malthuvius shifted back to the native tongue of the *T'et Faqin*. "You can release him." He dismissed Grimstar with a wave of his hand. "He will not go far."

Blackwing gave a barely perceptible nod and quietly spoke the spell to release the magical tether to Blackwing's staff, but not the band. Grimstar had no indication that he was no longer tethered.

"How long will it take for you to fulfill your contract?" Malthuvius asked Blackwing.

"No more than another phase cycle, I should think," Blackwing said, after making the mental calculations and padding the result.

"Unacceptable." Tension crept into his quiet voice.

Blackwing shrugged. "It could be less, but I would not expect it. It will take as long as it takes."

Malthuvius rose and began pacing. "Rest. I need to think and consult with others. I will watch Grimstar," he said, after a few trips across the room.

Blackwing gathered his duster around him as he settled into the chair, feet on the table, legs crossed at the ankle. After lowering his hat to cover his eyes, he crossed his arms and became quiet and still.

2

WIZARDS AND PLANES AND GATES (OH MY!)

Blackwing watched as the woman that had held his interest for the past several days came to the door. He had observed that she came here every morning, at the same time, and left long after dark. She obviously was a storekeeper of some kind, but the type of store had confused him. It had few customers on a daily basis, and he wondered what was sold there.

The woman was nice to look at, by the standards here, as he had observed several males turn and watch as she walked past. She had dark, rust-colored hair, and a pale complexion. She was lithe and moved with a certain grace that grabbed his attention. He had seen some wood nymphs who shared her general characteristics, but a closer inspection would have to be made to determine if she was one from the Fae.

From a distance, his left eye had indicated traces of the Source. It was her, or something she had touched, that had left the trace.

He noticed the woman looked sharply to the left of the door as she touched the handle to pull it open. He didn't know if it was a local ritual or something else. Something religious, perhaps. He had noticed several customers not performing the ritual, so he was uncertain. As he watched, he saw her turn on a small sign with strange drawings before sitting on a high chair behind a transparent case.

The building was distinct from others around it. It was small, with only two floors, and out of place among its much taller neighbors. This one was brick and had little glass in the front. Its neighbors were towers of glass that reflected light in a disquieting, unnatural way, in Blackwing's opinion.

He believed this Plane to be very strange and the people in it even more so. It had unusual conveyances of all sizes. For what purpose, he had no idea. Some were large and extremely noisy and spewed noxious fumes. Some were smaller and quiet as a whisper. A few flashed red, white, and blue lights and made sounds so loud and shrill that it hurt his hearing. These conveyances passed between him and the small store and traveled on the hard surface that was lower than the similar surface he was standing on. He saw people cross between white lines when a sign flashed white. On poles that held the smaller flashing signs was a silver button that people pushed, often several times, obviously to give them something to do while they waited for the sign to flash white.

He had been careful, in his observations, to cast a reflection spell, which allowed his surveillance without being observed. He had seen enough to approach and make initial contact, so after crossing to the door he dispensed with the spell and entered.

Suzanne Hawks exited the door that led to the upstairs apartment of her building and proceeded to open the store for the day. Hawks' Emporium had been a legacy from her father and grandfather, as was the building. It had managed to support her, so far. She had many offers from the major developers, who'd planned to demolish the building for another high rise, but she had refused them all. She knew, however, that the Tacoma City Council had been raising the property taxes in order to get her to default or sell to the developers. She had heard many of their arguments for updating the downtown area and getting rid of all the *eye-sore* buildings in favor of the modern high-rises. She had no idea how much longer she could hold out against their onslaught.

As she walked the few feet to the store's main entrance, she had a distinct feeling that she was being watched. The same feeling she'd been having for the past three days. As she reached for the door handle, she turned to look left of the doorframe so the retinal scanner could identify her and unlock the door. This particular upgrade had cost her dearly, but had been worth it, in her opinion. She felt safer, as the neighborhood was deteriorating at an alarming rate. To try to get her to sell, the city council had also reduced police patrols in her immediate area, and with the reduced presence had come the criminal element.

After entering and turning on the *Open* sign, she sat in her chair behind the counter to continue reading one of the old books her father had purchased just before he died, when a loud ding came from the electronic chime above the door as a man entered.

"May I help you?" she asked, congenially, as she tried to ascertain if he was customer or criminal.

The man was strange-looking, dressed in all black leather and a patch over his left eye. Inwardly, she cringed at the sight of the ugly scar that ran from under his hat, above his nose, across his left eye, down to the left side of his neck. The man spoke, but she didn't understand a word of it.

"I'm sorry, but I don't speak German," she said.

She had no idea what language he spoke, but it sounded like German to her. It was then that the man produced what appeared to be a three- or four-inch diameter crystal globe that glowed warmly. For some reason she couldn't take her eyes off the globe, and reached to take it from the man.

As soon as she touched the orb, her mind was filled with images of strange battles, of people riding what looked to be dragons or huge lizards, and flashes of fireballs, blue energy orbs tossed at each other, and flaming swords of various colors. As the images flowed, she heard a pleasant voice whispering, "I am not from your Plane and I need assistance. Will you help?" Her attention was on the images, but the voice repeated and echoed. After what seemed to be hours, she heard, "Yes," in her own voice. It was then that the images stopped and she shook her head to clear it.

"What happened?" she asked the man standing in front of her.

He was smiling warmly. "Am sorry, mizz, need help to spoke," he said, in broken English, with what sounded to her like a heavy, German accent. "I name Blackwing. You name?"

"Um… Suzanne… Hawks," she replied, her brain still foggy. *What the hell are you doing! Don't give out that information.* "You look like you could use a place to rest," she heard her voice continue. "I have a little empty space in the storeroom you could use for as long as you need to." *Shut! Up! You're going to get killed by this… person.*

"Mooch tanks for use storeroom for few… hors!" the man said.

"Okay. Follow me." Suzanne led the way to the basement door.

As she walked, she didn't hear him following her, and turned her head enough to see him out of the corner of her eye. Once at the door to the basement storeroom, she opened it.

"You can find a place to rest down there. Just make yourself at home!" she said, as he passed by her and descended the stairs. As Blackwing reached the bottom of the stairs, a part of Suzanne wanted to lock and bolt the door. Instead, she closed it gently and returned to the counter and sat back in her chair. Once there, she was startled by the sudden thought that a stranger had entered her shop. After a cautious glance around, she satisfied herself with the thought that there was no one there but her.

As Blackwing descended the stairs, he heard the door close gently behind him. As his eye became accustomed to the dim light, he saw a room filled with boxes of various sizes and some furniture. He found a straight-backed chair and settled in to rest.

He took out his tankard and some dried meat before removing the globe to set it on a box where he could reach it easily. As he munched some of the dried meat, he took off his hat and set it on a nearby box beside the globe. *I am tired and my scar and eye are giving me grief.* He washed down the meat with sips from his tankard. *At the rate I'm consuming them, I'm going be out of medicine soon and ale shortly after that. I'll need to find new sources before long. My supply line is unreliable, at best.*

"Sorry, my friend, but one of us had to go. Better you than me." The message he had received via the globe upon awakening here three days ago, replayed in his mind. *"Have no fear. I will complete your contract for you and see to it you get the credit and the fare for it. The good news is you have been promoted, as evidenced by the added gold ring."*

Blackwing fingered the rings at the left side of his throat. He now had three gold rings, not that it mattered much to him.

"The bad news is you are now stationed there to preserve the integrity of Plane Eight and the gate, by order of the High Council. As you are aware, Plane Eight was deemed off limits, so we know nothing of the creatures living there. You are to gain knowledge of them and their ways while you seek a few known violators, identities and breeds unknown, of the ban. There are not many of them that we know of. You are an invaluable resource to your grandfather, the General. Apprehensions and custody changes will be by way of your entry point. Message exchanges and reports will be by the globe, as is usual. I do expect daily reports, but knowing you, that is asking too much. Twice a week will be sufficient, for now. Do your duty and try to stay alive."

As he recalled the message, he felt the anger grow within him once more. Anger at his grandfather, who had assigned him this task, and anger at Malthuvius Nighthawk for the manner it was thrust upon him.

As Suzanne Hawks went through her day, she remembered bits and pieces of what had transpired that morning. She lacked quite a few of the details of what the person called Blackwing looked like, but some of it she remembered. Her plan was to ignore that he was in her storeroom.

If he isn't awake by the time I close, I'll tell him to leave, after questioning him, of course. If he refuses to leave, I'll just call the cops and have him removed. What wore on her was how he'd managed to swing the invitation. *True, I'd extended the invitation without his asking, but I know that was reckless of me. I would never trust some stranger to use my storeroom.*

As she glanced at the clock on the far wall, she heard someone walking toward her from the storeroom. She hadn't heard the basement door open or close and it bothered her that she wasn't more aware of her surroundings.

"Feeling better?" she asked, with sarcasm.

"Much, thank you," Blackwing said.

Suzanne noticed his German accent was almost nonexistent.

"Would you mind telling me who you are and what you want of me?" she said. *Am I angry with this stranger or with myself for being so trusting?*

"Socrates Blackwing." He bowed, with one foot slightly ahead of the other, arms out.

Who still does that?

"As I said before, I am a stranger here. Information would be gratefully accepted, as would some assistance to your ways."

Blackwing was standing at the counter and seemed to loom over her. She guessed his height at six-six, but because of his long, thin fingers and a more skeletal nature of his body, he seemed taller. Dressed the way he was, and because of his *basso profundo* voice, she found him to be intimidating. She could sense he was dangerous.

It was his eyes that made her uncomfortable. The patch, covering who knows what horrors, and the accompanying scar. The other was so pale she felt like he was seeing deep into her soul.

"For starters," Suzanne said, "how're your creds? You're going to need lots to survive here."

"Creds?" Blackwing asked, and Suzanne could see the confusion on his face.

"Money, credits, cash," she snapped. "Food and a place to sleep aren't cheap here. If you are, as you say, new here, you're going to need an ID and a means to earn a living."

Blackwing put a hand in one of the pockets of his duster. "Would this be acceptable payment?" He placed a gold coin on the glass counter.

From long years of dealing with people with items to sell or trade, she looked at the coin but didn't pick it up.

"Do you mind if I examine it?" she asked, once her heart quit pounding. *Looks like gold.*

Blackwing nodded. After sealing her hands, she picked up the coin. It was quite heavy for its size, circular, and had lots of strange markings stamped into it, close to the edge. She pulled out her small digital scale and placed the coin on the tray and made note of the its weight. She placed a right-angle scale on the counter, put the coin inside the angle and took a snap-shot of it, both sides, for sizing. She then put in a jeweler's loop and inspected it more closely.

"The coin weighs 1.1 Troy ounces. If this coin is solid gold and not just gold plated or alloy, I'd say it's worth is close to fifteen thousand credits, at today's market value. As a curiosity piece, it would be worth more, maybe twenty thousand, as long as there aren't too many in the public domain." She removed the loop and handed the coin back to Blackwing.

"It is solid gold," he said. "Is it of high value? You can keep it, for your kindness."

Suzanne was shocked at the generosity. "To put it another way, lots of people would slit your throat for it."

Blackwing reached into another pocket and pulled out an ornate pewter tankard and started to drink from it.

"That's quite a coat you have there," she said, with raised eyebrows. "Is it a coat, or a wearable vault?"

"It is a coat," Blackwing replied, with a deadpan expression. "True, it does have some... special properties, but the main function is as a coat."

It was then that Suzanne noticed his voice was barely above a whisper, but she heard him plainly. *His voice is so deep I can almost feel it in my bones.*

"How do I get more of these credits you speak of?" Blackwing pulled out another pewter tankard and placed it in front of Suzanne.

"Well, you'd have to have an ID, an Identity Device, for it to do you any good." She raised the tankard to her lips.

She could smell the liquid inside and it smelled sweet and a little like honey and caramel. As she slowly tipped the tankard, she let a few drops hit the end of her tongue. The liquid had a slightly sweet taste, not as sweet as it smelled. As she drank the small mouthful, it felt creamy and smooth in her mouth, with a pleasant level of alcoholic content.

"What is an Identity Device?" Blackwing asked.

"This." She turned her head, lifted the back of her hair, and pointed to a small silver spot on her neck close to the base of her skull. "The government tags everyone when they're born. It allows a lot of the tech that most of us use every day to work, and you can't buy or sell without one. It's powered by the electrical activity in the brain and is specific to an individual's DNA. Do you have one?"

"I have nothing like that," Blackwing said, as he shook his head. "What is DNA?"

"Deoxyribonucleic acid. It's a molecule that holds genetic encoding and is unique to every living organism. The government uses it to track everything you do and everywhere you go. Sixty years ago it was part of the anti-terrorist agenda. Now, though, it's an intrusion."

"That does not sound like a good thing to me." Blackwing took another sip from his tankard.

"I don't mean to be rude, but what are you and where do you come from?"

"I am me, and me is what I am."

"Flowery answer. And it tells me nothing."

Blackwing frowned. "It is difficult to explain. Me and my kind are called many things in many places. Generally we are called *T'et Faqin Q'estirions*, which simply means we are the *Called of Q'estiria*. Some call us Storm Riders or Storm Bringers, and some call us Dark Enforcers."

"I've never heard of Ka-eh-steer-ia. Is it a country or something, and why would they call you all those other names?"

Suzanne finally noticed the man's ears. *I've never seen ears like those on anyone.* From what she could see, the ends of his ears went under his hat.

"Are those real?" She indicated his ears. *You're definitely not from around here.*

"They are real. The places that call us Dark Enforcers are referencing our clothing and what we do. We dress this way and we enforce the edicts from the High Council. Those who call us Storm Riders or Storm Bringers do so for good reason. We are not generally well-received, especially among those who violate the edicts."

"Are you an elf?" Suzanne's mouth was agape and she threw her hands up to her lips to keep any more words from coming out.

It was what she was thinking, but she didn't intend to voice it.

"I'm so sorry! How politically incorrect of me. I didn't mean to be so blunt or offensive."

"What is *anelf*?" Blackwing said.

How do you explain a reference to a book that someone from out of town would have no clue about? As they talked, she had an image in her head of Elrond, from *Lord of the Rings*. But Blackwing wasn't as fair as her mental image of Elrond. *Not by a long shot!*

Suzanne glanced at the clock again and decided it was time to close the store. As she got to her feet, she placed the coin on the counter and walked around it to lock the door.

Joe Johnson aka Crackin', Tom O'Toole aka DA Tom, and Trevor Peterson aka Shooter, were watching the shapely red-headed woman in the small shop when they saw the gold coin. They had orders from their handlers at the Tacoma Police Department, to *explain* to her that she should move her shop out of their neighborhood. Consequently, they knew the cops wouldn't show to spoil their fun. They could do whatever they wanted.

As the woman was heading toward the door, Shooter pulled his Glock 19, making sure to rack a round, and Crackin' got out his Louisville Slugger. DA Tom pushed his way into the shop, followed closely by his compatriots.

"You jus' back it up, missy!" Crackin' pointed the thick end of the bat at her. "I knows you was told to clear outta here. You shoulda went." He looked around the store, then went to the counter and palmed the coin. "Go check ta see if anyone else be here, DA Watch her, Shooter."

Crackin' had been tapping the bat against his palm and was drawing back to hit the glass case, when they all heard a deep, menacing laugh coming from the middle of the store.

Everyone turned to look, and saw a hideous demon covered in blue, white, and yellow flames. It looked to be twenty feet tall and was hunched down to fit under the ten-foot ceiling of the shop. The demon had huge bulging muscles and its face looked like hell itself, burning red coals for eyes, a huge maw with dripping fangs, and enormous horns coming out of the side of its head.

As the demon reached out with its huge clawed hands, each of the would-be robbers scrambled for the door.

3

TO T'GORN E'FAL... PERCHANCE TO DREAM

Suzanne's face betrayed her shock and fright. "What the hell was that?" She turned toward Blackwing, who was still standing where he was before the three thugs pushed their way into her store. "Did you do that?" she said, when Blackwing didn't answer.

"We were having a pleasant conversation before we were rudely interrupted," Blackwing shrugged.

Suzanne narrowed her eyes. "Are you some kind of wizard?"

"What is wizard?"

"You know, like Gandalf." *You're definitely not a Harry Potter.*

"I do not know who or what that is. Or what you mean."

"Of course you don't." Suzanne paced frantically. "Why would you? You're not from around here." Having rounded the corner of the counter, she picked up her phone and Blackwing heard three distinct tones. "I want to report a robbery," Suzanne said, into the device. "Just now. Three men pushed their way into my store, threatened me, and stole a rare coin. I'm here now. When? *Fine!* I'll see the officer tomorrow." She slammed the phone down.

Blackwing could see that Suzanne was still trembling, but he couldn't tell if it was from the three men or from seeing the demon.

"You appear to be upset," Blackwing said. "What are you upset about?"

"I haven't been robbed in years, and then you show up and the shit hits the fan! And you're no help. I ask a straight forward question and I get a blank look from you. I can see why someone would call you a Storm Bringer. You bring a shitstorm."

"Who did you talk to on that device?"

"This," Suzanne picked up her phone and showed it to Blackwing, "is a cell phone. I called the police to report a robbery. They stole your coin. Don't you care?"

"Why don't you sit and try to calm yourself." Blackwing indicated the chair she had been occupying.

As Suzanne sat, she picked up her pewter tankard and tipped it up, but it was empty. She slammed it back down on the counter.

"If you would like more, just tap the handle three times."

"And what's that supposed to do? Send me back to Oz or Kansas, or something?"

She looked at Blackwing, who returned her gaze with a blank look of incomprehension.

After a few seconds, she tapped the handle three times with her index finger.

"There, I did it. Nothing hap—"

Suzanne stared at the tankard as it refilled itself.

"What the hell?" she said, with her own look of incomprehension.

Blackwing gave a wry smile as she took another sip. "I am unconcerned about the coin. It will return to me soon enough, and those who took it will pay a price for doing so."

"Hey, I just thought of something," Suzanne blurted, after she'd calmed down. "Those thugs didn't see you. At least, they didn't talk to you and didn't indicate that you were here. Why is that?"

"They saw what they wanted to see." Blackwing shrugged and snickered. "You were their primary target and they were too focused on you to notice me."

James McConnel, Law Enforcement Technician for the Tacoma Police Department, was sitting at his desk. The wall directly in front of him was covered with the images coming in from the surveillance cameras located in businesses, on street corners, bank exteriors, the bullet train station, and the Under Sound Subway stations. He marveled at the technological advances that had trickled down from the now defunct NSA and its surveillance programs of some sixty years ago. It may be old technology, but it served to keep a close eye on all the criminal activity in the city.

"Did you turn off the cams on Court C and 11th?" said Brian Trevail, the desk sergeant currently on duty.

"Sure did, just as I was ordered," McConnel replied. "Is there a problem?"

"No. That Hawks woman just called in a robbery," Trevail said, with some concern.

"I thought she was supposed to go to the hospital?" McConnel asked.

"That *was* the plan," Trevail snapped.

Suzanne looked at Blackwing, skeptically. "Well, I'm tired and need to sleep. Where are you going to spend the night?" She tipped her tankard and finished it before setting it in front of Blackwing.

"What is sleep?" he said, with a blank look.

"You know, sleep. Lying in a bed, closing your eyes and going to dreamland? You don't sleep?"

"Earlier today, I performed *T'gorn E'fal*. I will not need to do so again for some time."

"Well, you can't be inside the store when I'm not here, and I'm leaving. As much as I appreciate your help with the thugs, I just met you. I hope you understand. You're free to come back tomorrow, but you can't stay here."

"I will be back when you once again return." Blackwing gathered his belongings and strode out the door.

Suzanne didn't watch him leave, but quickly went through her lock-up procedures and exited the door shortly after Blackwing left. As the door locked behind her, she looked up and down the street for any sign of him, but didn't see anything.

"Gone already? Why am I not surprised?" she said to the empty street. *Was he really here, or was it my imagination.*

When Blackwing left the door of the shop, he reinstituted the reflection spell and became invisible once more. He managed to find a deserted alleyway, and performed the summoning spell that would bring the young man who had taken the coin, and the coin, to him. While he waited, he reviewed all the information the sphere had retrieved while in the store.

He discovered that the sphere had detected something called the Global Web and had copied it. This allowed Blackwing to research references Suzanne had made during their conversations. He was well into his research on wizards and elves, when he was alerted to the approach of his quarry.

Crackin' had pocketed the coin without telling the other two about the prize. *Why should I? I founded it and its mine. The storekeeper ain't gonna need it where she's gonna end up.*

From the time he and his cohorts left the small store, he had been fingering the coin in his pocket. The more he touched it, held it, the more he needed to hold it and touch it. The coin felt smooth, cold, and heavy in his pocket, but seemed to warm him from the inside whenever his skin contacted it.

He had been wandering around not far from the scene of his score. Periodically he would take the coin out to look at it, to feel its weight in his hand, to see it shine in the fluorescent lighting that held the darkness at bay.

I was supposed to report to my handlers at the cop shop, but there's plenty of time for that later. I'm not gonna tell them of this prize, either. I found it. It's mine.

Crackin' hadn't been paying attention to his meanderings and was shocked when his steps took him to an especially dark doorway in an especially dark alley.

"Enjoying your prize?" a deep *basso profundo* voice rumbled at him.

Crackin' jumped back. "You's lookin' fer trouble?" He slipped the coin back into his pocket as he pointed the bat toward the doorway.

"No, not looking for trouble. Looking for you," the voice said.

Crackin' felt the timbre of it in his bones, although it wasn't loud, just deep.

"What's that s'pose ta mean?" said the skinny, streetwise urchin.

"It means you are no trouble. Not to me, anyway. I need information and you are going to tell me what I want to know."

"Am I now? Why don't cha' step out where I can see ya an' we'll see who's gonna tell what." Crackin' grinned like he always did.

He was used to having the upper hand, even with the blue boys.

He heard scuffling of feet on the ever-present gravel. Then a huge hand grabbed him. What came at him from the dark was the same demon he'd seen in the store. It picked him up and held him eye-to-eye with it.

"Who sent you to that store?" the demon said.

Crackin' squirmed against the grip of the demon, trying to escape. The grip was tightened to the point that he swore his ribs were breaking.

"I can't tell ya that, b'cuz I don't know," he managed, finally.

The demon chuckled and Crackin' heard a car alarm set off from the rumble of it.

"Sounds like Crackin' is cracking."

"Ya can't make me spill," the young man screamed.

The demon tossed him into the air. When Crackin' looked down, he saw the ground coming up to meet him. His fall was arrested by pain in his ankle, where the demon caught him, his face inches from the hard pavement. The demon swung him up and caught him around his chest again, and once more brought them face-to-face. He could feel the demon's hot breath scorching his clothes.

"You will tell me." The demon chuckled.

Still being held, Crackin' could see the monster growing. Then there was a flash and Crackin' looked around. He could see the street far below. The monster was holding him over the edge of the roof of one of the skyscrapers.

"I can make you spill, Joseph. I can make you spill the information, or I can spill your guts all over the pavement down there."

"How did ya know my name?" Joe said, in a panic. "No one knows my name."

The demon let out a loud laugh which sounded to Joe like a

thunderclap close to his head. The demon tossed him again, higher than the last time, and over the street. Joe panicked when he started to fall again and saw the edge of the building the monster was on pass by with no indication that he was going to be caught. He heard screaming. It took him a second to realize the sound was coming from him.

Just before he hit the pavement, Joe passed out.

He woke up in a hospital bed. When he looked around, he saw Sergeant Trevail looking down at him.

"Welcome back to the land of the living, Crackin'," the TPD sergeant said.

"How'd I get here?" Joe asked, groggily.

"You were picked up on the street, screaming about a demon of some sort being after you. They're running your blood for drugs. Want to tell me what you took? It must've been some bad shit."

"I don't do no drugs. There's a demon after me. He grab me so hard I heard m'ribs breakin'. He tossed me around like a ragdoll and hurt m'ankle when he caught me after tossin' me inta the air."

"That's what you were screaming when they rolled you into the emergency room, but they saw no bruising. They did X-rays and found nothing broken or cracked. I did, however, have to confiscate your Louisville Slugger. Nice bat, by the way."

"I dropped it in the alley. How'd it end up here? Always did like a nice piece of hickory. Do I get it back?"

"You were carrying it when you were found." Sergeant Trevail chuckled. "I'm not convinced it's yours. The bat you were carrying is made of maple, not hickory. It's being tested for trace evidence, in case you used it on somebody recently. If it tests negative, then we'll see."

"I din't use it on nobody and I want it back. Am I under arrest, or can I leave?"

"Well, we did get a robbery complaint earlier. Someone matching your description stole a coin. Tell me about that."

Joe looked sideways at the sergeant. "Don't know nothin' 'bout that. I want a lawyer."

"If you didn't do anything, then why would you need a lawyer? Anyway, we searched you before you were transported and you had nothing of value, except the bat. They're thinking about enrolling you in the laughing academy. They say they have a special chair for you there, with wrist and ankle restraints."

"I ain't wacked. They cain't do that ta me."

"Oh, but they can. They've documented everything since you were found, and the docs are saying you need an assessment. So tell me again how you don't want to cooperate?"

"I never said that."

The sergeant smiled at him. "Sure you did. Right when you lawyered up."

As the sergeant left, Joe got a look in the mirror across from his bed. He saw the demon looking back at him and he heard it laugh, inside his head.

Suzanne opened the store, as usual. Shortly after doing so, Blackwing showed himself. He strode in and sat in the same chair he'd sat the previous evening.

Suzanne turned to look at him and he slid a coin across the counter to her.

She looked at it for a couple seconds. "Is that another coin?"

"No, it is the same coin. It returned to me shortly after I left. So there is nothing to concern you with its removal."

"I had a hard time sleeping last night." She tried to read his face. "I had dreams of a fierce battle—flaming swords, fireballs, dragons, and lots of people who look like you. When it woke me, I tried to shrug it off as a fantasy I'd read as a kid. But now I'm not so sure."

"I researched some of the references you made last… night? Night. To ease your mind, I am neither elf nor wizard, as your kind would refer. On the other hand," Blackwing took a deep breath, "I do have elements of those creatures."

Suzanne looked at him, raising an eyebrow. "Next, you'll be telling me you're from outer space."

"Not exactly, if I take your meaning."

Suzanne's mouth was agape. "Want to explain that?"

"I would prefer to leave that subject for a later time. It appears someone is coming."

The electronic chime sounded and Suzanne turned to see a police officer walking up to the counter. As he was walking up, she nonchalantly pocketed the coin Blackwing had left on the counter.

"Can I help you, Officer…" She looked at his nameplate. "McConnel?"

"I'm here to investigate your report of forced entry and robbery. Do you prefer miss, mizz, misses, or something else? Is this where it happened?" The officer took out his electronic notepad and a stylus.

"Miss is fine, and yes, I was locking up last night and three thugs pushed their way in."

Suzanne glanced at Blackwing as he sat quietly at the counter. *Can't this cop see him? He didn't even look toward Blackwing. I think I need a CAT scan.*

McConnel raised his hand and smirked. "Calling someone a thug is considered offensive, *miss*. Do you have any proof that they were devotees of the goddess Kali? Saying so could be considered racist. Are you a racist, *miss*?"

"No, but I *am* a victim. Three perpetrators—"

"I'm sorry *miss*, but you can't call people that. You have no idea if they've committed a crime."

"Okay, then, three guys—"

"Did you know that they were all of the male gender? Could one or all have been female, or identify as some other gender? It appears to me that you have a gender bias, and you can be arrested for any of the violations you've stated so far." McConnel frowned at her.

"Three individuals. Kraken."

"Can you spell that?" McConnel said, as he wrote.

"How the hell would I know how they spell their names? Kraken—what mother would name their child after a Norwegian leviathan—DA Tom, and Shooter pushed their way into my store while I was locking up. Is *that* better?"

"I'd change your *tone* when talking to me, *miss*. Please continue."

Each time he called her *miss*, Suzanne felt he was using the word as a weapon, to strike at her, like a verbal slap in the face.

"The one called Shooter held a gun on me while Kraken was getting ready to smash cases."

"*Miss*, you can't make those assumptions. How do you know the gun was real or what someone is going to do?" McConnel exhaled loudly to show his exasperation with her, while shaking his head.

"Anyway, they saw a de… um, something that scared them off."

"When you called, you said something about a rare coin? Was it yours or someone else's?"

"I was appraising it for a potential customer. He was here, but must've taken it back when the three… uh, individuals rushed in. He has it now."

"So why did you report it stolen? Accusing someone of theft is a serious matter. Who was this supposed customer with a rare coin? What was he doing in this neighborhood when there are plenty of reputable rare-coin dealers around? If I didn't know better, I'd think you're dealing in stolen property. Are you a fence, *Miss* Hawks?"

"I'm not a fence! That's a terrible thing to say."

McConnel was shaking his head as he ran through his notes. "I don't know… maybe I should have our robbery division come down and investigate you for stolen property violations. Admittedly, we have no record of any complaints about you, but there is always a first time. Second, your allegations against a person, or persons, unknown seems thin to me. Scaring a young person is felony child abuse, and you could be held liable for all their medical costs incurred through that abuse. And in light of the false allegations, gender bias, and racism, you'd be lucky to have a store left when the courts are finished with you."

"What about your surveillance? Isn't there video of any of it?"

"Our surveillance system has been down the last couple days. So no, there's no video."

"Convenient."

McConnel looked at her, sternly. "I'm sorry, *miss*, but was that an accusation against me or the department, or a disparagement? I have enough here to run you in, you know."

"No, no accusation or disparagement intended." Suzanne closed her eyes and exhaled loudly.

"I think I have everything I need." McConnel closed the notepad. "If we have anything further we need to ask, we'll send someone. I'm adding you to a travel ban so you don't leave town."

Officer McConnel turned sharply and exited the store.

After McConnel left, Suzanne walked over to Blackwing and poked his shoulder.

"Excuse me?" he said.

"Sorry, but I had to check. That's twice others have been here and failed to see you. I was starting to think you're not real, or not really here."

"Your recollection of the facts concerning last night was… interesting."

"I tried to give that cop the information without all the facts. Facts that, quite frankly, would get me a reservation at the closest looney bin."

Blackwing looked at her, stoically. "I do not understand."

"So you think I should've told him that yesterday an elf walked into my store, speaking German. He held out a glass sphere and I touched it and saw things right out of *The Lord of the Rings*. That allowed this elf, who turned out to be a wizard, to understand me, and I to understand him, and I let him sleep in my basement. After he woke up and tried to pay me for doing him a kindness, three hoodlums pushed their way in here and a huge demon covered in blue and white flames scared them off. Is that what I should have told him? They would've locked me up and thrown away the key."

"Do you have eight pieces of paper?" Blackwing said, after Suzanne had wound down. "Size doesn't matter."

She got out a notepad and tore off several pieces of paper.

"Number them so you know which is which."

She did as he had asked.

"Now take the first and second and put a hole through both. Put holes in all the pieces so from number one to number two there is one path, from two to three there is only one path, and so on."

"Why am I doing this?" she said.

"You asked me where I am from, so I am going to try to explain it. Imagine expanding one of those single sheets to the size of your universe here. That is what we call a Plane. People from my Plane know of seven Planes... eight Planes, now." Blackwing stopped to allow the sphere to search for the right words. "Call them Planes of Reality. Your Plane is not mine and mine is not yours. The tiny holes you placed would be what we call gates or portals. If they were tubes, you would understand better. This allows those that know how, to traverse from one Plane to another. On each of the Planes is what you call Earth. Not the same Earth, but unique. Some are similar and some aren't. For a long time our... um... scientists have known of seven Planes of Reality. They recently found yours, which would be number eight."

"So you're telling me there are eight different Earths? Why are there only eight. Why not ten, or twelve?"

"Eight that we know of. There could be more. Probably are."

"Okay, so why are you here?"

"In the seven known Planes, the people established a High Council. The High Council recently found out that your Plane existed, and ruled it off limits to anyone from the other seven Planes. From the research I've done here, there have been others aware of your Plane for some time and have been using it for their own purposes."

"For how long and for what purpose?"

"Who knows." Blackwing shrugged. "Tens of thousands of years, probably. Which explains why your culture is so replete with legends, myths, and folklore, most of which have a correlation to creatures of the Known Seven. Q'estiria is only one of what you call Earth. I am *T'et Faqin Q'estirion*, or loosely translated as Wizard Warrior, or the Called of Q'estiria, in your language. Organizationally, we seem to be close to a combination of your military and justice systems."

"I knew space was going to get in there somewhere. And wizarding, to boot. And I assume magic as well?"

"Yes. You seem to be taking this better than I thought you would."

"Well, I *am* a modern girl in a modern world. I grew up in this bookstore, around wonderful creatures such as elves and wizards. I must admit, I never thought I'd meet one, though."

4

BECOMING K'OBI SHA SHIN J'OI FAQIN

Two months after his arrival, Blackwing had become well versed in the ways of humans, in Suzanne's opinion. They had found a way to camouflage his appearance, through the use of spells that altered what others saw, more modern clothes, and other accouterments.

Suzanne was working on getting him some identifying documents. The sticking point was going to be his Identity Device.

She hadn't known Blackwing very long, but she knew him to be stubborn, and he refused to take the ID.

"I can't have your Identity Device implanted," Blackwing said. "If I do, I can't return to my own Plane, and I intend on returning someday. The electronics will interfere with my abilities and will make me a permanent ordinary resident on this Plane."

"Well, Sox, I have no argument for that," she told him. "Added to that is I'm unfamiliar with the criminal element that might be able to furnish us with a counterfeit. They're notoriously hard to copy or modify. If we don't get it from the government, then we don't get one."

Socrates had managed to master the language enough to use contractions, finally.

"It makes you seem more... human," she'd told him once, as a joke.

But he hadn't taken it that way, and said, "I see no reason for you to insult me."

It was a cold evening, and as they often did, Suzanne and Socrates sat on the roof of her building. They had taken to coming here lately, and spent many evenings in companionable silence or light conversation as they watched the stars. Or at least, that's what she believed they were doing.

The roof was only marginally more peaceful than the street. Casting her gaze to him as he stood looking up into the growing gloom, she could see the tension in him.

"You seem to be upset about something."

She finally broached the topic she'd considered raising for the last few weeks. Each night his mood had seemed darker, more troubled, she knew she had to ask before whatever was troubling him consumed him.

"Can you tell me what's wrong?"

"I'm about out of medicine," he said. "I need it to control the pain of my disfigurement. The medicine is horrendous stuff, but the local mead is helping with the taste. I like it better than the stuff that is sent to me, but the alcohol alone isn't enough to keep the pain at a tolerable level."

He raised his hand to caress the edge of his scar. Even now, he could feel the growing pain burning beneath his skin.

"You've never said how it happened," Suzanne said. "I'm not prying, just letting you know I'm here if you want to talk about it. I'm willing to listen."

He nodded, but said nothing else on the subject.

A week later, he was resupplied with the dried meat, his medicine, and his honey beer.

"How were you resupplied?" Suzanne said, when she saw his mood lighten.

"With this." He indicated his coat.

"I don't see how that would work." She carefully scrutinized the coat.

"Come over here and put your hand in any of my pockets." He grinned.

She chose one of the outer pockets and stuck her hand in. She didn't know what to expect, but she put her hand in his pocket as far as it would go, her wrist still visible, and found it empty.

"Okay, there's nothing in there," she said.

"Observe."

He put his hand into the same pocket, all the way to his elbow, and pulled out his eight-foot-long staff.

"How the hell did you have that in there? Your pocket wasn't deep enough to hide that."

"Each pocket is tied to a room in my Plane. When I stick my hand in, it travels through the interdimensional space and I can access what I want or need."

"I don't buy it. Why didn't it work for me?"

"There is, for lack of a better word, an enchantment that allows me, and only me, to access my supplies. If someone were to steal my coat, they wouldn't be able to get at anything I have stored."

"What happens if someone tries to cut it up?"

Blackwing took his staff, and with a quick up and down motion, it turned into a sheathed sword. To Suzanne, it looked to be a katana.

He handed the sword to her. "Cut my coat. Anywhere you like."

She took the sword and did her best to try to cut the leather of his duster. It failed to cut or even leave a mark. She handed the sword back to him. Blackwing produced an apple-like fruit and tossed it into the air. He made two quick slashes in the air and Suzanne caught the pieces. She noticed the blade sung as it sliced through the fruit.

The next day, Blackwing placed a polished silver coin on the counter. Or that's what it appeared to be, at first glance. As Suzanne reached for it, it flattened into a band and secured itself to her wrist. It fit snuggly, and after a while, she found it was comfortable to wear. It shone brightly. She turned the band around her wrist several times, but saw no seam.

"What's this for?" she said.

"It makes you *K'obi Sha Shin J'oi Faqin*. Trusted friend to wizards, loosely translated. I use gold ones to tether prisoners to my staff. It calls them to me. Makes transporting less hazardous, but they can't be removed. This is different. This you can remove anytime you want. It also allows you to call me to you."

As Blackwing gently stroked the edges of the bracelet with his thumb and forefinger, he whispered, "N'tia K'ojin Shaq," close to her wrist, and the bracelet loosened enough to remove it. He slipped it off her wrist, showed it to her, and then replaced it. It immediately retightened.

"N'tia K'ojin Shaq," Suzanne whispered to the bracelet, and felt it loosen. She slid the bracelet off and gave it a close inspection, and blanched. "I can't accept this."

"Why not?" Blackwing appeared dispirited.

"This is *platinum*," she said. "It's worth eighty of your gold coins, and

I'll have everybody and their brother trying to get it." She blushed. "And besides, it makes me feel engaged or something."

"But it won't come off. There are no seams or catches, and it fits too snug to just slip past your wrist."

"What's to stop someone from cutting off my hand to get it? It's not going to be easy to wear more than a million creds."

Hours later, Suzanne was sitting at her keyboard, trying to figure a way to monetize a portion of Blackwing's gold.

The Government has deemed that large quantities of precious metals require a license. In fact, the amount of gold is so small that a marriage license becomes a license to own the gold in the rings. I know enough to know that what I'm contemplating is against the law, and I've never broken the law, any law, before. But now I am. I should've turned in Blackwing when he first showed up, and now I can't. I'm not certain, but I think it's something that a K'obi Sha Shin J'oi Faqin wouldn't do.

"What's bothering you?" Blackwing said, seeing the furrowing of her brow as she stared at the screen, deep in contemplation.

He set a tankard in front of her.

"Oh, nothing much. We're experiencing a negative cash flow period." She took a sip from the tankard. "Which is interesting because there's no more cash." She giggled, and saw the blank look on Blackwing's face. "Long ago, there used to be cash money. People carried it and bought things with it. Now we have the cred system. Banks hate it, which is why the people want it. Under the old system, banks could perpetrate various frauds on people through the use of math and computers. Our new system stopped those frauds, but it also stopped the ability to convert money into something more usable." She took another drink. "One of your gold coins, for example, is worth somewhere in the neighborhood of twenty thousand to forty thousand creds. The higher worth, being the aesthetic value. Both federal and state governments have deemed the amount of gold in one of your coins to be illegal without a license. I don't have a license and neither do you. We need money for food and other necessities.

Under the old system, you could sometimes find someone willing to share the value with you in return for cash, but they were usually helping someone who stole something as well. I've thought of taking a coin to a bank, to try for the aesthetic value. That idea is out because of all the questions and testing and reporting regulations. Reducing it to a bar shape would only raise more questions, because the bars are marked a certain way, from certain sources. Without the marks, it becomes questionable. Private individuals with the kind of money to buy one of the coins will require the same documentation and will probably test it. Museums would just want you to donate it." She took another sip. The other problem is your gold itself. If they run the right tests, they may find that it is of a different isotope than is found on this Earth, which will draw even more unwanted attention."

"Maybe the answer is to buy something of value with the gold, without spending it or losing track of it," Blackwing said.

"Mr. Thomlinson, your three o'clock is here," Jeff Thomlinson heard from his intercom.

He got up, looked in the mirror, straightened his gold tie and opened his office door.

"Miss Hawks and Mr. Socrates?" he said, at the threshold.

As they came toward him, Thomlinson greeted the young, shapely, auburn-haired woman—obviously a true red-head, from her coloring—and a much older blind man with long hair, carrying a white cane.

"What can I do for you?" He shut his office door.

The young woman led the man to a chair and they both sat as Thomlinson returned to his place behind his desk.

"We were led to believe that you may be able to help us," the young woman said. "This is my uncle." She hooked her arm around Mr. Socrates' arm and patted it while smiling. "He has recently returned from living in the jungles of Brazil. He has no documents and needs to live here, for medical reasons."

"So far, I see only minor difficulties, but nothing in my purview," Thomlinson said. "I'm an investment counselor. What you need is a lawyer."

"As you say. But hiring a lawyer requires large amounts of creds, of which I have few and he has none. All we have is this." She handed him a small wooden box.

Thomlinson took the box and opened it. His eyes widened as he stared in at the three gold coins.

"Where did you get these?" he said.

"My uncle… acquired them, in his travels, and wishes to put them up for collateral. He wishes you to take half the value of one of the coins and invest it, on my behalf, with funds placed into this account." Suzanne passed Thomlinson a slip of paper with a handwritten account number.

"How am I to know if they're real?" Thomlinson narrowed his eyes.

"Test them, if you like. As long as it's in our presence. You can weigh them all and test one for purity. I weighed them myself this morning, and they each weigh precisely 1.1 Troy ounces."

Thomlinson sat back in his chair to stare at the couple and to think.

"How am I to see if they are solid gold? You could be trying to pawn off gold-plated tungsten on me."

"Thus the reason why we suggested you invest half the value of one of the coins. You may drill or melt one coin only—your choice which one—to be certain it isn't a scam. However, we do expect all of this to be done in our presence, and we retain ownership of all of the gold, so the loss in testing is minimal and we are aware as to amounts."

Suzanne and Blackwing looked at Thomlinson while he was lost in thought.

"Well, first things first." Thomlinson rose from his chair and walked to the door of his office.

He mumbled something to his secretary and closed the door again.

"I told my secretary to call a friend of mine and have him bring over his testing kit. I'm not committing myself to anything, but we can see what we're talking about."

Thomlinson resettled himself in his chair and put on a jeweler's loop to inspect the coins while they all waited for the tester to arrive.

By the time the tester, a Mr. Abercrombey, arrived, Thomlinson was drooling over the three coins. They all watched as Abercrombey weighed the coins and inspected them with his own jeweler's loop. Not long after, they all trooped to Abercrombey's lab, where even more extensive tests where run. One of the coins was melted, and watched, and poured into the shape of a small gold bar. Once it was cooled, it was stamped with the weight and put back into the wooden box.

"So, Abs, what do you think?" Thomlinson asked him, in the corner of the lab, out of hearing of Suzanne and Blackwing.

"It's real gold, all right!" Abercrombey said. "Purest gold I've ever seen. I'd say its value is… um… thirty thousand for the melted one. The others are double that."

"Well, write it up and send it to my personal e-mail." Thomlinson turned and saw Suzanne standing very close.

"No reports, gentlemen," she said. "The testing was for Mr. Thomlinson's benefit, to prove it wasn't a scam. Therefore, no pictures, no reports, and no results stored anywhere."

Thomlinson, Suzanne, and Blackwing were sitting in Thomlinson's office.

"So Mr. Thomlinson, do we have a deal or not?" Suzanne said, after some time.

"It *is* a tempting offer. What is it you expect from me?"

"We expect you to do your best to invest as wisely as possible." She smiled at him. "The account I sent you is a dividend account only. We need money in it as quickly as possible, so do what you do best."

"I'll invest twenty thousand creds against your three coins, but I hold the coins. They will be locked in a box that requires two keys to open. You'll have one and I'll have the other."

"And after a year," Blackwing said, "if you've made us money, you'll get the melted one as a bonus. If I like something, Miss Hawks will call you and tell you, and you can buy it. You're free to invest in anything I come up with."

"Agreed!" Thomlinson offered his hand to the older man.

"You're not trying to cheat me, are you?" Blackwing took the younger man's hand.

"Not at all. You can trust me," Thomlinson said, as they locked the coins away.

"How long do you think it'll take?" Suzanne led her older *blind uncle* out of the high-rise.

"Less than a year, certainly," Blackwing said. "Probably six to nine months."

"What do you think the return will be?" she asked.

"It depends. If Thomlinson is as good as he thinks he is, I'm sure it'll be sizeable."

Upon returning to the shop, Blackwing presented Suzanne with a necklace. The pendant was one of his gold coins.

"Wearing one of these is considered good luck," he said. "Wear it always and keep it in contact with your skin."

Since Suzanne put on the necklace Blackwing had given her months before, her ability to predict the markets became uncanny. Most of the time, her mind was focused on market volatility and trends. Consequently, she dabbled and managed to rake in a tidy sum on her own, which she kept separate from the investment account.

Suzanne checked the investment account daily, and in less than a week money was starting to trickle into it. After a month, the credits were fairly pouring in. At six months, she wasn't rich by anyone's standard, but she wasn't hurting either. In the eighth month, little or nothing came into the account.

Blackwing knew the time had come to dissolve the partnership.

Suzanne and Blackwing were sitting in Thomlinson's office, under their guise of blind uncle and dutiful niece. After a few minutes of waiting, Suzanne got a phone call.

"Hello, Thomlinson." She put the phone on share so Blackwing could listen.

"I should be there momentarily." Thomlinson panted.

"Well, my uncle and I have been waiting for quite some time. You're not skipping out on us, are you?"

"What? Never. As I've said, you can trust me. I just got a little jammed up in my schedule today. I'll be seeing you and your uncle soon. Bye."

Thomlinson had just hung up the phone, when his rental, a vintage Gulfstream G200, was ready for takeoff.

Those rubes got nothing on me. He felt the old plane pick up speed. *I made them all the creds they wanted and more. I know they're going to take back the gold—my gold. They had no idea the box had four keys, and I've had the coins out several times from the beginning. Now they want them and they belong to me. They won't get them.*

As the plane became airborne, he relaxed. *I'm on my way to Canada, where no one can find me.* With his eyes closed, he suddenly felt that something was wrong. When he snapped his eyes open, he saw Mr. Socrates sitting across the plane from him. No longer blind, but wearing an eyepatch and looking markedly different, more disheveled.

"What are you doing here?" the young man said.

"You lied to us, Thomlinson."

"I did what I said I'd do. I made you lots of credits."

"But you also stole the coins from us. You said we could trust you."

Thomlinson rose to his feet, his fists balled at his side as he faced Socrates. He glared at the figure and lashed out his fist to strike him squarely in the jaw. Only, instead of Socrates, his punch connected with the vintage aircraft's window, with a terrifying force, breaking the seal. Alarms blared throughout the plane and several of the crew tied him in his seat.

"We did get our coins back, you know." Socrates' image smirked. "You gave them back when you lied to us. Be sure to check as soon as you can. You'll find that the gold isn't in your possession."

Suzanne saw the flashing notification of a breaking news story on her tablet.

"*Breaking news,*" she heard, as she viewed the notification. "*A vintage*

Gulfstream G200 was forced to return to Pacific Northwest Airport when one of its passengers became unruly and destructive. The aircraft was on a private charter to Canada. The co-pilot aboard the flight reports, 'We had just taken off when the passenger started ranting. Then he hit the window and broke the seal. It took everyone on board to subdue him and return him to his seat.' The passenger was identified as Jeffrey Thomlinson, longtime resident and investment counselor from Tacoma. Mister Thomlinson was taken to the Pacific Northwest Medical Center for psychological evaluation."

5

IT'S WHAT'S ON THE INSIDE

Detective Jessica Sylvillagys, Tacoma PD, entered the precinct and walked to her desk. She set her tablet on the desk and it automatically started to sync with the network. She sat and watched the screen, studying the alerts as they popped up, and perused each, making notes on her tablet as she sipped her coffee.

Nothing really piqued her interest as she scrolled through them. *Same old bullshit. Idiots killing idiots.*

The first one pertained to Joe "Crackin' " Johnson, Thomas "DA Tom" O'Toole, and Trevor "Shooter" Peterson, in a brief report on a forced entry.

The second related to questioning of Johnson in the E.R.

A third pertained to Jeffrey Thomlinson, resident and investment counselor going crackers while in a private plane.

The newest one got her attention. She set her drink aside to study it closer. It listed Peterson as a possible victim in a homicide. The computer had flagged them because of a name common to all the reports. All the alerts were linked, in various ways, to a Suzanne Hawks.

Jessica sat back and took another sip of her coffee and did a quick background check on Hawks. *Why would common street thugs do a forced entry on a bookstore?* She scanned the screen. *And what would an investment counselor have to do with an owner of a marginally profitable business?*

She scanned through the most recent preliminary investigative report while continuing to sip her coffee. *That's odd. How does a body end up inside out?*

Suzanne had opened her store, just like any other day, and was checking investments on her handheld when Blackwing entered.

He sat in his normal spot at the counter. "I may need your assistance with a few purchases."

"What kinds of purchases?" she said, without looking up.

"Books, of course."

"We're in a damn bookstore. What kind of books are you trying to purchase?"

"Old books." He pulled out his tankard and took a sip.

Suzanne started rubbing her forehead with her thumb and forefinger. "I figured that out already. What are the subjects of the books?"

"Magic. What you'd call magic, anyway."

She stopped to look at him and noticed he was in his blind uncle disguise.

"You're serious?" she said.

Blackwing shrugged. "Of course."

"Are these books going to be for sale?" she asked, irritated.

"Part of my mission here is to secure magical objects. So no, they won't be for sale. I've noticed from watching you that people sell old books without really knowing what they have. I have contacted a few people who have very old books on magic. It'll probably come to nothing, but you never know."

"How do you know they're magical?"

Blackwing paused for a second. "Anything with magic leaves a… residue behind. This," he touched the temple of the dark glasses by his ruined eye, "coupled with my sphere, enables me to see the residue. The more residue present, the more magic."

"And if it's a person?"

"If you could look through this," he touched the temple of the dark glasses again, "and see me, you'd see what I mean. A person of magic glows with it, to the point of being blindingly bright. It is, after all, the source of magical power."

"And what do you see when you look at me?"

"I see your *K'obi Sha Shin J'oi Faqin T'orqute*," he indicated her bracelet, "and your *Sha Shin T'orqute*." He indicated her necklace.

"Bracelet and necklace?"

"Yes, bracelet and necklace. They both shine brightly."

"And me?" She raised her eyebrows.

"When I first entered your shop, I saw something very dim on you. It indicated that you had touched or been in contact with something, or someone, magical."

"Well, that's a relief. Sure wouldn't want any residue on me."

"I'm going to meet someone. If I find something promising, I'll tell them to come to the shop and see you about the purchasing details. I shouldn't be gone long."

You really know how to hurt a girl. She watched him leave the store. *All girls want to feel magical.*

An hour later, the electronic chime went off and Suzanne looked up, expecting Blackwing. Instead, a leggy blonde wearing a tight, black, combat unitard, which hid little, strode—or was she slithering—into the store and Suzanne could see, by her aggressive walk and her dress, that she was a cop. Suzanne turned on the video function on her phone and set it aside.

"Detective Sylvillagys," she flashed her credentials, "Tacoma PD. You are—" she checked her tablet, "Suzanne Hawks?"

"Yes?"

"I understand that you know—" the detective consulted her tablet again, "a Jeffrey Thomlinson?"

"Yes."

She checked her device again. "And a Joseph Johnson?"

"I'm not familiar with that name."

"No? How about a—" she consulted the tablet yet again, "Trevor Peterson?"

Suzanne shook her head. "No, that name doesn't sound familiar, either."

"Ah, well, you probably know them by Crackin and Shooter." The detective narrowed her eyes.

"*Those* names are familiar to me." Suzanne paled.

The detective set her tablet on the counter and Suzanne could see the light indicating that this encounter was being recorded.

"Can you tell me," she leaned on the counter, getting closer to

Suzanne, "why a financial counselor would know someone like you? I can understand the other two, given the state of this store and its location." The detective sniffed disapprovingly as she glanced around the store.

"What's that supposed to mean?"

"Come on, Hawks. I've seen your tax records for the last few years, and according to them you barely eke out a living here. What would you need with a financial counselor? I doubt you can keep any creds at all in this dump. As far as the location goes, I'd be surprised if you didn't know every criminal type in the city."

"My business is *my* business, not yours." Suzanne raised her voice. "What I need a financial counselor for is none of your concern."

"Until it becomes *my* concern." The detective flashed a wry grin. "According to our records, Joseph Johnson was admitted to the Pacific Northwest Med Center for psychological evaluation, as was Jeffrey Thomlinson. Add to that, this morning Trevor Peterson was the victim of a homicide. You are the connection between all of them, in my opinion." The detective glared at Suzanne.

Suzanne's face turned red. "First, I know nothing of those people or why they would be in the hospital. I had a few business dealings with Thomlinson, but I have no idea what caused him to do anything. The other two are only known to me because they decided to push their way in here. Second, if you had any proof about a connection to me, I'd be in custody until you sorted it out. That tells me you have nothing and are trying to intimidate me. I've told you what I know, so now, you need to leave!"

The detective grinned at her, smugly. "I think I'll order a safety check on this place. I'm thinking there may be a chemical leak, or something similar, causing all the problems. They would shut you down until it's completed." Her grin broadened. "It would take at least a year for the paperwork to get started, but they would close this place immediately, as a threat to public health and safety."

"You could," Suzanne said. "I've been recording this entire conversation, full audio and video streaming, to my attorney's office."

"You have an attorney, too? Interesting. But that doesn't bother me. I have the City behind me and your attorney wouldn't even make a good snack. No, as you said, I have no proof connecting you to anything illegal. Not yet, anyway. But I'll keep digging. You can count on it." The detective handed her a card. "In case you decide you want to chat."

Suzanne watched as the detective strode out of her store.

James McConnel was sitting at his desk, watching the heated discussion between Jessica Sylvillagys and Suzanne Hawks. Brian Trevail was standing behind him.

"You know she won't quit digging." McConnel turned to face Trevail. "She'll dig until she finds things she shouldn't."

"Her case has nothing to do with the Hawks woman," Trevail said. "There's nothing on that trail to find."

"But what if she does? I'm not going down for anything you have going on."

"She won't. I'll see to it that she stays focused on her case and not on us or our dealings with Hawks. Don't worry."

McConnel shook his head as he turned back to his screen. "When somebody says *don't worry*, I start worrying."

When Blackwing returned, he found Suzanne waiting and upset.

"What did you do to all those people?" she said.

"What people are you talking about?"

"The police were here today. Shortly after you left, in fact. Did you know that one of the assholes who tried to rob me was killed?" Suzanne watched his reaction, thinking she'd know if he were lying. "Another of the gang is in the hospital with psychological problems, along with Thomlinson. Did you know that?"

"No, I wasn't aware of those developments."

The sphere in his pocket was flashing quickly and Blackwing had information displayed about psychological problems.

"So Thomlinson and the man are locked up and being treated?" he said.

"Treated! Don't make me laugh. Damn doctors, anyway. Two hundred years of trying to find a cure for cancer and they can only *manage* it. They don't want to cure anything. Thomlinson is probably locked in a padded cell, wearing a straitjacket and getting his brain fried with drugs or electricity until he doesn't know who he is. I don't know, but they used to do lobotomies, so who knows what they're doing to him."

Through her tirade, Blackwing had his eyes closed, concentrating on the incoming information the sphere was providing.

"Surely not!" he said, after a short time to digest the information. "How did the other guy die?"

"I have no idea. I was trying to monitor the news, but found nothing. The police probably have a media blackout on the subject.

"Do you remember the cop's name?"

"Detective Jessica Sylvillagys," Suzanne read from the card.

Jessica Sylvillagys threw herself into her chair and slid her electronic notepad across her desk. On its trip to the far side of the desktop, it clipped a plastic coffee cup a third-full of ice-cold coffee from three days prior, spilling the rancid black liquid across Detective Sergeant Jon Crawford's desk.

"Hey! Watch it, Jess. This is a new suit for my retirement."

"Sorry, Jon, but how can you tell it's a new one and not just a spruced-up version of an old one? Did you check it for bullet holes?" She smirked. "Besides, you're too young to retire."

"Most days I feel like I'm a hundr'd and fifty instead of the sixty years I actually am." Crawford dabbed the liquid from his desktop. "So what's up? Why the tantrum?"

"This case has me annoyed. No one saw anything in the area of the homicide. The coroner's report doesn't tell me shit, either. They have no idea how someone can be turned inside-out, and live."

"Live? You mean, he survived it?"

"They guess he lived for less than thirty seconds. Just until his heart gave out, his lungs collapsed, and the massive aneurysm hit his brain. One of the techies said something about a rough trip through an interdimensional vortex. I've got pictures, if you want to see."

"What does that even mean?" Crawford held his hand up, shaking his head. "Do you know who he is?"

"DNA matches Trevor Peterson aka Shooter. They did say he was juicing, though. They even cut open his leg. Do you know what they found? Skin! How is that even possible?"

"You're asking the wrong guy. By the way, Cap'n wants to see you."

Jessica stood before the opaque closed door of the captain's office and took stock of her appearance before passing her left wrist over the scanner in the doorframe. She heard nothing, but waited patiently for the door to slide open. When it did, she took a deep breath and entered.

Captain Marshall Trooper sat behind his desk, glaring at Jess.

"Tell me about the homicide," he said.

"We know who he was, but not how he was killed or by whom."

Jessica kept it brief. She had put all the particulars in her daily report and she knew the captain always read her reports.

"I have been informed that you questioned the Hawk's woman."

Jessica could see his jaw muscles flexing.

"Yes, sir. I thought she could shed some light on the matter and that she may have info on other open cases."

"Did you see anything that would lead you to believe she had anything to do with the homicide?" the captain said, in a gruff tone.

"No, sir. I thought—"

"You thought! You're paid to *do*, not to *think*. You're supposed to bag 'em and tag 'em, and we'll worry about the rest if someone important asks questions. You're to leave the Hawks woman alone. No talking to her. No surveillance. No harassment of any kind. Understood?" By the time he'd finished, he was standing, with his palms flat on the desk, his face so red it looked like it had been sunburned.

"Yes sir, I understand."

"Sorry, Sylvillagys. I like it less than you do, but it comes from higher up."

"Understood, Cap'n." Jessica grinned. "So you want me to drop the case?"

Captain Trooper plopped into his chair, put his elbows on the desk, his head in his hands, and exhaled loudly.

"No." He finally looked up at her. "Just leave the Hawks woman alone, okay?"

"And if the facts lead me to her?"

"Unless you see her doing it, *and* have it on video, hands off."

"Got it, sir."

"Get out of here and do your job for a change." Trooper smirked.

He still wants me to continue digging. Jessica left the captain's office and the door closed. *His bosses want me to back off. Someone has tentacles into the PD.*

As Jessica was leaving the precinct, she saw someone in the shadows between the buildings ahead of her. A flick of the wrist and her stunner assembled itself in her hand.

"Thirty million volts available," the weapon said.

"I'm not here to hurt you," the shadow said, with a deep penetrating voice, "but you can fire your weapon if it will make you feel better."

She felt the timbre of his voice in her bones and it scared her. Reflexively, she fired and four metal darts, each packing two hundred fifty thousand volts, shot out. They struck the shadow's coat and bounced off.

Jessica raised her weapon close to her mouth. "Nine!" she said, and the weapon reconfigured itself.

"Nine millimeter. Fifty rounds available," the weapon said.

Jessica pulled the trigger again and nothing happened. Dumbfounded, she looked at her weapon and then to the shadow, which was holding out a plastic card.

"Yours?" it said.

She took the card and saw it was one of hers. "Yes, it's mine."

The shadow closed its hand and another card popped between his fingers. She gingerly took it. It was plastic, similar to hers, but the background was so black it was like looking into a void. In red script that seemed to be suspended in the void, she saw *Blackwing*. Below the red letters, writing with realistic flames appeared—*Wizard*.

"Pretty fancy card. Must've set you back some." Jessica tried to regain her composure. "What exactly is a wizard?"

The card, which she'd been grasping between her fingers, disappeared.

"I understand you have a case that is… unusual?" the shadow said.

Jessica tried to concentrate on the shadowy figure, but it appeared to be on the verge of vanishing. Almost like a ghost. Not that she believed in such nonsense.

"I have a homicide that is hard to explain, at the moment. Do you know anything about it?"

"What caused the demise?" the shadow said. "Do you have pictures?"

"We don't know yet."

Without thinking, she produced her tablet and scrolled to a picture of Peterson's mutilated body, and turned it to the shadow. She hadn't intended to show or tell this specter anything.

"This was not intentional," the shadow said. "This appears to be a person who was too close to a closing portal."

"A what?"

"A closing portal," the shadow repeated. "Someone on this Plane opened a portal. This individual was caught in the… backwash, is the best word."

"So you're saying this was accidental? Are you sure, or are you offering a theory? If it was intentional, how could you tell?"

"It could be intentional if there were a third party to push this person into the edge of the portal just at the right moment. But that would be unconscionable for anyone who had the skill to open the portal in the first place, or of anyone with the knowledge of portals."

"This all seems sketchy to me. I need you to come to my office and give us a statement."

"I just did."

"No, I mean a statement on the record. Something official."

"This is as *official* as I get. Take it or leave it. It matters not to me."

"How do I contact you again?" she hurried to ask, as the shadow started to disappear.

"Advertise for a wizard." The shadow vanished.

6

RELUCTANT PARTNERS

The next morning when Jessica arrived at the precinct, she headed for the break room where all the techies hung out. She found the one she wanted and dragged him to a corner table. For the first time she noticed his nametag on his lab coat—*Strange*—and had to stifle a chuckle. *He certainly is.*

"Yesterday you said something about an interdimensional vortex," she said. "What exactly is that?" When the Tech was reluctant to answer, she said, "It's for a case."

"I don't know what an interdimensional vortex is… exactly," the techie replied, nervously, pushing his safety glasses up onto the bridge of his nose. "It's a theory, mine or someone else's, that the universe here—our universe—is like a single sheet of paper in a ream of paper, or universes. And theoretically, a vortex could be created to pass between the universes. Why do you ask?"

"Last night I met someone who talks just like you do, except he used the term *portal* instead of *interdimensional vortex*. I'm assuming they're the same thing?"

"Yes, well, theoretically," again pushing his glasses up, "they are the same. Who was he?" His eyes reflected his awe.

Jessica glanced around and leaned toward him. "A wizard named Blackwing," she whispered.

Strange tried to stifle his chuckles. "You're joking with me, aren't you? Someone put you up to this?" He looked around to see who was watching and if anyone was laughing.

"What do you know of the standard stunner? Is it possible for the darts not to penetrate?"

The techie thought about it for a second. "Kevlar or carbon nanofibers, maybe, if they were treated properly. Why?"

"The wizard took four darts and they bounced off a coat that appeared to be leather. At least, it moved like it was."

"What did you do?" Strange said, with rapt attention.

"I tried to fire a few nine-mill rounds, but my gun wouldn't fire."

"Did he do something to you? Did he hit you with a spell or a light from a wand?" Strange chuckled.

"No, nothing like that. My weapon transformed normally, but wouldn't fire."

"Bring it to my lab and I'll check it. Your service weapon is extremely tough, and shielded. It should work, as long as it's not vaporized."

They both rose and left for the armory lab.

After an hour of testing, Strange found nothing wrong with the service weapon.

"I don't know what to tell you. Your weapon works and fires in all modes, just like it's supposed to." He shook his head.

"I'm not lying or playing a joke," Jessica growled. "I wouldn't do that. I fired the darts and then tried the nine-millimeter and it wouldn't fire. I didn't freeze or hesitate. I followed protocol and my training."

The techie shrugged. "I wasn't there and I have no idea what you did. Did you see anything else?"

"He showed me his card."

Strange's eyebrows shot up.

"And before you ask, it disappeared while I was holding it."

"What did it look like?"

"It looked like an abyss with red lettering and flames."

"I can do that. Most professional printers can."

"No. I mean it had actual moving flames spelling out *Wizard*. I've seen all the printers work and this was not something they can do. It looked like a solid hologram, but without anything external for the projection."

"Impressive! Did he say how you can get in touch with him again? I doubt he has a phone or any tech that we're familiar with."

"Why do you say that?"

"If he really is familiar with interdimensional portals, our simple tech would interfere with it. Something as simple as an ID would probably kill the wearer if he should get too close to a portal's event horizon."

"Great. That'll make him easy to find."

The morning after Blackwing's meeting with Jessica Sylvillagys, Suzanne opened her store and then started pacing. Thirty minutes later, Blackwing walked in without his disguise.

"Where the hell have you been? I've been a wreck, worrying about getting arrested," she blasted, before he even sat down. "That cop can come back at any time and haul me away. Where would you be then?"

"I would be getting you un-arrested," Blackwing replied, stoically. "I'd not let you languish in a dungeon."

"Um… they don't use dungeons anymore. They lock you behind bars. If I was arrested, how would you know? You gave me this thing and never told me how to call you with it." She showed her bracelet.

He looked at her blankly and set a pewter tankard in front of her.

"How do you fill that?" He motioned to the tankard.

"I tap the handle. Is that all I have to do? Tap the bracelet?"

"Yes, tap it three times."

"What is it with you and the number three?"

"Your history is replete with instances of triads. Three dimensions for object descriptions, triangles, three sides to a story, to name a few, and you ask me about threes?"

"So three is a *magic* number?"

"In many cultures, yes, it is."

"What happens if someone else taps my bracelet?"

"Nothing. It's keyed to you and only you."

Blackwing's sphere sent an alert to his left eye, of an ad placed seconds ago. *"Blackwing, same time, same place, tonight,"* it said.

"As far as the detective goes," Blackwing said, "I'm doing what I can to deter her from investigating you any further."

"I wish I could believe that," Suzanne mumbled ruefully.

Detective Sylvillagys was pacing outside the precinct. She'd been waiting longer than she liked for Blackwing to show.

"Yes?" she heard, from a shadowy doorway. "You called this meeting, so speak."

She recognized the voice by the timber and the chill it gave her.

"Is there anything you can do to direct me on the portal murder?" *I hate asking, but it's my only chance for a lead.*

"I could observe the scene of criminal activity," the voice said. "That may shed some insight into the matter."

"Great. I have a vehicle over here—"

"Just tell me where it is."

"Fifteenth and South G Street," she said, after a loud exhale.

She immediately felt dizzy, and queasiness in her stomach. When the dizziness passed, she looked around at the familiar street corner. The scene of the crime was in a desolate part of the city. To her it looked like it was bombed out.

"How did you do that?" she asked, with some fear in her voice.

"Show me," the shadow said.

As they walked, Jessica got a glimpse of her companion from a distant street light. All she saw was dark hat and coat, with spindly legs and arms, and it was tall. At one point during their walk, she did glimpse a hint of a nasty scar as well.

"Here it is," she said, when they reached the police barricades which indicated the crime scene.

She saw Blackwing produce a walking stick, seemingly from nowhere, the end of which glowed and cast a deep blood-red hue over the area. She saw ghostly images of people, and a huge vortex. She saw someone enter the swirling tunnel, and as it closed, a very short person pushed another into the edge of it. The victim began to be turned inside out, in a gruesome fashion.

"It appears," Jessica said, when the show ended, "that we were both right. It was due to a portal, and Trevor Peterson was pushed by a third party. That is, assuming of course, that what I saw is what really happened and wasn't some sham."

"You confuse me," Blackwing said. "You asked for help and I've given it. I've shown you what happened, and still you doubt what you've seen."

"You're an enigma wrapped in a mystery. How can I trust someone who can play with reality? Am I to take what you say on faith?"

"You saw the placement of the body, and the vortex," he boomed. "Does that coincide with your facts?"

"It does, and you showed me that I'm looking for two individuals who are connected to the incident. All I have to do now is prove everything, using our tech."

"You can try."

"What's that supposed to mean?" Jessica said, in a gruff tone.

"It means the person who opened and used the portal is beyond your reach. I know of the other, and you won't catch him."

"The portal could re-open here again. So you do know the third person."

"I know *of* him. I don't know *him*. And portals of this kind seldom re-open in the same location. The reason is… technical. If you somehow managed to apprehend that particular individual, he'd escape. He is for me to apprehend."

"You can handle him?" She chuckled. "You couldn't handle anyone. A strong wind would send you reeling. He looked to be rather substantial."

"Believe what you will. You're free to search or test or whatever else you do," Blackwing turned to leave.

"Wait. Don't go," Jessica said, contrite. "Since we'll be working together on this, I would like a better means of communication. How can I call you if I need you?"

"I've not agreed to work with you on anything. However, you have access to resources that may prove to be advantageous."

"Advantageous to whom?"

"Both of us. There is a means available, if I can trust you."

"To be frank, I'm only concerned with closing this case. Your skills would be an asset, but if there's any arresting to be done, I'll do it."

"I find those terms agreeable," Blackwing said, after a second of thought. He reached into a pocket and produced a gold coin. "Push up your sleeve a little."

"Why?" Jessica asked, even as she complied with his request.

She heard him mumble something.

"Hold out your hand," he said.

When Jessica held out her right hand, Blackwing dropped the coin onto her palm. Stunned, she watched as the coin, of its own accord, liquefied once it contacted her skin, and transformed into a band just above her right wrist. She held up her arm to look at the band, and saw no seam.

"How does this work?" She felt for a seam somewhere on the band.

"You tap it three times and I'll locate you."

"You were late, by the way." Jessica pulled her sleeve down over the band and slipped her hand into the strap that kept the sleeve in place, covering the back of her hand. "It's a hell of a way to start a partnership." She chuckled, shaking her head.

"I wasn't late. I was there long before you arrived. I had to be certain it wasn't a trap."

"It would appear that there are some trust issues going both ways."

"It appears so," Blackwing said.

They both disappeared and re-appeared where they started. Jessica was disoriented again, but less than the first time.

"You know something about the third person, don't—" Jessica looked around for Blackwing, but he was already gone, "—you?"

It was late when Jessica arrived at her apartment. The door opened at her approach.

"*Good evening, Jessica,*" the apartment said, as she entered.

"Lights, soft," Jessica said, as the door closed behind her.

She strode through the living area and kitchen, into her bedroom.

"Shower, hot." She took off the unitard and went into the bathroom.

The shower was already up to the temperature she liked when she entered the shower stall. A few minutes later, she was drying off and noticed the gold band. She had almost forgotten it was there. As she looked at it, her mind was wandering back to the events that led to her having it. After she finished toweling off, she stood in front of the mirror with the towel wrapped around her hips. When she looked up, she saw Blackwing in the mirror, and quickly turned to find... nothing.

"Just to be clear," the image said, "if there are any more... unnatural events, I expect to be notified as soon as possible."

"How are you doing this? Can't a girl have a little privacy?" Jessica stormed at the image.

"The how is unimportant. The why is. Do you agree?"

"Yeah, sure, whatever. Just respect my boundaries. This is crossing those boundaries."

The image of Blackwing, in the mirror, faded and was replaced with her own.

Blackwing, sitting in the basement storage of the bookstore, pondered the events of the previous evening.

The images were faded and blurred from the amount of time that passed since they occurred, but I recognized the user of the portal. Why would one of the T'et Faqin Q'estirion be opening a portal from here? A brown faerie either in league with him or just present. Either way, they were both breaking the edicts. Who of the T'et Faqin could open a portal? He knew he couldn't, and the magic required was beyond his capabilities. *I have to get the Sh'o Sook J'eid to open a portal.*

"And the wood nymphs are hard to get past, with their obsession with male beauty." He touched his scar. "If it weren't for this, I would have set up my own household long ago."

Suzanne had heard the basement door open when it was just a few hours from closing. When she looked up, she saw Blackwing, in his blind uncle disguise, come over and sit at the counter, in his usual spot.

"Have a nice rest?" She was concentrating on what was on the screen in front of her.

"No. I did rest, but recent activities have distressed me." He pulled out his tankard and another for Suzanne, as he usually did.

"Want to talk about it?" She took a sip from the tankard.

"Maybe later, after closing. You have a customer," he said, without looking toward the door.

The electronic chime sounded and Suzanne looked up and blanched.

"Detective Sylvillagys, what, uh, brings you here?"

"Relax, I'm not here for you. I'm here researching something. Who is this?" Jessica asked, upon seeing the older blind man sitting at the counter.

As she looked him up and down, she noticed the white cane and disheveled clothing. He was slumped over, sipping something from what appeared to be a very old ornate tankard.

"This is my uncle Socrates. What are you researching?"

Jessica pursed her lips, leaned on the counter to get closer to Suzanne, and looked side to side.

"Wizards," she whispered, glancing up at the surveillance camera.

Suzanne blanched again. "My uncle has more expertise than me to answer your questions or direct you to the proper books."

Blackwing sat a little straighter and turned to extend his hand toward the detective.

"Pleased to meet you, miss," he said.

"Detective. Pleased to meet you, sir." Jessica trapped the thin, long-fingered hand that had been waving around trying to locate her, and shook it. "Is there somewhere private we can talk?"

"Why? It's just the cops listening and watching. You're a cop. Besides, that thing's off more than it's on." Blackwing chuckled.

"Why don't you two use my office," Suzanne said.

"We could do that, too," Blackwing said.

As he got to his feet, he was careful to stoop and swing the cane from side to side as he proceeded to Suzanne's office, with Jessica following closely.

"How can I help?" Blackwing asked, after he'd sat in Suzanne's office chair and Jessica had closed the door.

"I need to know if there really are wizards," Jessica said.

"I suppose there are," Blackwing said, after a brief pause. "I'd like to think there are, anyway. Did you know that most wizards are portrayed as old codgers because it would take them a lifetime to learn what they'd need to know?"

"I didn't know that." Jessica gave a wry smile. "I guess I'd never thought about it. Do they have any weaknesses?"

"Hmm… wizards are like anyone else, and we all have our weaknesses." Blackwing waited until Jessica exhaled loudly. "Why are you really here? I mean, I enjoy the company of a pretty girl as much as the next man, but I get the feeling you came for some specific purpose and don't know how to broach the subject."

Jessica paced across the small room several times.

"I think I met a wizard," she said, finally.

"You think? You mean, you don't know?"

"I've never met a wizard before and I only know a little from books. I used to chalk it all up to utter nonsense, until two days ago."

"What happened to change your mind?"

"I met a shadow with an impossible business card," she whispered.

"What did he look like? Did you get a good look at him?"

"Not a good look, but he was tall and thin and dressed in black. He says he's a wizard, but how can I tell?"

"All I know is from old books, and from what they say wizards are very old and secretive. They are jealous of their privacy, and if they want to talk to you, they have their ways and their reasons. If someone says they're a wizard and you see proof, usually in the form of them doing something you can't do, then believe it, at least to the point that they show you otherwise."

"But how do I know if I can trust him?" Jessica pleaded.

"How do you know you can trust anyone?"

"That's easy." Jessica gave a wry chuckle. "You can't."

"You may be a little jaded. Sometimes you have to get outside of the normal and comfortable and take a chance. Trust your instincts. In the end, it's all you have."

"You're saying I should trust him?"

"I'm saying you should trust your own judgment. On another matter, what are you going to do about my niece? Are you going to shut her down?"

"No. I was directed to leave her alone, and that's my plan. Unless, of course, something happens to change my thinking."

"That's as fair an answer as we can ask for. Is there anything else I can help you with?"

"Not at the present. If I think of something, or something comes up, can I return? I would appreciate any light you can shed on the wizard, if you wouldn't mind. I've searched the web and found very little on the subject. I thought with all your books you may find something useful."

"You can return anytime you like. During business hours, of course." Blackwing smiled.

"Of course." Jessica flashed her own smile.

How long has it been since I smiled? Maybe I am jaded.

7

THE OGRE COMETH

After the shop was closed, Blackwing and Suzanne were sitting at the counter, each with a tankard.

"So what's going on with the cop?" Suzanne said.

"We're working on a case. She was assigned to the murder of Trevor Peterson. He was the one called Shooter," he added, seeing her confusion with the given name.

"Was he? Murdered, I mean."

"All the facts concerning his death aren't known yet, but it would appear that beings from my Plane have been crossing back and forth."

"So why does that disturb you? You knew that was happening shortly after your arrival."

"He died from the backwash of a Gate. That indicates that someone, one of my brothers, may be involved. They're definitely involved in violating the Council's edict. What bothers me about it is I have no idea how that was accomplished. My kind isn't supposed to be able to create a portal. We rely on the *Sh'o Sook J'eid*. You would call them wood nymphs. They're Keepers of the Gates, preservers of portal knowledge. Added to that, there's a brown... gnome here."

"A gnome? That doesn't sound too intimidating. A little gnome." she chuckled.

"The little gnome you're chuckling about can grow to be six-feet tall, under the proper conditions, and are thickly muscled, very tough. Usually they're five-feet tall. They have a tendency towards nasty dispositions. Under normal conditions they can be subdued without too much trouble, as long as you keep your wits about you."

"So a youngster can grow that big," she shrugged. "I doubt they would involve a youngster, would they?"

"I think you're misunderstanding me. If you over-feed them, you end up with a huge gnome, at any age."

Suzanne stared at him in shock. "I think I understand. If they're overfed, you have a big problem. At least there's only one."

"I only saw the evidence of one. They usually run in packs of thirty to forty. When you see one, there are more close at hand."

Suzanne hung her head. "Sorry I made light of the situation. I didn't comprehend the enormity of it."

Blackwing exhaled audibly. "I know. You *are* helping me, you know, by talking about it. Our conversation is helping me to order my thoughts and attempt to put together a plan."

"Would it be better to talk to Sylvillagys about this, to make a plan and to inform her of the danger?"

Blackwing could see the concern in her expression.

"That raises another complication. My operating parameters are to maintain what you would call a low profile. You're *K'obi Sha Shin J'oi Faqin*." Blackwing shrugged. "You're the one I should be talking to about this."

"Well, I brought it up because I'm no tactical genius. She would know more about this situation than I would. Speaking of which, should we be talking about this?" Suzanne glanced to the surveillance camera.

"Since you locked the door, I've made us invisible from the outside and from their prying eyes and ears." Blackwing sipped from his tankard.

When Jessica arrived at the precinct, she sought out Strange. She found him in his lab running some tests.

"Good evening, Detective. What can I do for you?"

"What time are you finished?"

"I'm on unpaid overtime as it is, so I could be done now. Why do you ask?"

"Let's get a drink. Meet me at Tony's when you're done."

"Sounds good to me." He appeared shocked at the invitation.

An hour later, they were both sitting in a secluded booth at Tony's Bar & Grill. Jessica was still in her combat unitard. Strange in his street clothes, jeans, and a light shirt. Both looked like they had come in straight from work, which they had.

"As nice, and surprising, as this is," Strange said, "I can't help wonder what you want. So, tell me."

"Can I trust you?" Jessica asked. "I mean, can I trust you keep what we talk about to yourself?"

"Sure, you can trust me with anything. Nobody talks to me anyway."

"I chose this place because it lacks surveillance and we need to talk." Jessica took a deep breath and exhaled slowly through puffed cheeks. "My *friend* has informed me that Trevor Peterson was murdered."

"Really! Someone actually had the means to turn someone inside out?"

"Sort of."

She glanced around before leaning on the table, and Strange did the same.

"He was pushed into a closing vortex," she whispered.

"How do you know that?" Strange whispered.

"I saw it… sort of. My *friend* and I went to the crime scene and he showed me."

"How did he do *that*?"

"It's my working theory that he showed me the residual energies. It was all very stra—umm… unusual and eerie. Is my theory plausible?"

"A vortex, like the one we've been describing, would require vast amounts of energy, and thus, would leave behind quite a bit of residual energy. But it would dissipate quickly. People would leave behind some as well. We don't have that kind of tech, but if you were shown, then I would believe it. Can I meet *him*? I would really like that!"

"I'm sure you would," Jessica replied.

"Anything else?"

Jessica took another deep breath and slid her sleeve up to reveal the gold band.

"He gave me this," she said, as she exhaled.

Strange leaned to inspect the band. "Is it real?"

"Very, and I think it's alive."

"How do you mean?"

"Try to get your finger under it." Jessica offered her wrist.

As Strange tried to get a finger under the band, he felt and saw it close down tighter on her wrist.

"That's a neat trick!"

Jessica turned her arm so Strange could see it completely. "There's no seam, either."

"How did he put it on you?"

"He pulled out a coin, mumbled a few words, and dropped it in my hand. The coin melted and then transformed itself around my wrist."

"Nah." Strange chuckled. "The melting point of gold would be enough to burn off your wrist. It's just under two thousand degrees Fahrenheit, so I'm skeptical."

"Why would I lie? What would it gain me? You're the only one I can talk to about this, so why would I lie?"

"I'm not saying you are. I'm skeptical of my own senses. I'd like to see if I can cut it off or get a sample, at least. Anything else?"

Jessica could feel herself blush. "He was in a mirror in my apartment."

"Really? Could you communicate?"

"Of course. Weird, huh?"

"You talked to him in such a manner as to eliminate the possibility of it being a recording, a hologram, or a projection of some sort?"

"It was my medicine cabinet mirror. I could see me and his ghostly image. The wall it's on divides my apartment from Edith Johnson's. That old biddy wouldn't let anyone in her place for any reason."

Strange sipped his scotch, contemplating.

Jessica sipped some of her own drink. "So what are you thinking?"

"I'm thinking we have an honest-to-goodness wizard on our hands. Did he tell you what the purpose of the band is?"

"He said I could let him know that I wanted to talk to him with it."

"How do you let him know with that?"

"He said to tap it three times."

Later, after escorting Strange back to his lab, Jessica exited the precinct-provided ground car in the underground parking of her building, and headed toward the elevator. She hadn't gone far when something hit her from behind. When her head hit the pavement, she lost consciousness.

When Jessica came to, before opening her eyes she tried to take stock of her situation. She was sitting, naked, in a heavy wooden chair. Her hands and feet were restrained. Her right wrist burned terribly. She slowly opened her eyes. Flashes of pain ran through her brain, causing her to wince and close them again.

"I know you are conscious, Sylvillagys. No need to pretend," a voice said, from behind her.

She heard no shuffling feet or anything else to indicate there was someone else there.

"What do you want with me?" she asked.

"Information… for now," the voice said.

"What information could I possibly have that anyone would be interested in?" Jessica struggled against the restraints.

She tried to think if she'd heard that voice before. There was something familiar about it. It had the same deep timbre that Blackwing's voice had. There were a few differences, though.

"What is the nature of your association with the wizard?" the voice said.

"What wizard?"

"You know of what I speak. You bear his banding. He has marked you. Are you a toy?"

"I'm no one's toy!" Jessica spat.

"Then, free woman, tell me what I want to know. What is the nature of your relationship?"

"That is none of your business!" she spat again.

"So you lied. He *is* your master."

"There's no relationship. He's assisting me with a case."

She heard a deep booming laugh.

"You expect me to believe that you are his master?"

"I'm not his master, nor is he mine. We're working together."

"I believe that is what you tell yourself to ease your conscience. I fail to understand your recalcitrance. My questions are not difficult."

Jessica glanced down at the chair. She didn't know her woods, but it appeared to be black mahogany. It shocked her to see she wasn't restrained to the chair. She was restrained *by* the chair. On each arm were two ornately carved claws wrapped around her wrists, immobilizing her. She assumed the same was true for her legs. She had no idea what was restraining her head, but something was wrapped around her throat and just below her ribs.

If I could only reach the gold band.

After he'd returned to his lab, Strange got a call from Jon Crawford.

"Have you seen Detective Sylvillagys?" said the detective sergeant. "The captain wants her, right now."

"I saw her a while ago. Have you tried her personal phone? She should have gotten home by now."

"Of course I have, you moron! I'm a detective!" The sergeant ended the call.

I hope she's okay. Strange put his phone in his pocket and busied himself in the lab.

An hour later, Detective Sergeant Crawford stormed into the lab.

"What have you done with her, you little dweeb? If you've done something to her, I'll… I'll… I don't know what I'll do, but you won't like it."

"Relax, Sergeant," Strange said, calmly. "I've done nothing to her, and wouldn't."

"We've checked her home and tried to call her several times. We've come up empty. Find her!" The sergeant stormed out.

For years it's been fix this or fix that. Finally, someone asks me to have a drink with them, and now I'm supposed to find them and I have no idea where to start looking. It's all my fault. I just know it.

After pacing for some time to try to calm himself, it dawned on him to see if her electronic pad was on her desk. He ran upstairs, burst through the squad room door and hurried to her desk. Her pad was on it. After getting access, bypassing her password, he found the ad she'd placed.

"The damn message doesn't say anything about where," he mumbled.

With deft fingers, he posted another ad with Jessica's account that said it was an emergency and to meet in the alley. He hoped it would be enough.

Shortly after finishing his tankard, Blackwing's sphere sent him a message.

"*Blackwing. Emergency. In the alley.*"

He quickly stowed his tankard. "I need to go. There's an emergency. I'll be back when I can."

"Is there always an emergency?" Suzanne said, but there was no one to hear her.

Irving Strange walked away from the precinct via the alley. It was dark and he said nothing until he was sure he was out of range of the ever-present cameras and microphones.

"Blackwing, it's an emergency," he whispered, in the dark alley. "Blackwing? Blackwing!"

He felt like something was lifting him off the pavement. *What have I gotten myself into this time.*

He tried not to look down, but a few times he couldn't help himself. He kept rising. At the top of a high-rise, he was set down on the roof.

"Why did you summon me?" said a deep booming voice, from the shadows.

"Blackwing, is that you?" Irving said.

"I am Blackwing," the shadow boomed. "Tell me why I shouldn't drop you back where you came from."

Irving panted. "It's an emergency! Jessica Sylvillagys and I went out for a drink and now she's missing."

"Calm yourself and start over." Blackwing looked perplexed. "Who are you?"

"Irving Strange, lab tech. I've been helping Jessica with some things pertaining to her case. I know what you say you are, and now I believe it. She told me in confidence, which I'll keep. Last I knew, Jessica was on her way home and now she's missing. Her boss was looking for her and no one knows where she is. Can you help?"

"I don't see *that* as an emergency," Blackwing said, calmly. "Maybe I should turn you into a toad, for unnecessarily dragging me out."

"Please don't. I wouldn't have sent for you unless it was an emergency. I didn't even know if that would work, since you gave Jessica the gold band. Police protocol is that everyone is to be available twenty-four-seven. Someone has to know where you are at all times.

"They've tried to track her location using her ID and her phone, and have nothing. I got worried and figured I'd give you a try."

"In other words, your ways don't always work." Blackwing shook his head. "How did she get home?"

"I don't know. I think she drove, but I'm not sure."

"Is there a way to trace her conveyance?"

Irving smacked himself in the head with his palm. "I should've thought of that." He pulled out his pad and entered a few numbers. "She lives on Hyada Boulevard Northeast on Brown's Point, and her ground car is there."

He showed Blackwing the map and their destination's relative location to them.

Suddenly, Irving felt sick and retched the contents of his stomach. When he felt better, he looked around in amazement. They were in Brown's Point.

"Well?" Blackwing said.

Irving looked around to orientate himself with the map on his pad. "Her building is over there." He pointed.

They both rushed over, Irving watching his pad.

"It looks like her vehicle is parked underground," he said. "That's not good."

"Why?"

"It means surveillance cameras, pass-coded gates, maybe even a security guard."

"Well, then get busy," Blackwing said. "I want to see if she is in her vehicle or lying unconscious on the pavement."

"I can't get us past the gates or the cameras. I'm not a burglar or a hacker."

Blackwing looked impatiently at him. "I'll get us in. You shut up." He mumbled something. "Are you up to a short hop?"

"Sure," Irving replied, not knowing what he meant by a short hop.

A second later, the pair were inside the underground garage.

"Find her vehicle," Blackwing said.

Irving got out his pad and followed the signal. "Whew! What is that stench?" he said, when they were close to their target.

"I smelled it some time ago," Blackwing said, "as we entered this space." He furrowed his brow. "I know what that smell is. I've smelled it plenty of times before. Look here."

He called Irving's attention to what appeared to be a sizable blood spot.

"It's blood, all right." Irving knelt down to inspect the pool. "If I had my sampling kit, I could tell you if it's human blood and if it's hers."

"We can't retrieve your tool. We don't have that kind of time. Neither does she, considering who has her."

"Who has her?" Irving waited. "You need to tell me," he said, when Blackwing didn't respond.

"You don't want to know. Besides, you wouldn't believe me."

"After tonight, I'd believe almost anything."

"Ogres. Ogres have her."

Jessica heard the voice behind her say something in a foreign language. She could hear scraping on the concrete. There was an odor so foul it almost made her retch, and it triggered a memory of being hit in the garage area under her building.

She heard something lumbering toward her, slowly. She tried and failed to turn her head enough the see what was coming. *It's coming for me! This is gonna hurt... a lot.* The anticipation was maddening. Her pulse raced, muscles strained, and adrenalin caused her body to tremble, and she began to sweat. *How bad can it be? I've seen more horror than anyone should.*

Finally, the beast came into view and she gasped at the sight of it. It was huge and ugly, with bulging muscles. Long fingers and toenails, like claws. Its enormous mandible was overshot and had tusks protruding upward, and it drooled. The worst was the smell. Being a cop, she'd smelled some horrendous things, but this beast was by far the worst.

It smells like month-old roadkill drenched in the perfume of a hundred skunks.

When it was close enough, it tried to remove the gold band that was still attached to her right wrist. As the monster tried to pry it off, the band tightened, causing her to scream from the pain of it. Her wrist felt like it was slowly being crushed.

The voice said something from behind her and the beast left the band alone. She saw the beast raise its massive fist above its head. Jessica closed her eyes and turned her head away as she tried to pull her body backward. *I don't want to see it coming. Just get it over with.*

The beast struck her left arm between the claw-like restraints. She felt her bones shatter with the impact. The pain was tremendous and forced her eyes wide open. Her vision turned black as she passed out.

8

AN UNEXPECTED HERO

It took some time for Jessica to regain consciousness. When she did, the throbbing pain from her shattered arm sent a deep ache through her upper body, making it hard to breathe. Her vision was blurry and grayed and threatened to go black at any second. Her brain finally came to the realization that the chair she was sitting on had been reconfigured. She was now sitting with her legs and arms splayed, legs extended in front of her. She didn't hear the monster moving, but she knew from the pungent odor it wasn't far away.

"Are you ready to answer my questions?" the voice said.

"I have answered them and you shattered my arm. What incentive is there for me to answer more?" she said, groggily, trying to appear braver than she felt.

"I want to know everything you know about your master, the wizard," the voiced boomed.

She couldn't tell if he was in the room or not, but the volume level was high enough that the low timbre made her shattered arm ache even more.

"From the sound of your voice, you have more in common with *him* than you do with me. Why don't you ask him yourself?"

"All in good time, all in good time. For now, I want to know what you know of him. Where he sleeps, where he eats, who his allies are and where they can be found."

"The only ally—if you want to call it that—I know of is me." *I can't do anything. If they release me, which I doubt, maybe then I can do something, and only after my arm gets fixed.*

"How do you communicate with your master?"

"I've told you, he's *not* my master," Jessica spat. "At this point, I'm sorry I know of him at all."

There was another command given that Jessica didn't understand, and once again the monster moved to her.

"I really wish you would bathe this thing. The stench is horrendous."

She saw the huge fist come up once more, and then it fell on her right thigh. She heard and felt her femur crush from the blow as the pain, barely felt by the already overloaded pain receptors in her brain, caused her to pass out again.

"So where is she?" Irving pleaded.

"Why are you so concerned?" Blackwing said, his back to the much smaller man.

"She is a co-worker."

"Is that the only reason?"

"No," Irving replied, sheepishly. "She was nice to me."

Blackwing chuckled.

"It may not be a big thing to you, but in the last ten years no one has ever invited me out for a drink, or asked my opinion, or even been nice to me. To me it is a big deal."

"What are you willing to do for her?"

"I'll do anything."

"Anything? That covers a lot of ground. We shall see. Jessica is being held by dangerous creatures and is likely severely injured. She is trained and expected to enter dangerous situations. You aren't. It isn't your job to go. If you accompany me, I can't guarantee your safety."

"If you're trying to talk me out of it, you won't," Irving said, in a gruff tone. "You may need my help and I'm ready."

"I doubt that. I'm making sure you know what the situation is so you can prepare yourself mentally. It isn't going to be easy and there is no shame in not going."

"In for a penny, in for a pound."

"If I take your meaning, I agree. Tactically, we will have the advantage. Ogres are slow moving, but deliberate. They are large lumbering creatures and can sustain a lot of damage, so your job will be to protect Jessica. Do you have a weapon?"

"No. Lab techs aren't issued one. But I'm still willing to go."

"I need to be assured that what you see or hear will remain between us. You already know far too much, but that can't be helped now."

"I can keep a secret, if that's what you mean. Are we going to get Jessica, or are we going to stand around talking about it?"

"Don't be in such a rush to enter the battle. Push up a sleeve and hold out your hand."

Once Irving pushed up his left sleeve, he held out his left hand. Blackwing spoke to something in his hand and then dropped a gold coin into Irving's palm. The coin liquefied and transformed into a gold band around his left wrist.

"That is in case we get separated," Blackwing said. "I can find you with that."

"Will it let you know if I tap it three times?"

Blackwing looked at the smaller man, shocked, and narrowed his eye. "Told you, did she? Unexpected. We'll deal with that later."

He reached into an inner pocket of his coat and produced what looked to Irving like a wakizashi.

"That's to aid you in your protection duties. It's for defense only. Try not to cut off anything important... important to you, I mean. It is quite sharp."

Irving looked at the blade in awe. He doubted it was an authentic wakizashi, but the differences were unimportant to him.

"Ready?" Blackwing said.

When Irving nodded, they disappeared.

When Jessica roused again, she was thankful. *If it wasn't for this chair, I would be lying on the floor in too much pain to move.*

"Welcome back," said the voice behind her. "You are quickly running out of extremities. There will be a point that no one will be able to repair. I would recommend cooperation over obstinacy."

"I don't know what I can say," Jessica replied, groggily. "If I knew anything, I would've told you long ago. I think you're doing it because you like seeing someone in pain."

"That is possible," the voice chuckled. "It might also be that I classify you and your kind as insignificant. No better than the brutes you cage in your open areas. From my perspective, you are causing your own pain and suffering by failing to answer my simple questions. My pet requires feeding and I am having trouble... restraining him. His kind tends to rend their victims. But enough of the pleasantries, tell me what you know. I doubt the wizard has given you a reason for your loyalty."

"What do you want to know? Or do you even know," Jessica spat. "I can tell you his name, but that's about it. Is that what you want? His name? If you would've asked me, I would've told you long before you broke my arm."

"I already know his name," the voice boomed. "That is not what I want."

He already knows Blackwing's name? He knows Blackwing? Is he the one I saw going into the vortex? Just my luck, though. I find him and can't do anything to apprehend him. This beast is definitely not what I saw pushing Peterson into the vortex, so it's likely there are other cohorts around.

"All I know is I was investigating your handiwork, and when I had no further leads he provided me with a couple." She fought to remain conscious. "I have no idea who he knows or where he lives."

"You know nothing else?"

"Nothing," she said, wearily. *I hurt all over and just want to get out of here.*

"Hmm… it would appear you have come to the end of your usefulness."

Jessica heard him give another command, and then she heard the beast coming again.

This is it. I always thought I'd go out in a blaze of glory. I never thought I'd be crushed and ripped apart by some smelly monster.

She saw the meaty monstrous fist rise. She closed her eyes, not knowing where or when the strike would come.

I really don't want to see it coming. I just want the pain to end.

Blackwing and Irving materialized inside the chamber in time to see the Ogre, with his huge fist raised, about to strike Jessica. Irving rushed to her side and managed to stand his wakizashi on the arm of the chair just as the Ogre's fist was about to strike Jessica's right arm. He held on to his blade as the Ogre roared, staggered back and drew away its injured hand.

"It's okay, Jessica. We're here," Irving whispered, as her eyes popped open at the Ogre's deafening roar.

He turned his back to her, putting himself between her and the beast.

Gold coins hit the floor in front of the Ogre. As the Ogre's feet covered several coins, gold shackles formed at the beast's ankles and a chain form, tripping the beast. When it hit the floor, its hands covered several more coins and they formed shackles around the beast's wrists, complete with a chain. The Ogre struggled and roared.

Irving did a quick inspection of Jessica's restraints and drew a blank on how to free her.

"Stand back," Blackwing said.

Irving complied and saw a deep-red beam of energy come from the end of Blackwing's staff and hit the back of the chair. The restraints released.

"My uniform," Jessica said, weakly.

Irving, still carrying his short sword, went to a table behind Jessica's restraining chair, grabbed her combat unitard and brought it to her.

Blackwing heard a door unlock and creak open.

"We're going to have company," he shouted. "Hurry it up!"

"Get my right arm into my sleeve," Jessica said.

Irving slid her Ogre-blood-covered arm into her unitard sleeve. Jessica activated her service weapon.

Lifting it close to her mouth, she said, "Breaching."

"Twelve-gauge autoloader. Double aught buckshot. Ten rounds available." The weapon morphed into a hard sleeve covering her right arm, nearly to her armpit.

Irving and Jessica turned to see a river of angry beings swarming into the room. They heard a *boom!* After turning to look at Blackwing, they saw a soundwave kick up dust from the floor, traveling toward the horde, and knocked those that the wave hit from their feet. His staff transformed into something ornate with a large red jewel attached.

As the beings closed in on the trio, Jessica pointed her weapon toward the rushing horde and started firing. After the first two shots, they seemed to think better of going after the humans, as their numbers where being decimated.

Those that went after Blackwing found their legs failing and they collapsed as a wide red beam traveled over them.

"My right leg and left arm are shattered," Jessica said to Irving, once her weapon ran out of shells. "Default," she said to the weapon, and began firing the metal taser darts. "I need to get to the hospital. I feel like I'm… going to… pass out."

"Blackwing, we need to leave," Irving yelled, to be heard over the din as he did his best to get Jessica stood up.

She stood on her left leg, with her right arm over his shoulder. He held her close with his left arm around her waist. Blackwing strode toward them. When he was close, all three disappeared.

As Jessica was regaining consciousness, she remembered that her leg and arm were crushed, but she had no pain. As she opened her eyes, she saw Strange standing at the rain-streaked window, looking out at Puget Sound.

"My hero," she croaked, and chuckled.

"Jessica! You're awake." Irving turned toward her and rushed over to the bed. "Everyone at the precinct was worried about you, and they've visited you several times," he said, quietly, looking down at her with a worried expression.

"How long have I been out?" she managed to croak.

She tried to reach for a water bottle on the side table, with her right hand.

"It's been two weeks since your accident." Irving opened the bottle and handed it to her. "I was starting to wonder if you were ever going to wake up." He tugged at his earlobe and raised his eyebrows. "The doctor has told everyone that there was no reason to visit or to worry. He assured everyone that you were in good hands. I just couldn't leave." He shrugged.

Jessica covertly looked around the room as she drank the water. She noticed the surveillance cameras in several locations, and knew the probability was high that she was being recorded. She handed the water back to Irving. He reached for it with his left hand and she noticed a glint of gold around his wrist.

"The doctor says you're in for a long recovery, but he'll be in later to see you and explain the extent of your injuries and such."

"My uniform—"

"Is secured at the precinct and will be cleaned and waiting for you when you return. Don't worry. It's all taken care of. From what I hear, everyone is most curious as to what happened."

"It's all jumbled in my head right now. What did happen?"

"I have no idea. I found you half in your car at your apartment building. Your injuries were consistent with being hit by two heavy objects. It looked like something, maybe a truck, t-boned you and crushed your left arm, and when you attempted to get out, another hit the front, causing the steering wheel to crush your right thigh."

Neither Jessica nor Irving said anything for thirty seconds.

"The level of our technology never ceases to amaze me," Irving said. "By the time I found you, the nanobots had repaired your vehicle to the extent that you can't tell there was ever anything wrong with it. They're looking for the trucks, or whatever hit you, though." He glanced at his phone. "I need to get to work. You just lay back and take it easy, okay? I'll stop in after to check on you."

Jessica's mind was whirling as she watched Strange leave her room. *Without appearing obvious, he managed to calmly explain away any questions someone would ask about my unusual injuries. I doubt I could do better. Trying to explain how I really received my injuries is going to be difficult, at best. I'm surprised he's now a member of the Blackwing club. I feel sorry for him. I'm sure membership is going to bite him in the ass one day.*

It was mid-afternoon when a tall man wearing a white unitard entered Jessica's room. She could tell by the unitard that he was a professional, just as her unitard indicated she was a professional. From the color, he was a medico.

"Good afternoon, Jessica. I'm Dr. Morton, and I will be your attending physician for the remainder of your stay." He pulled out his electronic pad and made some notes from the indicators that were on both sides of her bed. "How are you feeling?" He crossed his hands in front of him.

"Sore."

"I'm not surprised. You've been through a lot of trauma. Any trouble remembering what happened?"

"Some. More confusion as to how long I've been here and why I don't remember it."

"You've been with us for two weeks. We had to place you into a medically induced coma to allow the nanites to repair your bones and soft tissues. They work better when the patient is unconscious. It took them some time to reassemble and fuse all the bone fragments. Usually it only takes a few hours to repair a simple fracture. Do you remember what happened?"

"No, I don't. Is that normal?"

"Considering the amount of trauma, I'd be surprised if you did remember. However it happened, you still have extensive bruising on your left arm and right thigh. Mind if I take a look?"

"I don't mind. Why am I trussed up like this if the nanites have already repaired everything?" she asked, as the doctor uncovered her right thigh.

"They didn't repair everything while you were unconscious. In the past two weeks, they managed to get your bones fused and repair the veins and arteries. Your bones are far from being fixed, as you put it, but the nanites do eliminate the need for surgery to put in pins, screws, and plates. You have to let your body heal itself and form new bone over all the fusions."

The doctor observed her injuries through the clear cast that ran from her hip to her ankle. He checked her foot by having her wiggle her toes, and tested nerve function by doing a Babinski reflex test. He checked her left arm and tested her fingers.

"You have a lot of healing to do." He covered her once more. "If you can restrain yourself, you'll be released home in a few more days if you have a caregiver lined up. The nanites will be removed before you leave."

"How long before I can return to work?"

"Hmm, that's difficult to predict. Barring any re-injury, and if you follow the rehabilitation schedule, maybe a month for restricted duty. A lot depends on how long it takes your body to heal. If you have no further questions, I'll let you rest."

The doctor left and was replaced by a nurse, also dressed in a white unitard, but with royal blue stripes down the outside of the sleeves and the outside seams on the legs.

"Afternoon, Jessica," the woman said. "I'm your nurse for the next few hours. Is there anything I can do for you?"

"Yes. I need my phone and pad. Do you know where they are?"

The nurse went to the side table on Jessica's left side and opened the drawer. She took out a phone and placed it where Jessica could reach it.

"I have no idea if you had a pad, or where it is. You might want to check with the guy who brought you in. Strange, I think was his name. Anything else?"

"No, thank you." Jessica picked up her phone and started to search through her contacts.

It took her a while to find Strange's number.

"Hello, Detective," he answered. "How are you doing?"

"Do you have my pad?"

"Your pad is being held here, along with your unitard, at the precinct. They say it's police property and it couldn't be secured by the hospital. I'm coming up to see you in a bit. I'll bring you dinner, unless I'm presuming too much. I could pick you up a personal pad, if you'd like."

"Well, I haven't been in hospital before and I've yet to be fed, so dinner would be great. If you wouldn't mind, picking me up a personal pad would be appreciated. I'm going stir crazy here."

"Okay, I'll be there in… three hours with dinner. Any preferences?"

"No, at this point I'll eat anything. I'm starving." She grinned.

I really do appreciate Strange. He's turning out to be someone I can count on.

When Irving arrived, he handed her the personal pad and started setting out their dinner. Attached to the pad was a card, which she opened immediately.

I hope you feel better soon, she read, silently.

"This pad should help to keep you from going crazy. Be advised, you're being watched and listened to. Be careful what you say and how you say it while in the hospital. You can rely on me. Irving."

"Irving?" she said.

"Yes?" He looked up from his task.

"Your name is Irving?"

"I know." He gave a look that told her he didn't like his name. "My parents had a sense of humor. And before you start, I've heard all the comments before, ad nauseam."

"Like you, I've been at the precinct for years, and I never knew your name. Maybe I need to pay more attention to those around me."

"Want to hear something funny?"

"Sure."

"My middle name is Melvin."

I.M. Strange ran through her mind and made her laugh, which caused pain in her arm and leg.

9

ROOMATES

Jessica was released from the hospital three days after she regained consciousness. Irving had bought her a casual outfit that would allow enough room to cover her casts, and she made ready to leave the hospital. *This is way too baggy for my tastes.*

At her apartment, Irving retrieved the motorized chair from the trunk of the rented ground car and positioned it for Jessica to move from car to chair. Once in the battery driven chair, Jessica started off to her apartment, with Irving coming up behind her carrying her few belongings. At the door, she touched the plate with her right palm and the door opened.

"Welcome home, Jessica," said the apartment's computerized voice.

Her living room, as adequate and unused as it was before her injuries, seemed much smaller than she remembered. *It's got to be the chair that's making it seem so small.*

"Can you pass me the pad?" Jessica asked Irving. "The rest can be put in on my bed." She pointed toward her bedroom.

"Tacoma PD Captain Trooper is at the door," the apartment announced.

"Allow entry," Jessica said.

"Detective Sylvillagys, how's your vacation?" The captain grinned.

"Some vacation," she said sarcastically.

"I know you were just released," Trooper said, as Irving came out of the bedroom, "but I wanted to let you know that we're all working hard on finding out what happened to you. Also, I wanted to let you know that I closed the file on Trevor Peterson. So there's no need for you to feel like you have to rush back to work before you're ready."

"Why did you close the file?"

"The coroner determined cause of death to be *death by misfortune*. No homicide. Therefore, no need for any further investigation."

"So," Jessica said, as Irving came up behind her, "you're saying he was just at the wrong place at the wrong time?"

"Not me, the coroner. Anyway, I need to push on." The captain crooked his finger in a come hither fashion toward Irving.

Jessica watched as both men left her alone in the apartment.

"How's she doing?" Captain Trooper asked Irving in the hallway, after the door closed behind them.

"She's still shaken up from her ordeal, sir. Some confusion."

"Hmm... that's to be expected, I suppose. See to it that she's well cared for. Jon Crawford wanted to come by, but I told him to give her a few more days to get used to the new situation."

"I think that would be best, sir. Thank you for stopping by," Irving said to the captain's back.

"That's disappointing," Jessica said, as Irving re-entered the apartment.

Once in the apartment, with the door closed, he said, "What do you want to do about dinner?"

"I have nothing here. Eating is not what I do here. I usually get something before I come home, or go out to get something."

"We could go to Tony's, if you want." Irving tugged on his earlobe.

"Sure. I usually eat there anyway. I think they can handle the chair."

"Let's find out." He grinned.

Neither of them said anything until they got to the ground car. Once Jessica maneuvered herself into the vehicle and Irving got the chair stowed and then entered the vehicle, they left and headed downtown.

When they reached the bar, they found a private booth and settled in.

"We need to talk to our mutual *friend*." Jessica scanned the menu.

"I've talked to him several times since your injury. He's asked about you." Irving scanned his own menu. "He's been quite concerned. Have you given any thought as to how you're going to bathe, or other things, unaided?"

"Not particularly. You have, obviously. What do you propose?"

"I could sleep at your apartment. That would mean I would be there to help you. It would only be until you can function on your own."

Thank God the waiter is here. Do I want to live with Irving? She still chuckled whenever she thought of his name.

"What am I to do when you're at work?" she said, after the waiter left.

"In-home caregivers are expensive, but with me there the rest of the time, I think it would offset the cost. We do need to figure something out so we can talk privately, mostly about our *friend*."

They paused when the waiter arrived with their food and drinks.

"I'd like to talk to him ASAP," Jessica whispered, after the waiter left again. "He needs to be aware of what happened."

"He knows what happened." Irving started to eat.

"He doesn't know what I found out. Nobody does, as I was unconscious shortly after leaving that torture chair."

"I wasn't aware you found out anything. I can meet with him and let him know we need a group meeting. I need to find out if they're having trouble with your surveillance equipment. Maybe I can build something to disrupt it."

"I like your idea about the living arrangements." Jessica said, while she ate. "It's logical. Besides, it's been a long time since I slept unarmed. I'm feeling… vulnerable… and anxious. Being kidnapped will do that to you."

Irving had stopped chewing and his mouth hung open, full of partially chewed food, obviously surprised at her acceptance of his idea.

"Just until I can manage on my own." She flashed a sly grin.

"I'm wondering if the ground car is hooked into the city's surveillance system," Jessica said, as they nursed the remainder of the bottle of wine.

"Partially," Irving replied. "They track us by our ID's. Just by that they can map our movements and see who we associate with. The audio and video are for our benefit. It's so we know they have a record and that we can be prosecuted for anything illegal. I work on the equipment, repair it sometimes, and never did anything illegal. From what I've figured out about our *friend*, I think we're breaking several laws just by associating with him. But without *him*, you probably wouldn't be here with me, sharing this nice bottle of wine." He grinned at her.

"I think you're a little drunk." Jessica chuckled. "I know *I* am. The doc said I shouldn't have any alcohol, but I didn't see anything wrong with wine."

"At least the car can drive us home." Irving chuckled.

"I think you need to go into the alley behind the precinct and make your call before we head home."

Irving checked his phone for the time. "I think I should. It's still early."

Within the hour, Jessica and Irving were sitting in the ground car in the alley behind the precinct, tapping their gold bracelets and laughing. They'd been waiting for some time.

"Are you two okay?" Blackwing asked, through the open window next to Jessica.

"Ther-r-re you are… aren't choo," Jessica said, with an eye closed, a big grin, and having to concentrate to keep from slurring her words too badly. "I jus wanna to tell yooo," she pointed her finger at him, "thank you for gettin' me outta that place, and t'say that the guy who ques'ioned me knows yer name."

"You two need to go home and sleep it off." Blackwing tried to keep from laughing at the pair.

Irving was strangely fascinated with buttons inside the ground car, and kept hitting his head on the steering wheel.

It was early afternoon when Jessica finally woke. She was still in the chair, which had been reclined, covered with a blanket. As she looked around, she saw that Irving was gone and she was alone.

She found her phone and saw she had a message from Suzanne Hawks.

"This is Suzanne Hawks. I'm calling to let you know that my uncle has found something you'd asked him to research. If you could come to the store about six this evening, he could pass on the information. Hope you're feeling better."

She made a mental note to let Irving know that dinner would be delayed until after they went to the bookstore. Then the phone rang.

"Hello?" she said.

"This is Home-Aid of Puget Sound. We received a call from a Mr. Strange about you needing some assistance. We have a few associates available today. What is your preference for an aid worker?"

"Female, and yes, I do need assistance."

"If you're free today, I can send one over."

"That would be fine. As soon as possible, if you could."

"Good. We'll send her over. Her name is Emily, and I think she'll be acceptable. If you have any issues, just give us a call."

She hung up the phone. *Irving, you're so efficient. Almost too efficient.*

At 5:55 that evening, Irving and Jessica arrived at Hawks' Emporium. As they entered, Jessica saw Suzanne and her elderly uncle sitting at the counter.

"Don't worry." Jessica rolled her chair toward the counter. "I'm not here to arrest you. I couldn't even if I tried."

Everyone except Irving laughed.

"So what did you find?" she asked the blind man.

She followed Suzanne with her gaze as Suzanne locked the door and returned to the counter.

"In good time," Socrates said to Jessica. "How have you been?"

"Good, considering. This is Irving Strange. He's a lab tech at the precinct and he's been helping me."

Irving shook hands with Suzanne, but couldn't reach the blind man to shake his.

"And this," the blind man indicated Suzanne, "is Suzanne Hawks. She owns this establishment." He turned to Suzanne. "Is everything secure?"

Suzanne nodded.

"Fine. The last time you were here," Socrates said, "you asked me about wizards."

"Um… should we be talking about this here?" Irving glanced at the camera and then toward the window by the door.

"We're fine," Socrates said to Irving. "Can I see your right wrist?" he asked Jessica.

She held out her wrist without thinking about him being blind. He gently took her wrist and whispered to the gold band. To Jessica's surprise, the band loosened and Socrates slid it off easily. He held the band in both hands and then stuck out his right fist and opened it, showing them a gold coin. Jessica's was speechless, her mouth agape.

"And you, young man? Will you step over here and show me your left wrist?"

"Um… I'd rather not," Irving said.

"Come, come. Let me see it."

Irving moved closer and cautiously extended his left wrist. The older man repeated the process. Irving's wrist was bare and Socrates showed the coin in his hand.

"How did you do that?" Irving said.

"The answer is quite simple."

Jessica and Irving watched as the older blind man stood and melted away, leaving Blackwing standing where the blind man had stood, pocketing the gold coins and placing his fedora on his head. The white cane had transformed into the staff the pair had seen him carry.

"I figured you two would like to meet a real wizard."

Jessica frowned as the realization of what she had just seen hit her.

"You lied to me," she said.

"Not really. I told you what I needed to without disclosing my identity. Surely you wouldn't fault me for that?"

"I don't mean to intrude, but we *are* being observed," Irving said.

"From the time you two entered, you have been unobservable to those that intrude."

"But our ID's are telling everyone who's looking where we are," Irving replied.

"Some distance away, your ID's quit transmitting your location, so, no, they aren't. Can I interest you?" Blackwing showed the pair a pewter tankard before passing it to Suzanne.

"Sure," Jessica said, still frowning. "I could use one."

"Sox, sometimes you're just too damned dramatic," Suzanne said as she took the offered tankard.

"It is, I confess, one of the little pleasures I have." Blackwing passed a tankard to Irving and Jessica.

"So how long have you been hiding in plain sight?" Irving also took the offered tankard.

"Drink that slowly." Blackwing handed a tankard to Jessica. "Not long, about a year."

"Do you *know* how much pain and suffering I went through for you?" Jessica said.

"Yes, I'm aware. Your loyalty is much appreciated. I'm sorry you had to go through that, but I had no idea you would be put through it. I was just trying to help with your case."

"You do know they closed the case," Jessica said.

"I didn't know." Blackwing frowned.

"Yeah, I found it out yesterday. My captain came to my apartment to tell me he closed it. The coroner basically said Trevor Peterson was just in the wrong place at the wrong time."

"So why are you here?" Irving asked Blackwing.

Over the next hour, Blackwing gave Irving and Jessica the quick version of how he came to be there and what parameters he was to operate under. Everyone listened patiently and rarely interrupted.

"So are you military or law enforcement?" Jessica said.

"Both. On my Plane, my kind performs both functions."

"What do you think of all this?" Jessica asked Suzanne, who was silent during the speech.

"For my part, I was just being nice in trying to help Blackwing. I had no one to talk to about it all, and I used to think that he'd caused all the things that befell me since his arrival. Now I know he didn't cause anything. I had the sense that there was something else going on in the background, years before he arrived. Things calmed down for a while, but now they're on the upswing again. I, for one, am glad he's here. He knows more about the individuals who took you and how to deal with them than anyone else. Do you really think it's all over now?"

"So are we on the outside?" Irving said. "Is that why you took our bands?"

Jessica looked at him and frowned. "Are you serious? You want to continue your association with him?"

"Speaking for myself," Irving said, "before the Peterson case I wasn't involved in any investigations. At least, not at this level. I had no friends and no family. Now I feel like I'm much more involved in something that could be important. Since my band was removed, I feel… diminished somehow."

Everyone remained silent for a long time.

"Have you two eaten?" Blackwing said.

Jessica and Irving shook their heads.

"Why don't Irving and Suzanne go get something to eat for everyone and bring it back here?"

"How far are you going?" Jessica said.

"Just around the corner," Suzanne said. "There's a little grill a block from here that has exceptional food."

"How safe are they going to be?" Jessica said, panic evident in her voice.

"They'll be fine," Blackwing said. "I've had wards up for quite some time in the area."

"Wards?"

"Protection spells, for lack of a better term. They prevent those that would do them harm from entering this area."

"You can do that?"

"Do you have your bracelet, Suzanne?" said Blackwing.

"Yes, I haven't taken it off for months," she replied.

"You'll be fine," Blackwing said, as Irving and Suzanne left the store.

Blackwing stood, watching as Suzanne and Irving walked out of sight.

"Irving is surprising." He shook his head, chuckling.

"What do you mean?" Jessica said.

"When you were taken, he shocked me by how adamant he was that you be found. He knew something was wrong and told everyone he could find about it. Did you know he was ready to jump into the fray, unarmed?"

"That wouldn't have been too bright of him."

"Maybe not," Blackwing shrugged. "But he was willing to do it, nonetheless. He stayed with you while you were unconscious. He didn't leave for any extended periods, until after you were awake. He is quite loyal to you."

"He's *too* loyal and too… clingy," Jessica said. "I've been alone for as long as I can remember. It helped me to focus on my career. I'm used to doing for myself."

"Now, you can't do for yourself. Can you allow him to do for you? He thinks he needs to. Besides, you may find you like not having to do it all yourself."

"I don't have a lot of choices, apparently. I have a feeling he's going to try to do what he can for as long as he can. Sometimes it's very irritating."

"Irving may be what you'd call, odd. But he is intelligent and he cares about you. That's something you should take a closer look at before you discard him. I don't think you're irritated with Irving. I think you're irritated with yourself. You're blaming yourself for having to be rescued. Big, bad Detective Jessica Sylvillagys. Relentlessly hunting down those who break the law, and you were rescued by a lab tech."

"I think you need to shut up," Jessica said, through clenched teeth.

"Why? Because it's true? Because that *is* the way you look at things? You're forgetting something very important."

"And what would that be?" She snipped.

"In this version of the Universe, as in my version, it's seldom all about us. More often than not, we're just tiny things that have little influence on the events that matter. Are you familiar with the Butterfly Effect?"

"I've heard of it. Why?"

"I like to think that if we change something small, it may have a greater impact on the whole, sometime into the future. The problem is we can't see far enough into the future to know if we're doing anything significant."

10

DISCLOSURES AND REMINISCENCES

After Suzanne and Irving returned and once all the humans had something to eat, Blackwing stood.

"I need to know who wants to remain in our group," he said, pacing.

"You need to ask?" Suzanne chuckled, shaking her head.

"I don't know where we're going or what will happen," Irving said, "but I want to remain in the group."

"I need answers." Jessica frowned.

"What answers do you need?" Blackwing said. "I'll answer what I can."

"What was that thing that crushed my arm and leg?"

Blackwing took a deep breath and exhaled slowly. "That was a *P'koosh*, what you'd call an Ogre. They are big, strong, dull-witted, and easily controlled."

"Not to mention, smelly in the extreme," Irving said.

"That's for certain," Jessica said. "Why was I singled out?"

"At this point, I have no idea. I half-expected to be taken, but I had no idea the rest of you would be targeted. The only thing that makes sense is you must have done something that brought you to their attention."

"I was working on the Peterson investigation before I linked up with you. That's the only thing I can think of. Captain Trooper said to leave Suzanne alone right after I was here. He's never done that before. I've thought that there was something going on within the PD."

"After the attempted robbery and assault," Blackwing said, "I instituted wards in this area. We haven't had any attempts since, have we?" He looked to Suzanne, who shook her head. "My conclusion is that it has something to do with the City trying to get their hands on this building."

"What were those things that swarmed into the room where Jessica was held?" Irving said.

"Those were *Brui K'sha U'ien*. Brown… gnomes, you would call them. They swarm like that. They're tough and can grow to be as tall as Irving, and are quite nasty."

"My shotgun setting seemed to give them pause," Jessica said. "What did you do to them with your staff?"

"I caused their leg bones to be turned to gel, temporarily, to slow their attack. My kind usually doesn't kill unless there is no other way. Just to let you know, after extracting Jessica to the hospital, I returned and found nothing to indicate anyone had ever been there."

"Where did they all go?" Jessica said.

"I have no idea. They could've escaped via a portal, but it was all clean before I returned."

"Do you know who was questioning me?"

"Did you see him?"

"Never did. It sounded like he was in the same room, but after my arm was shattered I wasn't sure of anything."

"When you and I made the trip to the um... crime scene, we saw someone enter the portal. I suspect he is the one who questioned you, and I may know him, but there wasn't enough to be sure who it was. I have reported it, but I don't know what will be done about it from my Plane. If it was one of my brothers, that report could... disappear."

"So what, if anything, can we do now?" Irving said.

"Ah... you've come to the reason for this meeting," Blackwing replied. "Not being a native of this Plane, I have no idea what can be done while remaining inconspicuous. I'm open to suggestions."

"I think you'd remain inconspicuous, regardless of what you do," Jessica said. "Most people don't want to know anything they don't have to and are willing to believe whatever they're told. If Peterson was killed for his involvement in the attempted assault, his fellows will also be prime targets for elimination. Johnson is somewhat safe in the loony bin, but O'Toole is exposed, as are we."

"There is one way that I can think of," Blackwing said, "to figure out who was questioning you."

"What way is that?" Jessica said. "You didn't hear or see him and I didn't see him."

Blackwing produced his sphere. "If you're willing, I may be able to recognize his voice. All you have to do is concentrate on your experience and his voice while touching this."

Jessica paled, but nodded.

"What you'll be experiencing will be memory and it can't harm you." Blackwing brought the glowing sphere closer to her, cradled in his hand.

Jessica closed her eyes and hesitantly touched the glowing globe.

She was back in the place of her interrogation, restrained to the chair. With concentration, she heard, "*I know you are conscious, Sylvillagys. No need to pretend.*" Another thread of memory. "*What is the nature of your association with the wizard?*"

Jessica opened her eyes when the images in her brain faded, and saw a frown on Blackwing's face.

"Did you recognize the voice?" she said.

"I did." He scowled. "I also have a record of it."

"Are you going to tell us, or is it a secret?" Suzanne said.

"Malthuvius Nighthawk," Blackwing said, with venom. "He sent me here to stop those entities from doing what *he* is doing."

Malthuvius Nighthawk was standing in a lavishly adorned room, looking at the back of Phelonius Blackwing, The General, as he was known in most quarters of the Seven Known Planes. Phelonius was standing, looking out a window at city lights far below him, hands behind his back.

"What of my grandson?" he asked, in the native tongue of *Q'estiria*.

He arched his back and raised his chin a few centimeters as he waited for an answer.

"He is as stiff-necked and obstinate as usual. His last report told of finding the residual of the vortex, along with the residuals of a *T'et Faqin* and a *Brui K'sha U'ien*. We knew he would, eventually. Whatever else he is, he *is* quite intelligent.

Phelonius chuckled. "He believed you about the orders you drafted. How bright can he be? How precedes the plan?"

"These *P'koosh F'aeul*," Malthuvius sneered, "are foul of mouth and mind, but are ripe for the picking again."

"I know that! *I* am the one who brought *you* in!"

"Of course, My General. This stage of the plan is progressing only slightly behind schedule, but the pace will pick up quickly."

"How are you planning to bring Socrates to our side? You do know that I had never intended to promote you over him. I see a lot of his father in him, be that for good or ill."

"I have not devised a plan for bringing him into your fold. I know him to be somewhat flawed, in that he actually takes his function seriously. He is not one to blatantly break our tenants, but he will bend a few if it benefits him."

"So you plan to weaken his resolve, using his allies."

"Innocents are his weakness."

"Why would he do that?" Suzanne said.

"Malthuvius Nighthawk is quite skilled," Blackwing said, "mostly in bowing and scraping to his superiors. My *illustrious grandfather*, ordered me here to guard and export those from the other Planes who come here for their own gain. Nighthawk is my grandfather's aide and confidant. If Nighthawk is here, my grandfather sanctioned it."

"It sounds to me," Suzanne said, "that you have… um… issues with your grandfather. Why is that?"

"He is what you'd call our… Supreme Commander. The Council appointed him during our war with the *Ha'Jakta Ha'Dreen B'kota*… um… Dragon Riders. He commanded legions of legions of my brothers. He decided, in his infinite wisdom, to send me and my father on an unnecessary reconnaissance mission into the heart of the enemy. My father was killed and I received this." He indicated his scar.

"Legions of legions?" Jessica said.

"Roughly 1.08 million to 36 million, depending on the numbers you use," Irving replied.

"That was some time ago," Blackwing said.

"That doesn't explain why," Jessica said. "Why are they here? What do they want?"

"In my estimation, power," Blackwing said. "That's all my grandfather values. Thus, that's what Nighthawk craves. Without knowing their plans, I can say that should they succeed, it would mean enslavement for all on this Plane."

"But you're part of his family," Suzanne said. "Why would he do that to his own family?"

Blackwing explained…

Socrates Blackwing's childhood was no different than any other child of his race and station. His earliest memories were pleasant enough, running through the stone hallways of his father's manor house, stealing sweets from the kitchen, being shooed out from underfoot by Cookie when he lingered too long.

The kitchen was his favorite room in the manor house. It always seemed to be filled with the smells of baked bread, cooking meats, and bubbling sauces and soups. He enjoyed the sounds of clattering pots and pans, the low tones of instructions given by Cookie to her interns and their helpers.

Cookie was always pleasant to him, even when he was getting in the way of her appointed tasks. More than once she had bribed him with a small piece of sweet bread to stay out when the staff was busy preparing a meal. Socrates had decided that he liked Cookie, and he enjoyed watching her in the supervision of the staff. He especially enjoyed the times he had gone to the kitchen and found her sitting on an upturned barrel outside the kitchen door, smoking her long clay pipe and supervising the care of the manor's herb garden, which was her pride and joy and the envy of the neighboring manors. Or so she was fond of telling him.

He'd failed to notice that Cookie appeared older than either of his parents, rounder than most of the residents in the household, and was a *Grum K'sha U'ien*. He wondered about her large, hairy feet and short stature.

Years later, he always grinned when he recollected the conversation about her weight.

"I am not fat," she had said, chuckling. "I am just short for my weight." And then she had laughed her hearty, earthy laugh which always seemed to warm him.

The Lady of the house, S'hyrlus, who Socrates had thought was his mother, was of a different race than Cookie. She was tall, thin, and majestically graceful. Her fair skin used to shine in the light of the moons when he had seen her on her balcony after dark.

Her usual demeanor—toward him, anyway—was of kindness, introversion, and reclusiveness. The few times he had seen her vexed, her striking deep blue eyes used to flash and her long red mane seemed to deepen with differing degrees of her anger.

To him, she was strikingly beautiful, and he was saddened when he found out she was not his mother. But that did not stop S'hyrlus from treating him as a son. She always had a soft, sweet smile and a soothing, gentle word for him.

His father, Neh'Krim, was stern but fair. The few times Socrates was allowed, he enjoyed mimicking his father's combat training moves when he practiced in the secluded training room in the house. At those times, Neh'Krim used to smile slightly and give some gentle corrections to his young son.

He used to wonder where his father journeyed, when he was old enough to understand that his father was one of the noble-born of Q'estiria and had responsibilities that took him to exotic places young Socrates could only speculate about.

Whenever the time came for Neh'Krim to leave, the entire household would turn out into the inner garden. Socrates used to puff up with pride at the sight of his father dressed in the black leather that marked a *T'et Faqin Q'estirion*. The black pants and shined boots. The black duster that hung below his knees and seemed to flow like water whenever Neh'Krim moved. The leather fedora with the flat brim, pulled down in the front to shade his pale, blue eyes. His long, braided, black hair circling his neck, offset by the three polished, three-quarter-inch wide gold rings that held his braid at his throat. The all-important wooden staff topped off the effect of a no-nonsense agent of the Council on an important mission.

They would all walk after him through the grounds and stop at the outermost gate. It always made his heart flutter with excitement when he watched his father take two more steps to exit the gate, and then vanish.

The morning before his seventh birthday, Socrates was summoned to his father's private room. He was dressed in clean beige work clothes, as he had nothing else. When he entered after knocking, he saw his father in his black leather pants and a white linen shirt. He was just finishing braiding his hair.

"Socrates, sit please." His father patted the unmade bed beside him.

Socrates sat on the bed and attended his father. He had never been in this room before and was uncertain with its strangeness.

"You know what tomorrow is?" his father said, and Socrates nodded, not wanting to speak or disturb his father in any way. "You will be off tomorrow morning to attend the Academy at Q'estiria. A comrade of mine will arrive sometime today, and he will be resting most of the day. You are to treat him with the same respect you give me."

"Yes, Father."

"You will spend the rest of today saying your goodbyes to Cookie and S'hyrlus and anyone else you feel you need to. This evening will be a party and I expect no sad faces."

"Yes, Father." Socrates scrunched his face.

"Questions?"

"What if I fail?"

Neh'Krim rose, paced back and forth for a few seconds, and then stopped in front of Socrates.

"You are my son. Never forget that. I expect you to do your best. If you can stand before me and truthfully say you did your best, then that is all I can ask."

"How long will I be gone?"

"There is a high probability that you will never be here again. To be sure, you and I will see each other from time-to-time, but it is doubtful you will ever return here."

After being dismissed, Socrates left his father's room to seek out Cookie. He knew his birthdays had never come in the same season, for the previous five birthdays that he could remember. He wondered why that was, since a birthday was surely an annual event.

As he made his way to the kitchen, he felt that he was starting to miss the familiar halls of the manor. As soon as he entered the kitchen, Cookie spied him and met him just inside the doorway.

"What are you doing here, young sir?" Cookie said, with a mock frown. "I am very busy preparing a special dinner for someone. You should leave so I can do my work."

"I will not be here after tomorrow," Socrates said, with a catch in his voice. "I wanted to say goodbye and to let you know I will miss you."

He was doing his best to remain stoic, but felt it slipping the more he thought about leaving.

"I doubt that." Cookie turned away and went to the counter where the sweetbread was, and lifted her apron to her eye. "I think you will be too busy having adventures, meeting new people, learning new things, to think of an old cook you once knew." She handed him a small slice of the treat. "Just remember. You never get a second chance to make a first impression."

"I will not forget." Socrates took the treat. "And I will not forget where I heard it either."

"Away with you," Cookie said, her voice cracking. "I have too much to do and no time to do it." She quickly turned and went about her work.

Later in the morning, he meandered to S'hyrlus's door. He listened for a bit before knocking softly and waiting.

"Enter," S'hyrlus said, her voice muffled by the heavy oaken barrier.

It was then that he noticed that hers was different from any other door in the manor.

S'hyrlus was sitting next to a low table in an elaborately embroidered chair. Across from her chair was its twin, and she indicated that he should sit in it.

"To what do I owe this pleasure?" she said.

Her melodious voice always soothed him.

"Father said I should come see you. I'll be going tomorrow—"

"To the Academy, yes, I know."

"I felt I should come and—"

"Say goodbye?" S'hyrlus chuckled. "Am I last on your list?"

"Yes, but not least." His voice cracked.

"What is wrong, Socrates? You appear to be emotional about something. You are not emotional, are you?"

"Yes, I am."

"Tell me about it." S'hyrlus leaned back in her chair.

"I am afraid, I guess." Socrates was embarrassed at his weakness.

"You have been comfortable here, and knowing the comfortable will be replaced by the unknown is frightening." She reached out for his hand and he gave it to her. "Fear is normal. I would wonder about you if you were not afraid." She stroked his hand with her thumb. "You are going off to see wondrous things and to bravely perform whatever duties you are assigned."

The tone of her voice and the massaging of his hand slowly cleared away the fear.

"I am glad you are emotional. It is healthy." She gave a sad smile. "Your father gets emotional, too."

"Not Father!"

"Yes, your father." S'hyrlus chuckled. "Where you are going and what you will be doing will seem strange at first, but it will all make sense eventually. Just trust in your abilities and learn all you can."

"Thank you," he said.

"For what?" S'hyrlus chuckled again.

"For everything you have done for me." His nerves settled. "You have always been there for me and I feel I should thank you. It was appreciated." He kept his stoic posture.

S'hyrlus had a quizzical look on her face as she stood. "I do not think someone of my station has ever been thanked by someone of your station. You are a strange one, Socrates." She touched the end of his nose, smiling.

As he stood to leave, she said, "Your strangeness is a good thing. Do not let anyone tell you differently."

"I will not." He bowed and then left the room, closing the door behind him.

"*Ahem*... my kind are not like your kind," Blackwing said. "I was seven when I was taken to Q'estiria to begin my training, and never returned to my father's house. We don't keep any emotional or familial ties. We're told that we are all brothers and all are sons of Q'estiria. To my grandfather, my father was just another... um... soldier. As am I."

11

THE STORM CLOUDS GATHER

Detective Captain Marshall Trooper, Mayor Lester J. Worth, Police Commissioner Michael Behrnson, and City Attorney Diego Hernandez were sitting in the mayor's office.

"What is the status of that eye-sore building on Court C and 11th?" the mayor said.

"We've tried to persuade the owner that she needs to sell, but still no go," Hernandez replied. "We raised her property taxes and she paid them. We've cut her police services and the incidences of crime in her neighborhood have dropped."

The mayor leaned forward, elbows on his desk, one hand covering the other fist, scowling at the others.

"We've tried to hire someone to burn it down or blow it up, Behrnson said, "and everyone sent to appraise it for feasibility came back refusing the job."

The Mayor scowled more, directly at him. "This office will *not* be party to any means that are illegal, so bombings and burnings are off the table. So if any of that happens, I don't want to know about it and you better have clean hands."

"Well, there is always the eminent domain option," Hernandez said.

"Isn't that only for public use?" the mayor said.

"It is, but we can buy it from her, under *eminent domain*, for a park or a parking lot. Hold it for a couple years, then we sell it off to the developers after the planned use is found to be unfeasible."

"Hmm… look into that further as a possibility. Anyone else have any other ideas?"

"A small localized earthquake would come in handy," Behrnson said. "That old building would come down like shaking a table with a house of cards on it."

"Don't even joke about that," the mayor spat. "Certain… individuals could make that happen, but the cost would be too high. I don't want to pay it and neither would you, if you knew."

"We could try closing it down as a danger to public health," Hernandez said. "At the least, the owner would be tied up in court trying to re-open it."

"I want to know who kidnapped and injured one of my detectives," Trooper said. "She's one of my best and someone wanted her out of the way. I want to know which of you ordered it."

He looked around at all the blank faces. *None of them know what I'm talking about.*

The mayor scowled at him. "No one here ordered anything of the sort. She must've crossed the wrong path."

"I have a question," Irving said. "How does magic work?"

"Hmm… that's hard to explain," Blackwing replied. "Basically, what you call *magic* is a redirection of existing energies. There is something we call the *Source* which stems from lifeforms and tends to focus around magical objects or creatures. It behaves in ways similar to your electromagnetic radiation. Depending on the—for lack of a better term —*spell*, the energies required can be little or great. As an example, your gold bands drew some energy from you to remain seamless and unremovable, but the amount required was minimal. Roughly an hour of your life energy is used for every two years of wear, to maintain the spell. For me to perform the spell, I used about a day's worth of my life energy. You never get something from nothing. However, if the need arose I could replenish what life energies I use by drawing it from another lifeform as I use my own. Say a nearby tree or a small animal. Magic is a tool, and has a cost to its use."

"So you could speed Jessica's healing?" Irving said.

"That's a little different. I can redirect her life energy to focus more on her injuries. However, the cost to me would be greater. It would work out to be about six months from her and a year from me."

"Can you heal yourself?" Suzanne indicated his scar and his eye under the patch.

"The simple answer is no. On my Plane there are healers. They perform their *spells* with precision, to keep the costs a minimum. In my case, what could be healed already has been. If it were a fresh injury, it would come down to severity and the availability of renewal energies."

"Well, I'm willing to give up whatever life energy it would take to have Jessica up and moving," Irving said.

"What? Don't you dare!" Jessica said. "I don't want that on my conscience. I have enough already."

"As noble a sentiment as that is," Blackwing said, "it would only cut her recovery time by half. There is no instantaneous healing through magic." He looked out the main window of the store and noticed the lateness. "Before any plans can be made, you need to decide if you're part of our group or not. It will be dangerous and I'll do what I can to protect you, but the danger remains real."

"I'm in!" Irving said.

"I've been in from the start and I'm not about to stop now." Suzanne flashed a wry grin.

Blackwing looked at Jessica and waited for her to decide.

Sergeant James McConnel, Surveillance Technician, and Brian Trevail, Precinct Desk Sergeant, were in the main surveillance room looking at the wall of monitors. The monitors were all on but showed nothing but snow.

"You see?" McConnel said. "It's a mess. I've checked everything and there's nothing wrong with the equipment." He changed the feeds to a different area and the bank of monitors cleared and showed what was occurring in that area. "It appears to be only in that one area, but I'll be damned if I can figure it out."

Trevail looked at the wall of monitors and said nothing while McConnel changed the area back to the original, and the monitors again showed snow.

"What could cause it?" Trevail sighed.

"Something is interfering with the video. But it'll clear itself in a couple hours and then scramble again intermittently. I have no idea what would cause it." McConnel changed the settings again and nine monitors showed part of the city, with a bunch of moving red and blue dots.

As they watched, a few dots disappeared.

"This is the track of active IDs in the area."

"Why are they disappearing?"

"They shouldn't be. IDs operate differently than the surveillance cameras."

"Really? I'm not an idiot, so quit talking to me like I am."

"Sorry. IDs work differently, but they do report their location similar to the way our surveillance cameras do. Whatever's affecting the cameras is also affecting the IDs reporting capabilities, and I have no idea what could do that."

"What's the shape of the outage area? Can you show me that?"

"I'm sure the system can show that, but I have no idea how to get it to do it." McConnel blushed.

"Get one of the techs to show you how, and then you can show me." Trevail turned to leave.

"What would the shape of an outage tell you?" McConnel asked.

Trevail took a deep breath. "The shape of the outage should be roughly circular because of the electromagnetic emanations, with the source of the interference in the center or close to it. Once you figure out how to display the shape of the affected area, monitor it to see if it moves or changes shape."

Trevail left as McConnel called the technicians.

"Have you decided?" Blackwing asked Jessica, as Irving's phone rang.

Irving took the call and went across the room.

"Honestly, I'm embarrassed." Jessica didn't want to meet Blackwing's gaze.

"About what?" he asked.

"I was rescued by you and Irving... and I was naked. Why was my uniform removed?"

"From the perspective of Malthuvius, he was looking for any weapons that could be used against him."

"I think she's worried about the sexual connotations of being naked."

Suzanne moved closer to Jessica and put a hand on her shoulder and looked at Blackwing.

"To us that is something private, and reserved for someone… special," Jessica said.

"I sympathize with your feelings," Blackwing said. "But to my kind something sexual is far from acceptable between you and us. It would be akin to your kind and the bovines. Our… sexual habits and morals differ greatly from yours." His face became red.

"Are you embarrassed about the subject of this discussion?" Suzanne said. "I would've thought you were beyond embarrassment about anything."

"That is something that is also private to my kind. It's a subject that's not usually discussed in this fashion."

Irving walked over to the others. "We have a problem. I have to go into work. There's something screwy with the surveillance system and they want it fixed immediately."

"They know we're here?" Jessica said.

"No, and that's the problem. I think it has something to do with Blackwing's… spell to hide us. Can you see Jessica home?" he asked Blackwing.

"Before you go, bare your arm," Blackwing said.

Irving pushed up his left sleeve.

"No, bare the entire arm." Blackwing pulled out something from his coat pocket as Irving removed his shirt from his left arm. "Are you sure you're in?" He showed a silver coin.

Irving nodded and Blackwing placed the coin above his bicep. It flattened and formed a band that fit snuggly.

"I'll explain what this means later. For now just tap it three times to call me. I'm trusting that you will be discreet. And yes, one of us will see that Jessica gets home safely."

After putting his shirt back on fully, Irving walked over to Jessica to gently squeeze her shoulder, and flashed a smile when she looked up at him.

"I don't know him well," Suzanne said, as they watched Irving leave the bookstore, "but surprisingly he seems to be quite capable." She smiled and bent close to Jessica's ear. "He also cares for you," she whispered.

"Of course he does." Jessica frowned. "I'm an injured colleague."

"That isn't what I meant and you know it," Suzanne whispered, and stood. "I want to know more about S'hyrlus," she said to Blackwing.

"What would you like to know?" he asked.

"If she wasn't your mother, then what was she?"

"The Lady S'hyrlus was a... wood nymph. Her tree is the oak." Blackwing drew his staff from his duster. "She gave this to my father as a gift." He struck the butt end on the floor and it transformed into an ornate dragon's head. "My father's symbol was a... tiger."

"What I meant was, what was her purpose? Why was she with your father?"

"Hmm... I guess you'd call her a consort."

"So who was your father's wife?"

"My father had no wife, if I understand what you mean. Lady S'hyrlus accompanied my father at formal functions. She was his advisor in all things. She ran the household when he was away, and was his nurse when he was injured. She raised me, as much as was permitted."

"But why did she do all those things? What did she get from the... arrangement?"

Blackwing sat at his place at the counter and passed around tankards to Suzanne and Jessica.

"We're different from humans in that we enter a... breeding phase. At that time, if we're selected to enter the *T'et Faqin,* all of our seed, all that will ever be, is collected and stored. Those that bring dishonor to the *T'et Faqin* have their seed destroyed. Those that distinguish themselves may be selected to have a young one, but only if we have a companion. I once asked my father how he met Lady S'hyrlus. He said he was injured defending her, before he found out she was a wood nymph. While she nursed his injuries, she became enamored with him and selected him." Blackwing chuckled. "My father said she was with him because of a life-debt, but I think she had feelings for him and only she knows what she got from the arrangement."

"If your staff was your father's, how did you get it?" Jessica said.

Blackwing frowned. "When my father died, I was obligated to return it to Lady S'hyrlus. At that time, she gifted it to me but said the tiger symbol didn't fit my personality, and changed it to the dragon."

"So do you have a mate somewhere?" Suzanne said.

She saw Jessica frown in her direction and saw Blackwing become uncomfortable.

"No, we don't have mates or joinings. Not for my kind, anyway. We are selected, most of the time, by wood nymphs. But they are obsessed with their ideal of male beauty and I'm not acceptable. Besides, I have neither a manor house nor property to share."

"That makes me sad," Suzanne said. "Everyone needs someone, in my opinion."

"What did you put on Irving's arm?" Jessica said.

"One of these," Suzanne showed her a platinum bracelet. "It allows me to call Blackwing to me. It is something special. To me, anyway."

"What makes it so special?"

"It makes me *K'obi Sha Shin J'oi Faqin.*"

"It makes you what now?"

"Trusted friend to Wizards."

"Is Irving aware of what it signifies?"

"He hasn't been told yet, but he knows," Blackwing said.

Irving entered McConnel's office. "What's the problem?"

McConnel raised his hand toward the bank of monitors showing snow. "Fix it."

"Is it here, or is it at the locations you're monitoring? Looks like interference of some kind to me."

McConnel made some changes and the monitors cleared. "It appears to be at the locations." He changed the settings back and the monitors again showed snow.

"How long has it been doing that?"

"The interference has been occurring intermittently for most of a month. Also, there's this." He brought up the same view he'd shown Trevail earlier. "This is all the IDs in the affected area. If you watch, you can see them disappear. I've tried to narrow it down to show the point they disappear, but I can't. I need to know the shape of the interference."

"Let me in there." Irving stepped toward McConnel, who vacated the chair, and Irving sat.

He began running through menus and entering commands, but nothing changed. *If I fix it too quickly, they'll find the bookstore. And if they see the shape of the interference, same outcome.*

"There is no quick fix," Irving said, after a short time. "I'll have to create something to give you the information you require, and that'll take a while."

"How long?"

"Maybe a month, if the interference remains. You said it was intermittent. It'll probably clear up on its own long before I can get something to work. Are you sure everything is shielded at the source?"

"It was when installed. Would loose shielding cause this?"

"Definitely. I could work something up, but as I said, it'll take a while."

"Then get on it!"

"I'm sorry, sir, but the number of resources required will have to be cleared through Captain Trooper before I can begin." Irving vacated the chair. "And I would start with a crew to check the shielding of the cameras affected. If it is loose shielding, I'd be wasting time and resources to create something to help narrow it down."

Irving turned to leave and McConnel grabbed his arm.

McConnel was already on the phone. "Yes, sir. He says it may be a shielding issue. The other issue, he says, will take some time. Yes, sir, I'll send him right up. Captain Trooper wants to see you." He put his phone away. "Now!"

McConnel released his arm and Irving left.

After a short elevator ride, he was standing in front of the captain's door. He was about to signal, when it opened.

"Get in here, Strange!" boomed the captain, from his desk. "Are you trying to be difficult?" he said, after the door closed.

"No sir." Irving crossed the room to stand in front of the Captain Trooper's desk. "As I explained to McConnel, the issues may be caused by faulty shielding and without checking that first, I'd be groping around in the dark."

"I'm not an idiot, Strange. The issue with the cameras and the issue with the IDs aren't related. The Identity Device System works on the old GPS satellite tracking in real time and uses a different frequency. McConnel needs to see its shape. He needs it and so do I. How come there isn't something already in the system to do that?"

Irving shrugged. "Bad planning?"

"Really? I can't believe you just said that."

"Look, Captain, the IDS was something we got from the Feds. It's at least fifty years old, and at design time I doubt they took something like this into account. Either it wasn't important enough to handle or it was an oversight. Whichever it was, it amounts to bad planning."

"And you think it'll take a month?"

"It'll probably take a minimum of a month. It could easily take twice that long."

"Well, Strange, we need the system working immediately. So consider yourself otherwise occupied. I want you working on this, exclusively. Understand?"

"Got it, sir."

Captain Trooper glared at him for a few seconds. "Why are you still here?"

12

THE MORE THINGS CHANGE...

"Before you leave, I need to know if you're in or out," Blackwing said to Jessica.

Before she could answer, her phone rang. She answered, nodded a couple times, and then hung up.

"That was Irving. He's on his way here to take me home and he should be here shortly. I'm still upset with you." She looked at Blackwing. "You told me that wizards were old because it would take a lifetime to learn their skills. From where I'm sitting, you look to be in your late forties, maybe fifty."

Blackwing chuckled. "I said they are *usually* portrayed as old codgers, and they are. As to my age... let's say I'm older than I look. Does that satisfy you?"

Jessica didn't answer right away. "I don't know what kind of help I can be, but I'm in... if you understand that I'll continue to do my job, and you have to promise to train Irving, especially if you give him a weapon." She tried to move a little to get comfortable. "I was worried sick that he was going to hurt himself, or me, with that damn short sword." She chuckled.

Blackwing pulled out a silver coin and mumbled something to it. "Would above your left bicep be out of the way of your uniform?"

"It should be." She slid up a voluminous sleeve of her blouse, baring her left bicep.

Blackwing pressed the coin to her bare skin and it formed into a band around her arm.

"Now that I'm in," she straightened her blouse, "what makes this so special?" She indicated the band.

"I'll explain it when Irving returns." Blackwing flashed a wry grin.

"I have a question," Suzanne said. "What do your women look like?"

"That's a good question," Blackwing said. "I wish I could answer it."

"So you won't say?" Suzanne pouted.

"No, I can't say, because I don't know."

"What do you mean you don't know?" Jessica said. "What about when you were younger? Surely you've seen the little females at your school."

"The Academy is and always has been males only. There were no females of any race allowed on the grounds. The only students were of Q'estiria. The other staff members were male."

Suzanne stared, dumbfounded. "As old as you are, you've never seen a female of your own kind? Where did they say the young ones come from?"

"Maybe the cabbage patch." Jessica snickered.

"They said young ones came from... the Ministry of Husbandry."

Jessica looked at his innocent expression and chuckled.

Irving rushed into the store, panting. "We have trouble."

"What kind of trouble this time?" Blackwing said.

"Your spell to hide us from surveillance has triggered an outage of the cameras and any IDs in the area."

"That is what I intended."

"I was told to fix it and get the tracking program to show the shape of the ID outages. The outages, if outlined, can be used to find the center of it, and from that figure out that this bookstore is the source."

"They'll be on us in no time," Suzanne said.

"I managed to buy us a month or a little more," Irving said. "After that…" He shook his head.

"What kind of signal do they use and how do we block it?" Suzanne said.

It's been a week since I gave Strange orders concerning the IDS. I should check into his progress. Captain Trooper unlocked his office door and entered.

"Lights!" He set his tablet on his desk.

"Captain Trooper, I presume?" a voice said, from behind, causing him to jerk around and draw his service weapon.

"Who the hell are you and how'd you get in here?" the captain growled.

The man was well-dressed—black suit, no insignias, and wraparound dark glasses, the lenses of which were lightening, showing an outline of eyes. The air about the stranger screamed of government lackey.

"Who I am is unimportant—"

"You have the look of federal spook! Is that why you think you have the authorization to break into my office? Didn't you see the signs concerning unauthorized individuals and being shot?"

"Look," the stranger held his hands in view, "I'm from the government and I'm here to help. But if you feel it necessary, then shoot me."

"As a general rule, anyone from the government is never helping anyone but themselves." Trooper still had his weapon trained on the stranger, trying to decide whether to shoot or not.

The stranger slowly reached into a pocket and produced a small tablet. A three-dimensional document materialized in the air between them.

"As you can see by my credentials, I *am* associated with a federal agency." A large handheld weapon seemed to grow from the stranger's hand. "Your service weapon defaults to stun. I prefer something more... old school. I think I can shoot you before you shoot me. Yours will just stun me. Mine will blow a big hole in you and the wall behind you. That seems to be the only purpose of a fifty-cal." He grinned. "That and dropping elephants with a pistol."

"Okay," Trooper said, as his weapon disappeared.

The stranger put his back inside his jacket.

"Now that we're done with the dick measuring, same question, Trooper said. "Who are you?"

"You can call me John... Smith. That'll work as well as any, I guess. Our office received this." Smith tapped a few more keys and the 3D image changed to an e-mail. "I'm here to find out the whys and wherefores and to help... if I find it appropriate."

Trooper read the document floating in the air and looked for the signature.

Irving! "So you're tech support?"

Smith chuckled. "Not in the way you mean. I'd say I'm more... troubleshooter."

Trooper pulled out his phone and made a call. "Strange? Get your ass to my office. Now!"

Twenty minutes later, Irving was about to signal when the door opened. As he entered, the captain was sitting behind his desk and another man was starting to stand.

"This is Smith," said Captain Trooper, as the door closed.

Smith extended his hand. "Call me John. You're Irving Melvin Strange? Currently head technician? Graduated Magna Cum Laude from MIT and Caltech? Impressive, by the way."

Irving looked at the stranger skeptically as he took his hand. "How do you know that? Have you been spying on me?"

"I prefer to know who I'm dealing with. Call it due diligence." Smith smiled as they shook hands.

"Smith is here to help us with our IDS issues," Trooper said. "Walk him through everything, but do it in your lab. I have my own job to do. Besides, your geek-speak gives me a headache."

"Sorry if I embarrassed you in there," Smith said, as he and Irving walked to his lab. "I did it to get your captain to realize what he has. Our agency would be interested in having you, should you feel the need to, shall we say… branch out?"

"Um… I'm content where I am, thanks," Irving replied. A bead of sweat running down the side of his face.,

"How's your girlfriend doing?"

"What makes you think I have a girlfriend?"

"Oh, I'm sorry. I thought Jessica Sylvillagys was your girlfriend. After all, you have been spending a lot of time together and a lot of expense. I was just asking how her recuperation was going."

"I'm not comfortable with your prying," Irving snapped. "I'm a private person."

They entered the lab.

"I've noticed that about you."

"You know," Smith said, after an hour of explanations, "I only understood about half of what you said. You seem to have done everything hardware related. Is the interference still there?"

"No, it isn't. It disappeared after a few hours. As I said, it's intermittent, and how long it lasts varies. What the captain wants is to be able to see the shape of the outage, as I stated before. I sent a message to try to get the source code and the specs for the system."

Smith chuckled. "That isn't going to happen. We allow you to *use* the system only. Making changes to it would be a violation of national security. That being said, you have done all you can on your end." He used his small tablet to send something to Irving's phone. "The next time it happens," he ran through the different screens and pulled up a small input box, "come here and type in the code I just sent you, and you'll have what you need. It'll reset once you change views." He got up to leave the lab. "Before I forget, you're the only one authorized to apply the fix. So keep a close eye on that code." He opened the door and looked at Irving for a second. "Tell Jess I said hi."

Jessica and Irving were sitting in a booth at their favorite beanery, sipping drinks.

"We have a major problem." Irving put his drink down.

Jessica leaned in. "What kind of problem?"

"I had a visit from a Fed today. He gave me the code to give the captain the type of display he wanted for the IDS."

"Does our *friend* know?"

"Not yet. I was trying to think of a way to meet up without raising a bunch of alarms."

Jessica pulled out her phone and dialed. "Hi, Suz. We're at Tony's and would love it if you joined us. Okay, see you soon."

"Why didn't I think of that?" Irving chuckled, shaking his head. "On another note, do you know anyone working for the Feds?"

"I have no idea. In my life, I've known so many people and I have no idea if any work for the Feds. Why'd you ask?"

"This Fed, he called himself John Smith—"

"That's original."

"—and he acted as if he knew you." Irving frowned. "He seemed to know a lot about me, you, and our relationship."

"What relationship?"

"I think he was assuming you and I are… um… involved."

"I can see you're upset about it, but I wouldn't put much stock in it. Unless he offered information that he couldn't have found on the web, I'd let it go. Any remarks made about you and I are assumptions, because of the bills for my injuries and our living arrangements, and they're designed to get a rise out of you and to cause suspicion." She patted his hand. "Try not to let it get to you." She grinned at him. "On a brighter note, I'll be getting these casts off next week, but I'll still have to be careful."

Irving's eyes were downcast. "So you'll be back to work soon?"

"Couple more weeks and then I'll be riding a desk for a while." She stared at him. "I thought you'd be happier about that bit of news. What's wrong?"

He scuffed his feet on the floor and stared at his half-empty glass. "To be frank, I've become accustomed to taking care of you. Now you won't need me to help you."

"I'll always need a good friend around, and you've been that. I owe you a lot. Just know that all your efforts have been appreciated."

Irving brightened up as Suzanne came over to their table.

"What's up?" she said.

"We have to make other *arrangements*," Jessica said, as Suzanne sat. "We have less time than we thought."

"Hmm... I thought it was something like that. Things have been too quiet at the store. I've been having some strange feelings, like things are going to take a turn for the worse."

All three sat quietly for some time, each lost in their own thoughts on drastic changes.

Shortly after returning home from her impromptu dinner with Jessica and Irving, Suzanne was sitting at her table, working on her tablet. She tapped her bracelet three times and waited nervously.

"What is it you require?" Blackwing walked to the table and sat.

"Do you see this?" She turned her tablet towards him so he could see the displayed map. "If something... odd happens, go here." She pointed at a spot on the map.

"What do you mean by odd?"

"Before you showed up, the city had been trying to get their hands on this building. I've managed to keep possession of it as best I can, but recently things have been too quiet. I think they're planning something."

"Planning what?"

"I have no idea. It's just a feeling I've been having. I've diversified a lot of my holdings so that, short of total civil asset forfeiture, we should be all right. Maybe I should just sell the building."

"Would that solve the problem?"

"It would shift the target from me to someone else, and right now that's all I want. I'm tired of fighting with the City."

"Since I don't understand all your laws, do what you think is best for you. Since you live here, where would you go?"

"At this point, I have no idea. Maybe buy a place outside the city. You, of course, would be more than welcome to join me. I've been thinking about this for almost a year, but if you're going with me I need to know."

"I'll go with you until such time as you tell me to leave."

"I'll make the call tomorrow."

"Can it have a healthy, good-sized oak tree on the property?"

"I'll keep that in mind. What's your plan on dealing with Nighthawk?"

"First, I have no hard proof that he is doing anything outside our dictums. Second, my grandfather is behind whatever he's up to. And since they're my direct superiors, I'm not certain there's anything that I can do."

"Can you go to your Council?"

"Any of us can go to the Council at any time. However, without definitive proof, there is nothing they would do and it could hurt my chances later when I get proof."

"Irving let me know that they now have a way to locate the cause of the disturbances. Should you cast more spells to block cameras and IDs."

"That was faster than I expected."

"It wasn't something Irving did. It came from outside his purview."

After the meeting with Suzanne, Irving and Jessica were going through their nightly routine, at Jessica's apartment.

"Is there something wrong?" Irving said. *She's been uncharacteristically quiet since our meeting.*

"I'm tired of sleeping in this damn chair. I want to sleep in my own bed tonight. Problem is I haven't figured out how to accomplish it."

"I can help you, if you like." Irving blushed.

Jessica maneuvered the chair into the bedroom. "I need help getting to the bed and getting undressed."

Irving went into the small room and bent over so she could wrap her good arm around his neck. After some struggling, he managed to get her onto the bed and then wheeled the chair out of the room.

He returned and stood at her oak dresser, with his back to her. "What do you want to sleep in?"

"Before my injury, I used to sleep *au naturel*, but that may not be appropriate. Do you have any suggestions?"

Jessica could see his ears turning bright red, and she grinned.

"Umm... I'm not comfortable going through your drawers. If you tell me what you want and which drawer it's in, then..."

"Help!" Jessica said.

When Irving turned around, he saw that Jessica had gotten her cast tangled in the voluminous blouse she was wearing. She was stuck half-out of it. He went over to untangle her and removed her top for her.

"Can you help me out of this dress? If so, we can call it good enough and I'll just lay down, if you help."

A few minutes later, she was lying on the bed, on her back, with the covers pulled up over her.

"I'll be on the couch, if you need anything," Irving said, an uncharacteristic quaver to his voice, as he started for the door.

"I just thought of something. What if I need to pee in the middle of the night?"

"Just yell and I'll come in to help," he said, without turning around.

"Do you want to talk for a bit, or are you too tired?"

"We can, if you want. I just don't want to keep you awake. You're still on the mend, you know." He walked around to the other side of the bed and sat with his back to her.

"Lights off," Jessica said to the ceiling, and all the lights in the apartment turned off. "You can stretch out, you know. Get comfortable. I won't bite. Well, maybe a little, but I promise not to draw too much blood. Besides, I've had my shots." She snickered.

"What did you want to talk about?" Irving's voice trembled as he lay next to her on the bed.

"What exactly did that Fed say to you about me?"

"He asked how my... girlfriend was. I tried to remain calm and non-committal, but I may have confirmed his belief. Sorry."

"What are you sorry for, that someone pushed a button, or that it wasn't true?"

Irving was quiet for a long time and he was glad the lights were off so his embarrassment wouldn't be apparent.

"Both, I guess."

"You guess? You mean you don't know, or is it that you don't want to be *involved* with me?"

"Umm... I never said that."

Jessica could hear his voice crack.

"You know, I was upset with Blackwing. He gave you a short sword without training you. You could've been injured."

"I didn't know."

"I need a favor from you."

"What kind of favor?"

"Kiss me? If you want to, I mean."

13

CONTINGENCIES

Jessica and Irving left the Precinct through the back door after their shift ended.

"Wouldn't it be easier for you to take a car home?" Irving said.

"This is the end of my first day back to work and I want to go to Tony's before going home. It's not that far and I prefer to walk. I've been confined to that damn chair for too long and I need to stretch my legs a little."

"The doc said you should take it easy."

"I *am* taking it easy." She smiled at him and touched the side of his face. "You worry too much, Irv."

"And you don't worry enough, Jess."

"That makes things perfect, then." She grinned and continued walking.

As they continued, they became aware that they were in a dead spot for surveillance. Jessica recognized the spot as the one where she'd first met Blackwing, and she grinned.

"Could I interest you two in dinner?" said a familiar *basso* voice, which they both recognized, from the shadows.

"Of course!" the pair replied, and took each other's hand.

Blackwing walked up behind them, took Jessica's hand, and all three disappeared. The next second, they were in an under furnished living room, with Suzanne looking on.

"It's so nice of you to come," she said. "Welcome to our home." She grinned as she moved to each, giving a brief hug to the guests.

"This is nice." Jessica looked around the room. "Not much furniture yet, but it's getting there."

Irving looked around the room for cameras "This *is* nice."

"No need to worry, Irving," Suzanne said. "There's no surveillance here."

"Mind if I ask where we are?" Jessica said. "I was beginning to worry. We hadn't heard from either of you for weeks."

"We're about twenty miles south of the city—" Suzanne started.

"We're in the Badlands?" Irving said. "Why are you clear out here?"

"Irv." Jessica took his chin between her thumb and index finger, and turned his face toward her. "Have a little patience. We'll be told everything we need to know. Give them a chance to answer. Honestly! It's getting so I can't take you anywhere." To Suzanne and Socrates, she said, "Please forgive him. It's hard being with a genius. They can be so… irritating… and rude."

Suzanne glanced to Socrates and both smirked.

"Irving," she said, "three weeks ago I signed over the building to the developers. I felt there was something imminent and bad about to happen. It was a way to get the target off me."

"But out here?" he said.

"We had to live somewhere, and it had to be somewhere outside

Tacoma Proper. It took us two weeks to find this place. I was raised in the city, so this was all new to me. I had always been told that those who lived outside the city would murder you in your bed and steal you blind. That hasn't been the case, so far, and I feel it unlikely to happen. Those that live out here are just trying to survive."

"How did you get out of the city?" Irving said. "They say there are barricades and check-points to prevent anyone from leaving."

"There are, and it is a hassle to leave. But they let me, after a lot of argument and other rigmarole. This place has most of what we need. We have privacy, except for my ID, and people leave us alone." Suzanne turned to Jessica. "How have you been?" She squeezed Jessica in a hug. "It's been so long since I've seen you. I see you're out of your casts. And back to work, I assume?"

"Yes, no casts and back at work. Light duty, of course. I drove by your building a couple days ago, and I'm sorry to say it's no longer there. Demolished."

"It couldn't be helped." Suzanne's eyes began tearing. "Jessica, are you up to helping set the table?" She wiped away any emerging tears. "Dinner is about ready. I haven't cooked in a long time so don't hold it against me."

Jessica and Suzanne went into the kitchen.

"How have you been, Blackwing?" Irving asked.

"I've been well, thank you. I've been busy with moving, re-establishing the wards around the property, and returning most of the *Brui K'sha U'ien*—"

"The brown gnomes?" Irving nodded. "Did you find the Ogre or that other guy?"

"No to both. I suspect they have returned to the proper Plane for each. Whatever they're planning, causing chaos is high on their list of priorities."

The women called them to the table, and Socrates handed something to Irving.

"For later."

"That was… remarkable." Irving pushed his plate away and took up his tankard.

"It was just stew, which I made. The bread bowls were purchased." Suzanne grinned, taking up her own tankard.

"I agree with Irv." Jessica took a sip from her tankard. "It's been ages since I had homemade stew. But I'm sure that isn't the only reason we're here."

"You're correct, Jessica," said Blackwing. "You two were brought here to discuss what progress has been made, if any. Irving, if you don't mind." He signaled.

Irving reached into his pocket and produced two gold coins, made into pendants with string. He handed one to Jessica.

"Feel free to replace the string with a chain, if you want," Blackwing said. "Those are to be worn and kept in contact with your skin."

"What are they for?" Jessica asked.

"Early on," Blackwing said, "I gave one to Suzanne and she began to comprehend the arcane concepts associated with investments. It was something she wanted and needed to know. Now she is quite good at it. Those coins enhance your already existing strong points, as well as minor things that go with it. In Suzanne's case, with her understanding of business, she understood investments. And that feeling she'd get as to what to buy or sell, it helped to tip her off that something bad was going to happen if she didn't sell her building when she did. I have no idea what it will enhance in either of you, but I figured it would be worth a try."

Jessica slipped the pendant over her head. "So that's why you were so worried about something happening concerning your store?"

"For me," Suzanne said, "it took about twenty-four hours before I noticed that I was more focused and was grasping concepts that I was ignorant of before wearing it. The longer you wear it, the better it works. I found out early on that the effects last about twenty-four hours after you remove it. I've had mine on for quite a while, so it may take longer to wear off."

"Is this real gold?" Irving stared at his pendant.

"Yes, but they're gold from my Plane, so if they're tested, they'll probably test as a different iso… isotope. With Jessica, I expect her agility, strength, endurance, and eyesight to improve, along with an increase in coordination. With Irving, I'm expecting an increase in intellect."

"Oh, no! Making him smarter than he already is? He'll be insufferable." Jessica said, and they all laughed. "What did you do with all your stuff from the bookstore?" she asked, when everyone had calmed their laughter.

"It's all here," Suzanne replied. "Blackwing made the move simple. I got to see some *real* magic."

"How so?" Irving said.

"He pulled out a black cloth and tossed into the air. It unfolded itself to fit the room, and as it fell it covered things in the room. Those things covered disappeared, and it refolded itself once it hit the floor. It took less than thirty minutes to empty the building—the store, my apartment, the basement, everything. Then he just carried the folded cloth out in his pocket."

"Hmm… trans-dimensional storage?" Irving raised an eyebrow toward Blackwing.

Blackwing nodded.

"This property is more than adequate for our needs," Suzanne said.

"Ten acres enclosed by conifers with a small grove of oaks close to the middle, a four-bedroom house, and a large Gambrel-style barn. It only cost three times what I got for my building in the city."

"That seems expensive," Jessica said.

"Well, it cost a third more because of the rushed paperwork, and I paid for it all upfront. No loan, so there was that penalty and fine. So it all came out to triple what I sold my building in the city for."

"I've made a little progress for our cause." Irving retrieved his small backpack and dug out three small devices. "I made these." He showed the others the devices.

"What are they for?" Suzanne said.

"I guess you could call them repeaters." Irving walked up behind Suzanne. "Since we can't remove the IDs, and because of the other functions the IDs provide that we need," he pressed one to Suzanne's ID at the back of her neck, "they'll show anyone monitoring that the particular ID is in a certain area, even if the wearer is not. I've set this one to your ID, Suzanne. Now, once you plug it in and it's on, you can go anywhere within a mile of it and it'll show your position as wherever the repeater is. You could leave the repeater in the living room and go to the barn and it would show you're in the living room."

"That's a nice piece of tech!" Suzanne said. "I can see where that could come in handy."

"Since I just returned to work," Jessica said, "I'm riding a desk, doing paperwork. I have monitored some reports, starting from the date of my injury, and I have seen nothing out of the ordinary. But I'll keep checking. Have you located Thomas O'Toole?" she asked Blackwing.

"Not yet."

"When I'm more up to speed, I want to interview Joe Johnson. He may know how to find him."

"How could someone disappear so completely?" Suzanne said.

Jessica chuckled. "Actually, it's easier than you'd think. If he moves out of the state, he would seem to have disappeared. Keeping track of everyone is difficult, at best. It takes too long to track someone through their digital footprint. Most jurisdictions don't care once someone leaves it. After one hundred fifty years, there's still no jurisdictional coordination."

"One of the other reasons we wanted you to come out here," Suzanne said, "was to extend an invitation. This house is quite large and has plenty of room, should either of you, or both, decide to quit the city. You have a place to go, if things get to be too rough or you need to get away for a while."

"That's a nice offer, Suzanne." Jessica smiled. "But right now I need to be in the city."

"A very kind offer, and one we'll keep in mind," Irving said. "But I, too, need to be in the city."

"Well, the offer's there," Suzanne said. "Feel free to come out anytime."

"With that," Jessica said, "I want to thank you both for dinner and a lovely time, but we need to get home."

"I'll return you," Blackwing said, as they gathered their things.

A short time later, Jessica and Irving were back where Blackwing had picked them up.

Three days after the small dinner party, Suzanne and Blackwing went for a walk and stopped at the oak grove. Blackwing stopped Suzanne and approached the central and largest tree, alone, and rested the side of his face and hand against the rough bark. She actually saw him grin a little.

"There is something I need to do here," he said. "It won't take long, but you're free to observe. Don't interfere. Hold your questions until later, okay?"

"Sure." Suzanne shrugged. *I have nothing else to do right now, and it's so nice here.*

She found to place to sit on the ground and leaned against a smaller tree. She saw a wild rabbit hop up to Blackwing's feet. As he reached down, the rabbit dropped dead, and Blackwing pulled out a small knife and started to clean and gut the rabbit. As he did, he shook the rabbit's blood all over the ground at the base of the enormous tree.

Once the rabbit was cleaned, he built a small fire a few feet from the tree and started roasting it. As it cooked, Suzanne heard him sing. His voice was deep, penetrating, and sounded like a distant thunder carried by the wind.

She didn't recognize the song, and the words were gibberish to her, but it was soothing and peaceful, with the smell of the cooking rabbit wafting around her. She closed her eyes and let his song pass over her, through her, and become part of her.

She didn't feel she was sleeping, nor did it feel like much time had passed, when she heard an answering lyric to the song, one that was definitely female. When she opened her eyes, she saw the bark on the gnarled surface begin to shimmer, the distortion slowly taking form, until the delicate figure of a female stepped from within.

The female entity was the most beautiful creature she had ever seen. Statuesque, with long, flowing flame-red hair and pale skin, dressed in leather with a flowing cape of leaves, and her feet were bare. On her head was a small, simple diadem of oak leaves that shimmered like platinum. More notable was that Blackwing knelt and hung his head.

Suzanne saw the female eat some of the roasted rabbit. Their conversation sounded like wind blowing through trees, carrying voices from far away. She understood none of what was said, but it didn't seem to matter to her. It wasn't long before the female entity stood. They bowed to each other, and she stepped back into the tree trunk and vanished.

Once gone, Suzanne found that she could move—not that she'd noticed the contrary—and stood as Blackwing came over to her.

"Who was that?"

"That was Lady S'hyrlus."

"*She* raised *you*? She doesn't look a day over sixteen!"

Blackwing chuckled. "She would say that she's looking old. Nymphs are ageless. No one knows how long they have been or their origins. She did say that she thanks you for being *K'obi Sha Shin J'oi Faqin* to me."

"I had a choice?"

"Of course you had a choice. You have a choice even now."

"Was that all she had to say?"

"I had asked for her opinion on how to handle Nighthawk and my grandfather. She said she doesn't get involved in politics or military matters, but she suggested that unseating the General will take a majority of the Council, each of which are heads of their own family. Meaning, if the current Blackwing on the Council—Cornelius, I think is his name—retires or dies, the General will be promoted onto the Council and could then be controlled, to a degree, by the other families."

"Who is Cornelius Blackwing?"

"He's the General's grandfather."

"So what are you going to do about Nighthawk?"

"The only thing I can do is defeat him, subdue him, and then transport him to Q'estiria."

"Have you noticed any differences?" Irving said. "It has been three days since you were given your pendant." He was lying on the bed, half-covered.

"Some, I guess." Jessica brushed her hair, in front of her dressing mirror.

She was naked, having just finished with her shower.

"Can you toss me my pendant?" she said. "It's on the end table, on my side of the bed."

Irving reached over for it and fired it her way without looking at her first. Jessica saw it and switched the brush to her other hand, and while looking in the mirror, reached behind her to catch it. She put it on before continuing to brush her hair. Then she stopped.

"I guess that answers my question," Irving said. "I hadn't intended on firing it at you that way, but I just knew where you were without seeing you."

"I know. It's funny, I always used to get confused when looking in a mirror, especially when trying to catch something, and yet I managed it without even thinking about it." She looked at him in the mirror and gave a flirtatious grin. "There are other changes in you."

"What do you mean?"

"I wouldn't say that you've filled out, but I would say your muscles seem to be more defined."

Irving laughed. "That has nothing to do with the pendant. That's all you."

Jessica placed the brush on the dresser top and turned to face him. "What's that supposed to mean?"

"It's the workout you keep giving me." He grinned at her.

"Complaining?"

"Not a bit! I may not be the smartest person in the world, but I am smart enough to know when I have a good thing going. You do look prettier since you've had your pendant, though."

"Flatterer!" She flashed a broad grin.

"As much as I possibly can." Irving put his hands under his pillow, got a self-satisfying grin on his face, and closed his eyes.

14

READY OR NOT

"Are you ready?" said Phelonius Blackwing. "The time for confronting my grandson is almost at hand."

"I am prepared," Malthuvius Nighthawk replied.

Phelonius turned towards Malthuvius, sniffed, and looked at him skeptically.

"I doubt that." He turned back to the glassed wall that overlooked the city far below.

"My minions have deprived him of his stronghold and separated him from his puny allies. I was trained, just as he was, and I have battled him before. I know him."

"I know how both of you were trained. I designed the training many years before either of you came to Q'estiria. But that training only shows techniques to the untrained. There are techniques and stratagems you pick up years after the training ends. Have you battled him or anyone outside of the required training? Your last statement betrays your overconfidence. You are foolish if you believe he needs a stronghold. Have you even read his reports?"

"I have, and I find them woefully incomplete and lacking details."

"What did his report on the Grimstar apprehension tell you?"

"It told me nothing. It was just one line saying he apprehended him. As I stated, his reports lack detail."

"How many *Grum K'sha U'ien* have you apprehended?"

Malthuvius dropped his head and looked at the ground. "None."

"That one line tells me volumes. I *have* hunted many of the *Grum K'sha U'ien*. They are not easy to apprehend. That one line tells me that Socrates did not quit. If he fails once, he will keep coming. He gets his tenaciousness from his father... and from me. Breeding will always show."

"I take it you have little confidence in my abilities," Malthuvius said, anger tingeing his words.

"I have confidence in your ability to persuade and seduce. You follow the edicts and procedures, and, to be sure, we need individuals like that. When I mention Socrates, what characteristic comes to your mind?"

Malthuvius's facial expression betrayed his disgust. "That hideous scar."

"How did he get it?"

"I was there. I know how he got it."

"You know, but I do not think you understand. At the time of the war with the *Ha'Jakta Ha'Dreen B'kota*, like you, Socrates was young and inexperienced. He took down three of the dragons and their riders before he was injured, and another five afterward. How many did you personally dispatch?"

"You know the answer to that. I was where I belonged, at your side, throughout the war."

"I know where you were, which demonstrates my point. You do know that he was given the opportunity to have the severity of his disfigurement mitigated?"

"I read the scrolls."

"Then you know that his refusal is a slap in the face to those who didn't perform as honorably, as bravely, as he did. He wears it as a warning to everyone."

"What warning is that?"

"Anyone who sees that scar asks themselves if they could, or would, continue if they were injured that way. In other words, underestimate him at your peril."

"You think I underestimate him? I can assure you, I do not!"

"I certainly hope that is the case."

Jessica had just arrived at the precinct when she received a message to report to the captain's office. She had no more arrived at his door when it opened, and she entered.

"Sylvillagys, are you okay?" said Captain Trooper.

"I'm fine, sir. Why do you ask?"

"You had your re-qualifications yesterday?"

"Yes, sir. I did re-qualify, didn't I?"

Captain Trooper exhaled loudly. "I don't know if you're aware that we keep several qualifications to make comparisons, in case there's a significant drop in proficiency."

"I wasn't aware. Did I pass or not?"

"I'm not concerned about your passing." The captain switched views to display the results in 3D, in the space between them. "Here are your shooting lane results."

Several pictures of target silhouettes flipped by slowly.

"They all look good to me, sir." Jessica shrugged.

"Did you notice anything?" Jessica shook her head, with a pouting expression and a raised eyebrow.

"Each one is at a different range. Each one is a head shot. More disturbing is the placement at those different ranges." All the pictures overlay each other. "Notice anything?"

"I don't understand what you're getting at, sir."

"Every shot from ten feet to two hundred yards is in the exact same spot. I've overlaid them one at a time and I don't see any significant deviation in placement. Usually the further away the more the impact points bounce around, but not yours. I want to know if you think this is funny."

Jessica cocked her head to the side. "I don't understand, sir."

"I know you cheated!" The captain stood and slammed his palms on the desk. "Fess up! Who put you up to this? I'm not at all amused."

"Sir, I didn't cheat, and if there's been any attempt to deceive you I'm unaware of it."

"Okay." He changed the pictures and cycled through them. "These are your last qualifications before your injury. Did you see any changes?"

"Yes, sir. The impacts seem to become less accurate with the greater distance."

"That is what I'd expect! Most trained officers can't hit center mass at one hundred yards with their service weapon. You included, apparently. So why is it that with your most recent test there's no drop in proficiency? Saying yours are accurate is an understatement. Did someone at the range change the ranges on the display, with the target being only ten feet away? Maybe the pictures are just copies."

Trooper's face was turning a dangerous shade of red.

"I say I didn't cheat. If you think I did, let's go to the range and see."

"Fine, have it your way!"

The captain stormed out of his office, with Jessica in his wake.

It didn't take long to reach the second sub-basement of the precinct, where the shooting lanes were located. The captain, still angry, had Jessica get into her ready position—service weapon pointed up and configured as a nine-millimeter, with her back to the lane. He took up the controller and entered the distance he wanted. The blank target slab ran downrange. He watched the readout as it traveled. When it reached 253 yards, it stopped.

"Here are the rules. You start in this position and end in this position. When I say go, you turn and shoot one round as fast as you can. Understood?"

Jessica nodded.

He clicked the countdown. "Go!"

Jessica turned, fired, and resumed her position. He clicked the countdown again once she returned to her starting position. He stared at the screen, giving the results.

In her peripheral, she saw him freeze and his jaw work side-to-side, the way it always did when he was highly irritated. He clicked *Save* and *Clear* and changed the range to 256.12 yards.

"This time, four shots as fast as you can, but still hit the target." He glanced at the indicator. When the ready light flashed green, he said, "Go!" and clicked the countdown.

Jessica pivoted and fired four quick rounds. As she pivoted back, she heard him click the countdown again to stop it.

"Is that sufficient?" she said, seeing his jaw moving side-to-side again.

"Yes. I'll start the processing, and we can review it in my office."

Captain Trooper clicked *Save* and *Process*. Then he turned and left for his office.

Once Trooper and Jessica were back in his office, he displayed the recent results. His jaw worked side-to-side again as he flipped to the next one. This time it displayed *Four Impacts Detected*, in red letters, and then displayed the coordinates of all impacts—all within thousandths of an inch of each other.

"Did you notice?" said Captain Trooper.

"Notice what, sir?"

"I moved the target further away and you still hit the exact same spot, at a distance that a rifle would have difficulty. Also, if you look at the reaction times from yesterday to today, they improve. I want an explanation, Detective!"

"To be fair, Captain, the distances are simulated, and if you check the indicated positions of the impacts I think you'll see that they aren't *exactly* in the same spot. The differential is greater in the four-shot result."

Trooper slammed his palms on his desktop. *Boom!* "You want to argue thousandths of an inch from a distance you shouldn't even be able to see the silhouette? One other tidbit you're forgetting to dispel—your reaction time?"

"I was... better rested?" Jessica shrugged. "Come on, Cap'n, I can't explain it and you know it. Does it really matter? Doesn't it just make me better at my job?"

"That's up for debate. It does mean you can protect yourself." Trooper's jaw was working again. "See here, Sylvillagys. There seems to be some funny bullshit going on here, and I won't have it! Understand? I'm not having any of it."

Jessica said nothing and waited to be dismissed. Trooper had his head down and she could see the early balding spot. After more than a few seconds, he jerked his head up.

"Detective?" he whispered, and crooked his finger at her.

"Yes, sir?" She leaned in.

"Is this *your* office?"

"Um… no, sir."

"Then why are you standing there?" Trooper jumped to his feet. "Get the hell out of my office! And take your prankster bullshit with you."

Jessica hurried out, only faintly catching the last words before the door closed.

After she was gone, Trooper pulled up her re-qualifying results again and studied them with a proud smile.

"Damn, that's good shootin'."

When Blackwing entered the house, by way of the back door, he saw Suzanne sitting at the table in the dining room.

"Sox, I have some questions," she said, without looking at him.

Blackwing sat across from her. "What do you want to know?"

"How did you kill the rabbit?"

"I called it and took its life force."

"How did your summoning spell work?"

"It wasn't a summoning spell. A summoning spell gives the individual summoned no choice. It was more of a… request… done in a chant. It was sung to be more coaxing than commanding."

"But why so softly? I couldn't make out anything that you were singing."

"If I whisper, aren't you more likely to come closer than if I yell?"

After a few seconds, "Have you decided what to do about Malthuvius?"

"I have to face him, if he will."

"But isn't he your brother in the *T'et Faqin*?"

Blackwing nodded. "And my commander. It will be… how you say… tricksie?"

"Tricky?"

"Yes, tricky. For us, we can challenge those above us, but it's dangerous. If he views me to be unworthy or impertinent, he can decline. If he deems that I'm worthy, and I've challenged him in a respectful way, then he has to accept. There are rules to the combat as well. Spells or enchantments that cause transmutations of either of us are not allowed. In other words, he can't change me into a toad and then step on me. I can, however, become the demon you saw in the bookstore. That doesn't count as a transmutation, even though it is. That is more of a show of strength, or a battle of strengths, if he does the same."

"Will he abide by your rules?"

"Probably not. Our spheres will record it, and it will be sent to the Council for review. He won't break the rules, but he will bend them to the point that they crack."

"Will he try to kill you?"

"No, that's something that isn't allowed. As I told you before, we store energy from the *Source*. If we run out of reserves we can die, and there is nothing that says we can't do that. There are rules against taking the other's life force, but nothing that prevents each of us from using more than we have available, which would effectively kill the caster. And therein lies the danger."

Suzanne said nothing for some time. "I think he'll do whatever he can to subdue you. Including breaking any rules you think are in place. This Plane is not your Plane, so if he considers that, your rules would go right out the window. You need to be careful."

"I intend to be cautious. It doesn't matter if he abides by our rules or not. I have to do what I have to do, and do it in a manner I can live with. Otherwise, what would be the point?"

Jessica and Irving had left Tony's and were walking back to the station after a pleasant lunch.

I wonder if Suzanne would like company, she thought, as they strolled along, holding hands.

With their minds elsewhere, they failed to hear anyone behind them.

The familiar grip on their upper arms didn't surprise them. A second later, at their destination, they became aware that something was amiss.

"What the hell?" Jessica said.

"This looks somewhat familiar." Irving scowled as he looked around.

They couldn't see much, but what they could see caused them to be concerned. A blinding light flashed and they could see the bare concrete floor, walls, and ceiling.

"Welcome back," said a menacing deep voice, from behind them.

When they both turned to look at the source of the voice, they saw a familiar tall, lanky figure with his head down. As the figure raised his eyes, they saw two pale blue eyes looking at them, with a menacing grin.

"Welcome to my impromptu arena," said the voice.

Jessica looked the person over and concluded that this wizard looked like a less disheveled copy of Blackwing. *Malthuvius Nighthawk!*

"I know we haven't been properly introduced—"

"Malthuvius Nighthawk," she said.

He nodded. "As I was saying, before being rudely interrupted, I am Malthuvius Nighthawk. You are Detective Sylvillagys." He looked at her. "But I do not recognize this one." He indicated Irving. "I do, however, know he is the one who affected your rescue before we could conclude our previous… conversation."

"Why did you bring us here?" Jessica snapped. "We won't tell you anything."

"I am confident I could elicit information from either of you, if that was my purpose. At this time, information is not my purpose." Nighthawk wandered around the open space.

Jessica moved closer to Irving. *I hope this encounter isn't going to be another torture session.*

"What *is* your purpose for dragging us here?" she said.

"One must always have bait when hunting." Nighthawk grinned.

"So we are the bait," Jessica said. "What is it, or who is it, you're hunting?"

"All in good time. We must not rush things. Our stage is not yet set. I am sure you remember my helpers."

Jessica heard scraping steps coming from shadows and doorways. She turned to see six Ogres of varying sizes, enter the open space. The Ogres made a big circle around Jessica and Irving. One of the bigger ones lunged at Irving, and Nighthawk gave a command and the Ogre backed away.

"I see that he remembers you." Nighthawk chuckled. "He remembers that you made him go hungry and ruined his fun with the detective. I never would have thought they had the capacity to remember anything. I did appease him, though, with one of your kind. The one called Thomas O'Toole seemed to satisfy his bloodlust for a while."

"You fed O'Toole to that thing?" Jessica said, with disgust.

"I had to feed him something. Besides, O'Toole was just a minion to be used by others. I think we may be ready now. Go ahead and summon your master."

"I told you before, I have no master," Jessica said.

"I remember, but call him anyway."

"Do you know who he's talking about?" Irving whispered.

"He wants me to call Blackwing," Jessica whispered back, "and I won't do it."

"Either one of you can call him," Nighthawk said. "One of you will, sooner rather than later."

Suzanne and Blackwing had decided to go inside the city limits to do some shopping. As they walked along the street, Blackwing in his blind uncle disguise and Suzanne guiding him as he gripped her elbow, she would see something interesting at a couple of the street vendors, and stop to look through some of the wares before coming back to guide him further. They were about to enter one of the stores, when they both disappeared.

When they reappeared, they found that they were inside the circle of Ogres with Jessica and Irving. Blackwing's disguise had dropped and he was in his full wizard regalia, complete with staff.

"Our *guest* has arrived," Nighthawk said. "And he brings me another to help appease my *P'koosh*."

"What are you trying to prove, Nighthawk?" Blackwing said, with a touch of dismissiveness in his tone. "They aren't food, and I won't let you turn them into such. This is between us. Leave them out of it."

"But how can that be? You involved them in this, and now they get to see what that involvement has wrought."

"*L'Tuin Auld F'allie,*" Blackwing called out.

Nighthawk laughed. "A ritual challenge? How predictable you are. We are not within the Seven Planes, and thus are outside the purview of the Council. I feel you have a need for an education as to how our worlds work. I am more than happy to teach it to you."

Blackwing's globe drifted over to Suzanne and she plucked it from the air.

"I assume the normal rules apply?" Blackwing said.

"Rules?" Nighthawk replied. "What rules are you talking about? There are no rules here. You have what you have, and I have what I have."

"Are you giving any assurances that my *friends* are outside of the conflict between us?

"The only assurances I can give is that, should you lose, you can count on your friends being *P'koosh F'aeul.*"

15

OGRE SLAYERS

As the three humans watched Blackwing take a few steps toward Nighthawk, they moved closer to each other, partly to put more distance between them and the Ogres, and partly to gain strength from proximity to each other, as they watched their friend prepare to do battle.

Nighthawk attacked first. It seemed like everything happened at once. He threw balls of blue energy, some targeting Blackwing and some targeting the humans, then turned into a fifteen-foot tall demon and grabbed for Blackwing.

With one hand, Blackwing cast a protection spell to cover his friends, and with the other cast a small shield of reddish energy with a prominent rune in the center to deflect the balls of energy that were thrown his way into one of the Ogres. And when Nighthawk grabbed for him, he sidestepped and changed into a twenty-foot tall demon and cuffed his opponent just below the horns, knocking him to the ground before stepping forward to stomp on Nighthawk.

Nighthawk rolled forward when he hit the ground, avoiding the heavy stomp. When he regained his feet and turned to face him, Blackwing grabbed a live Ogre by the leg and began pummeling Nighthawk with the hapless creature. After dozens of hits to the face, Nighthawk was dazed. Blackwing threw the Ogre at Nighthawk's head, and then picked up Nighthawk by the ankle and started swinging him around. Nighthawk hit the walls, concrete pillars, and the floor several times each.

While Blackwing and Nighthawk were engaged in their Battle Royale, Suzanne cautiously looked around at the closest three standing Ogres and noticed they were watching the battle rage. She nudged Jessica with her elbow and signaled with a slight nod and eye shift, to the standing Ogres.

Jessica nodded slightly and nudged Irving, who, like the Ogres, was too mesmerized by the battle to notice anything as innocuous as the barely perceptible nod of Jessica's head.

"What?" he said, irritated and loud, as he turned to look at Jessica.

Jessica whispered, "Be ready. If we get the chance, we're leaving."

"What about them?" Irving whispered back, and nodded toward the Ogres.

"I have a little surprise for them." Jessica nonchalantly touched the sleeve of her unitard where her weapon was.

"So do I." Irving touched his own sleeve and grinned.

The last time Blackwing swung him, Nighthawk was released into the far wall. He slid down it, rather than attacking. As he slowly got to his feet, Blackwing walked over to him. With a sudden burst, the two monsters grappled, each trying to gain an advantage. Blackwing turned his head sharply. One of his horns was about to gore Nighthawk, when he changed back into his wizard form, complete with staff, and slipped under the much bigger Blackwing and ran to a standing Ogre. Once Nighthawk reached the Ogre, he placed a hand on it and fired a pulsing blue beam from his staff, toward Blackwing.

Blackwing, who had also reverted while Nighthawk was making his way to the Ogre, had his own staff and a large red convex shield of energy to divert the pulsing beam just as it reached him. Nighthawk drew out the life force from the Ogre and his bean intensified in its pounding pulse, forcing Blackwing to strain to continue to block the intensified beam.

Irving saw Jessica give her right wrist a small flick, and he did the same. He saw her service weapon form in her right hand and felt the twelve-inch hilt form in his hand, and once it was formed, pressed the small tang located close to the guard. The blade unfolded to its four-foot length and the blade sections locked in place.

As his blade was unfolding, Irving looked to the remaining Ogres. He noticed there was only one close to him and decided that was his target.

"Now," Jessica said.

She didn't yell it. He presumed, to not want to warn the Ogres.

At the signal, he rushed up behind the Ogre that was his target and slashed behind the left knee, cutting both collateral ligaments. A slight side step and a return swing and he cut the ligaments of his target's right knee. The Ogre fell face forward to the concrete floor.

When Jessica saw Nighthawk take the Ogre's life force, she understood why the Ogres were there. *They're here to ensure Nighthawk wins. They're here to replenish his energy.*

Once her service weapon was formed, she fired the stun darts at the Ogre closest to Irving.

Holding the weapon close to her mouth, she said, "Nine."

Once the weapon made the minor conversion to the nine-millimeter setting, she fired two rounds in quick succession, at an Ogre close to Suzanne, hitting it in the head with both rounds. She adjusted her aim at another Ogre and fired two more quick shots, the rounds finding their target. She adjusted again and fired three more quick rounds at Nighthawk's staff.

I don't need to hit him. I don't think the rounds would have any effect, anyway. If I can deprive him of his staff, maybe that'll even things up.

The first two hit the staff, which was close to the gem. The third round hit the gem, shattering it. All the magical power that was flowing through it became uncontrollable.

Nighthawk and Blackwing were too focused on their own battle to pay any attention to the reports from Jessica's weapon. Blackwing was in the process of changing his shield from convex to concave when the first two reports reached him. He could see the deflected beam start to change to focus back at the source. By the time he heard the second set of reports, Nighthawk's beam was reflecting back at him and he had to produce his own blue energy shield to avoid the effects of his own beam.

When the first two rounds from Jessica's weapon hit Nighthawk's staff, it caused the dense wood to vibrate and it became hard to hold. As if in slow motion, he saw the end of his staff, holding the Blue Lapis-Lazuli-like gem in place, fall and he gasped. The third round shattered the stone and he dropped the staff, feeling the loss of the heirloom.

I have lost my father's staff. I have underestimated the primitives. And I have underestimated Blackwing as well.

The ensuing explosion of unrestrained magical energies lit the room in a deep blue light. The concussive force took everyone in the room off their feet.

Blackwing was the first to recover, and the jewel held by his staff glowed a deep ruby as he held it inches from Nighthawk's face.

"Yield!" he said, in a deep booming voice, while leaning over his opponent.

Nighthawk didn't reply. He grinned and thrust his hand toward Blackwing and a bolt of energy hit him in the lower part of his chest, inside his duster, knocking him back fifteen feet. Blackwing released his staff, but it didn't fall. It hovered, and Nighthawk thought it growled at him. When he tried to swat it away, it dodged, of its own accord, and continued to threaten him. When he finally grabbed Blackwing's staff, he tensed as if he were being electrocuted.

Blackwing was slow to recover, but when he finally got to his feet, Nighthawk had finally been able to release the battle staff.

Nighthawk slowly crawled to the disabled Ogre. As he reached down to touch the Ogre, Jessica, her weapon now in breaching mode, touched the side of his head with the hot barrel.

"This will take your fucking head right off," she said, through clenched teeth. "Give me a reason."

Nighthawk froze. He next felt a sharp point at his throat and saw Irving holding his sword. He tried to speak, but he had no means, as Blackwing had caused a golden plate to cover his mouth. Blackwing came up behind and affixed gold manacles to his wrist.

"You are my prisoner, Malthuvius Nighthawk, by virtue of the *Sh'tuk Q'estiria Faqin*."

Nighthawk, gagged, beaten and battle-weary, hung his head.

"Hang on to him," Blackwing said to Jessica, as he walked over to the Ogre that Irving had dropped.

When he reached the creature, he saw that it had bled out.

Just as Blackwing turned toward the others, an Ogre who had been hiding behind one of the concrete pillars rushed toward Suzanne. Irving saw the movement and interposed himself between the Ogre and its target. The Ogre swung a meaty hand toward him. Irving stepped closer and thrust his sword upward into the beast's abdomen. As it was dropping forward, Irving spun and swung the sword to remove the Ogre's head, and stepped away so the beast wouldn't fall on him.

Jessica and Irving did a quick body count of the Ogres. Satisfied that they were all dispatched, the pair put away their weapons.

Blackwing was barely moving and appeared to be injured. As they gathered to leave, Blackwing was hit from behind by an emerald energy ball and fell forward.

Jessica, Irving, and Suzanne looked at Blackwing with wide eyes and agape mouths as another wizard materialized. The recent arrival grabbed Nighthawk and they both disappeared.

Jessica dropped to check Blackwing.

Suzanne said, "Is he…?"

"He's still alive, but barely." Jessica tried to keep her tears from falling.

"What the hell happened?" Irving said.

"Another wizard struck Blackwing down and took Nighthawk," Suzanne said, tears streaming down her cheeks.

"Who was the other wizard?" Irving asked.

"What do we do now?" Jessica said.

"We take him out of here," Suzanne said. "We need to get him home. We can't take him anywhere else."

"How do we get him there?" Irving said.

"I can commandeer a truck, if we see one," Jessica said. "Can anyone drive a truck?"

"First things first," Suzanne said. "We'll worry about that after we get him, and ourselves, out of here."

Irving and Jessica managed to get Blackwing up by draping his arms over their shoulders. Suzanne, still holding the sphere, bent down and gingerly touched Blackwing's battle staff. When she wasn't jolted, as Nighthawk had been, she took it up.

It took several hours to transport Blackwing to Suzanne's home. Jessica managed to commandeer a pickup truck, and after several payoffs to border guards, they arrived at their destination.

"Get him out back by the big oak tree," Suzanne told her companions.

"Why out there?" Irving said, as he and Jessica got Blackwing up, and then headed to the tree.

I only hope I can call upon her. "It's the only thing I can think of," Suzanne followed, carrying the staff and sphere. "We need help. I only hope Lady S'hyrlus will… or can."

"How are you going to call on her?" Jessica panted as they carried Blackwing.

"I was there when Blackwing called to her. I heard the song he sang and I think I can reproduce it."

"Sounds like a long shot to me," Irving murmured.

"Have a little faith, Irv," Jessica said. "What've we got to lose? It's about all we can do."

Blackwing was gently placed on the ground under the massive tree's canopy. Suzanne placed his battle staff on the ground next to his body.

"Who has a knife?" she asked.

"I have my sword." Irving activated it and handed it to her.

"That'll have to do. When Blackwing called the Lady S'hyrlus before, he had a fire and was roasting a rabbit, but he first sprinkled the rabbit's blood. I can't explain it, but I seem to know what to do."

Suzanne grabbed the blade with her left hand and jerked. She felt the blade bite into her palm. She tossed the sword to Irving and started dripping blood on the ground.

"You two can stand over there. And don't interrupt me."

As Jessica and Irving moved away from the big oak, Suzanne was holding the sphere, getting her blood on the ground and smearing the bark, as she knelt between Blackwing and the tree trunk and closed her eyes.

"Lady of the wood, hear my call," she sang. "My need is dire as I humbly beseech you, the Lady S'hyrlus, to come to me. My need, great though it is, is not for myself, but for another of your followers. I beseech you, in the name of Socrates Blackwing. Come to me."

When Suzanne reached the end, she heard a growl and a whimper from the staff.

She started again.

"What is she saying?" Jessica whispered, standing next to Irving, just outside the tree's canopy.

"Sounds like a prayer of some kind to me," he whispered.

"I figured that, but what language is it? I've never heard anything like it."

"I don't know, but it sounds lyrical and nice. It's oddly soothing."

"Who calls upon the Lady S'hyrlus?" Suzanne heard, after the third time through her song.

She opened her eyes and looked to the tree trunk. "'Tis I, Suzanne Hawks, sweet Lady."

She could see the bark glow as if from the inside of the tree.

Lady S'hyrlus walked out of the trunk. "For what purpose do you call upon me?" she asked, softly. "Who are these others?"

"These," Suzanne indicated Jessica and Irving, "are also *K'obi Sha Shin J'oi Faqin,* called into service by Socrates Blackwing. He," she gestured to Blackwing, "was felled by a foul blow and we know not what to do."

S'hyrlus knelt and placed a hand on Blackwing's chest. "He will discorporate soon. What is it you would have me do?"

"My Plane is in desperate need of his integrity and protection. Is there something that can be done to ensure his continuance?"

"There is, but the price is high."

"If I can, I will pay the price," Suzanne said, through tears.

S'hyrlus looked to Suzanne gravely and caressed her face. "Understand, what can be done must be done quickly, and may not accomplish what we hope. His life force is badly depleted and he needs more. I can transfer yours to him and it may revive him to the point that he can increase it on his own. Whether it works or not, you will not continue."

"I understand and I will pay the price," Suzanne said, tears falling. "His continuance is more important than mine."

S'hyrlus motioned for Jessica and Irving to join them. Once they were kneeling on either side of Suzanne, S'hyrlus placed their hands on the sphere.

"Socrates has chosen wisely in the company he keeps. I am impressed with the three of you. For Socrates to continue, he requires a life force.

It may not work, but Suzanne has chosen to offer her own in an attempt to save his."

"No," Irving whimpered, tears flowing.

"Is there no other way?" Jessica asked, through tears.

"There are no assurances that this will work," S'hyrlus said. "It is a gamble of the highest order."

Jessica and Irving nodded solemnly. S'hyrlus motioned that they should back away. Suzanne placed the sphere on the ground next to Blackwing.

"In my room," Suzanne said to her friends, "is an old wall safe. The combination is four-eleven-twenty-forty. Take care of him."

S'hyrlus said something that none understood and clapped her hands over her head. Two more females walked from inside the tree trunk and started removing Suzanne's clothing.

Suzanne removed the platinum band from her arm and the gold necklace, and placed them next to Blackwing. There was some chatter between the strange females as they pointed to Suzanne's Identity Device. S'hyrlus touched the tiny silver dot and it worked its way out. It fell to the ground, its long spider-like filaments retracting into the device. When they were ready, they lay Suzanne on the ground next to Blackwing.

S'hyrlus knelt at their heads and placed a hand on each of their chests and leaned back, with closed eyes.

"Fear not, my daughter," Suzanne heard inside her mind. *"I am well-pleased with you. If this comes to fruition, you will become as I am."*

I am ready. Suzanne tried to remain calm.

She felt sleepiness starting to fall over her. The longer she lay there, the more she was convinced that she was unable to move. Shortly, she knew she was asleep, and then there were no thoughts at all.

Jessica and Irving were aggrieved. It felt like their hearts were breaking. Here was their friend giving everything for Blackwing. Neither could stop their tears.

Soon, they saw the newly arrived nymphs lift Suzanne's body and they all disappeared into the tree trunk. Then they were motioned over by S'hyrlus.

"You frient wit my kint now," she said, in broken English. "Hontor her sac'fice."

S'hyrlus re-entered the tree trunk and the glowing on the bark disappeared.

Blackwing inhaled deeply, like someone who hadn't breathed in a long time.

"Are you okay?" Jessica knelt beside him.

"I'm weak, but I think I'll be okay. Why am I out here? Where is Suzanne?"

Jessica stood. "We need to go into the house and have a discussion."

Jessica and Irving helped Blackwing into the house.

16

REPERCUSSIONS

"You were ready," Phelonius Blackwing chided. "Your definition of that term appears to be significantly different from mine." He turned his back to stare out the rain-streaked window, his hands clasped behind his back, tapping the back of one hand in the palm of the other.

A significant amount of time passed.

"So you have nothing to say?" he asked, without turning. "No excuses to offer?"

"His manner of battle is… unorthodox," said Malthuvius Nighthawk.

"And effective, apparently. I tried to warn you, but you decided to ignore my warnings."

"Then why did you send me? I obviously disappointed you."

"Oddly, you were not a disappointment. Your battle with Socrates went as I expected. Why do you think I was observing?" Phelonius's reflection in the glass grinned.

"His minions added… an unexpected element to the battle."

"I would be justified in promoting Socrates to your rank and dropping yours well below his current ranking."

"Without his minions, I would have won the battle."

"Let me summarize. You were there with six *P'koosh*. He had three… what are they called here?"

"Humans."

"Humans, yes. He had three humans. How many of his humans fell? I didn't see any, but maybe I missed something, since I am in my dotage. How many were…what did you call the weaker of their kind?"

"Females. And there were two of them."

"So out of three, two were these weaker females? You did tell me that they were weaker, did you not? And you had six strapping, virile bull *P'koosh,* and none of the humans fell. Am I correct so far?"

"Yes, my General, that is correct," Malthuvius whispered, while hanging his head.

"I am aware of their strange weapons and tactics, but still, I would like to think that at least one would have fallen." Phelonius made a deep sigh. "Did you have first-strike advantage?"

"Yes."

"And how long did you maintain that advantage?"

"Not long, but his tactics were so… so unusual. No one changes shield sizes and shapes while under sustained attack. He apparently knows techniques that I am unaware of. And that battle staff of his…"

"What was so unusual about his staff? I happen to know it was his father's, given to both of them by the Lady S'hyrlus of the oaken wood."

"I have never encountered a staff that could move and defends of its own accord."

"I think you have spent too much time in *Sh'tuksa Q'estiria Faqin* and not enough time in the faewyld."

Irving and Jessica helped Blackwing into the house and into a chair at the table. Then they both went out to gather the remainder of the objects that Suzanne had left behind. Upon seeing Suzanne's ID on the ground, Irving, out of habit, collected it with tweezers and put it into an evidence bag. The bag was then put with Suzanne's clothing.

When Irving had re-entered the house, he gave Blackwing his sphere. The staff, the gold necklace, and the platinum band were placed on the table, while Jessica took Suzanne's clothes to her room. Once she returned to the dining room, Jessica started to weep and turned away from Blackwing and Irving. Blackwing took out his tankard and several pieces of dried meat.

"What is that?" Irving said. "Is that all you eat? I've never seen you eat anything else, so I'm curious."

Blackwing dropped a couple pieces on the table in front of Irving. "I doubt it will harm you. I'm not sure if what you humans eat is safe for me to consume."

Irving picked up a piece and smelled it. Then he touched his tongue to it.

"Irving," Jessica yelled. "Don't you dare. You don't know what that'll do to you."

"I'll test it when I get to the lab." He dropped the pieces into his pocket. "At least I'll be able to tell you if our food would hurt you. Mind if I ask you some questions about what happened?"

Blackwing shrugged.

"Why didn't you stay in that... that demon state when Nighthawk changed back into his wizard form?"

Blackwing thought for a few seconds. "While in the demon form, I can't cast any spells and I don't have access to my staff. Changing takes very little magic, and while in that form, I gather more energy—a way of recharging, if you will—but it has limitations. If, while in that form, I would have been hit with an energy bolt or a sword, it could have been fatal."

"So while he was in his wizard form and you were in your demon form," Jessica said, "why didn't you just squash him?"

"What should have happened is I call out the phrase '*L'Tuin Auld F'allie,* and he would either face me or turn his back to me. By his facing me, all others—you three and the Ogres—would be off-limits, to use as either helpers or targets. What did happen was Nighthawk attacked first, and his first targets were you three and then me. In the ritualized version, lethal force is forbidden, but his attacks were all lethal. The deflected energy ball that hit the Ogre took its life, but it shouldn't have."

"So he cheated," Irving said. "Did that surprise you?"

"No, I expected it. I was hoping he would do things the proper way, the way we were both trained as acceptable, but I figured he'd do exactly what he did. I sometimes wish there was a way to show you what I'm talking about."

"How would that help?" Irving said.

"Just before I was struck from behind, the one doing it had to be partially visible at least. I think I know who it was, but some proof would help."

"I don't know what you mean." Irving shrugged. "No one had a recording device."

"What do you think this is?" Blackwing indicated his eyepatch. "My sphere records everything in its view if my eye is closed or blinking. But if my eyes are open, it prioritizes what to record and will merge images later."

"That little thing? What is it, three inches in diameter, maybe four? It's too small to store very much."

"It's big enough to hold a copy of what you call the Global Web. The sphere passes information to my brain, like when we talk and I don't know a word. Those pauses are the sphere trying to figure out what word I should use to get my point across."

Irving stared, mouth agape. "That would require hundreds of the fastest processors working at top efficiency to accomplish something similar, and it wouldn't work as fast as yours. Not to mention the memory required. I'm officially impressed."

"You were *officially impressed* as soon as you found out he was a wizard," Jessica said.

"True." Irving shrugged. "Let me think about it. I may come up with something."

"We, on the other hand, should get home," Jessica said. "We do have a truck to return, and you need to rest. We'll be back in a day or two."

Suzanne awoke with a start. She saw that she was lying in a meadow just off a dirt path. To her, it looked to be late spring. Balmy breezes, new grass growing, and a number of wildflowers were just starting to bloom. To the side of the dirt path was a huge oak tree with a canopy that overhung the path. Across from her, the path was lined with lilac bushes that were just starting to bloom and fill the air with their fragrance.

When she stood and looked at her loose attire, she found that she was wearing a dress in the style of a Greek toga—one that was just above her knees in the front and just above her ankles in the back. Both her arms and her right shoulder were bare.

"This place looks interesting. Where is it?"

Suzanne heard the distinctive female voice from behind her. When she turned, she saw the Lady S'hyrlus dressed as she was when Suzanne called her. The name *Balanos* popped into her mind.

A wistful look crossed S'hyrlus's face. "That is a name I have not heard for a long, long time," she said.

"Where is it?" Suzanne asked. "I'd have thought you'd know. It doesn't look like any place I've ever been."

"No, I do not know this place. What I can tell you is all this," S'hyrlus made a sweeping gesture with arms outstretched, "is in your mind. You are still becoming, and I have come to get to know you."

"Maybe it's a place I've read about." Suzanne looked around, confused, and strolled to the oak tree. "What is it you want to know?" She leaned against the rough bark, finding comfort in it.

"You misunderstand my meaning. This is more conversation than interrogation. I am curious, where my son is concerned."

"Your son? I was told you raised him until he was seven, but hadn't borne him." *How did I know she meant Socrates?*

"True, he was not of my body. For my kind that would be impossible. But I consider him my son, nonetheless. So why would you choose to give your life for him?"

Suzanne thought about her answer for some time. "He's given as much to me, as well as to my kind. True, he was sent to my Plane without his consent, but he's still given much to me and others. Even though most people of my Plane don't know him, he's willing to defend us, and he gave me companionship when I needed it."

"And you have given him companionship when he needed it the most. Otherwise you would not be here. Socrates is… different."

"I've never met anyone like him."

"I am sure you have not. But what I mean is, over the millennia I have known many. Humans, *Q'estirions*, others, and none had treated me kindly or respectfully, not the way Socrates has, and for his kind that is unusual, and much like his father. *Q'estirions* are usually vain, arrogant, and too consumed with the vulgarities of accumulating power."

"So you can understand my reasons."

"I can, but *you* need to know your own heart as to *your* reasons. Your decision should never be regretted."

"Will I be allowed to see my friends again?"

"Once you have become, you are free to do what you feel is correct. If you want to see your friends, then you can. You are, however, forbidden to do anything that would bring harm or dishonor to the rest of the *Sh'o Sook J'eid*."

"What am I becoming?"

"Before you were brought here, I told you. I said you would become as I am. In other times and places we have been called many things, but one you may know. Hamadryad. It may take a while, but with patience you will get there."

"If I remember correctly, Hamadryads lived in trees and could be killed by killing a particular tree—"

S'hyrlus laughed heartily. "You are still becoming, so you do not know. The *Sh'o Sook J'eid* do not live inside trees. Many ages ago, humans believed we were immortal and lived inside our trees. In actuality, we have a hidden Plane that is only known to us and can only be reached by us. The trees are our ritual places and the source of our power, but we do not live inside them. I live in a house, much like you do. The trees are our portals, which is why those ancients thought as they did. Though we are not immortal, we are enduring. None of my sisters or daughters have died of old age. Our mortality comes through accident, illness, or injuries. It is true that we can be killed by exterminating all of the trees, but to accomplish it they would have to do it on all Planes, known and unknown. Does that sound like something that could be accomplished?"

"Why is it that humans haven't seen you for many ages?"

"Why would we show ourselves to those that would abuse us and those who have turned away from the old ways? It has been ages since I heard an enticement from your Plane."

"How old are the Hamadryads?"

"We have been since the beginning."

Shortly after Jessica and Irving returned to the precinct, Irving went to his lab while Jessica went to her desk. As she sat, she received a message from the captain.

"You wanted to see me, Cap'n?" She entered his office.

"Sit please, Jessica," Captain Trooper said, without looking up.

Several seconds later, he looked at her from his place behind the desk.

"Did you have a nice lunch?"

Jessica blanched. *I'd forgotten how long ago I went to lunch with Irving.*

"I'm sorry, sir. I must've lost track of time. I just learned that a friend died."

Trooper looked at her skeptically at first, but then his expression softened.

"Sorry to hear that. That would throw you off. But that isn't why I called you in.

"As you know, Jon Crawford is retiring soon and I'm looking for his replacement. You've been working with him for the last few years, and you were the one I thought of to replace him."

"Thank you, sir."

Trooper raised his hand. "You earned it, so no need to express your appreciation. You can imagine my surprise, while checking your file, at finding you have yet to take the Sergeants' Exam." He stopped and looked at her expectantly. "You were eligible over a year ago."

"No sir, I haven't taken it yet. I haven't made up my mind if I want the position. There has been a lot going on in my life, lately."

Captain Trooper got to his feet, walked to the front of his desk and leaned back against it.

"Look, Jess, I understand your reluctance, but help me out here. I need a detective sergeant I can count on to get the job done. For the last several years that has been you. I can't promote you until you pass the exam. You're the best I've got, so get on it. Take a few days off to decide, and let me know. I have a new case for you, but I can't give it to you at your current rank. Have Strange put in for a week's vacation and you do the same. At the end of it, though, I expect you to have passed the exam, or I'll be forced to promote Taggert. And you know how incompetent he is. So do us both a favor and get your head together."

"Yes, sir. Thank you, sir."

"Now get out of here and do what you need to do."

"A week?" Irving said. "We have a week's vacation? Together?" He took a sip of his drink while waiting on his meal.

"I'm as surprised as you are." Jessica took a sip of her own drink. "Cap also wants me to take the Sergeants' Exam."

"You should. Isn't Crawford calling it quits?"

"He is, but with our new… um… responsibilities, I've been reluctant to accept a promotion. It may make getting away when we need to, harder."

"Well, I'm at the top of my pay grade, so no room for advancement. Taking the exam doesn't mean you have to take the promotion. I'm sure you could ace it." He stopped, noticing her demeanor. "Are you okay? You seem… down."

Jessica shrugged without looking at Irving. "Suzanne's passing has hit me pretty hard, I guess."

Irving looked around to see who was listening. "What *passing*? She isn't *gone* gone. From my understanding, she's with Lady S'hyrlus. I'm sure she'll be back for a visit, if nothing else."

"I heard what S'hyrlus said and got the same impression, *if* she survived. At this point, we don't know if she survived. I don't understand why she did it, though."

Irving looked at her with wide eyes. "You're teasing me, right? You know why as well as I do."

Jessica shook her head. "Sox isn't human. His kind looks down their noses at us."

"Maybe his *kind* does, but I don't think *he* does." Irving touched his band. "I, for one, am glad she made the decision she did. Otherwise, where would we be? Who can stand against Malthuvius? I doubt you or I could, not after seeing the battle we did."

"Maybe. But you need to understand, I've never had friends, as I do now. Losing one, for whatever reason, hits me hard. Harder than I expected. Maybe I should have stepped up…"

"I would've been quite upset if you had. I'm not done with you yet. In fact I'm barely getting started." Irving chuckled and winked at her.

Jessica smiled. "I'm enjoying you as well, Irv."

17

THE HAMADRYAD PLANE

Suzanne felt a soft hand on the side of her face and heard her name whispered. As her eyelids fluttered open, she could see trees looming over her, sunlight streaming through the high boughs. When she sat up, she noticed that she was in a depression in the middle of a grove of ancient oaks, judging by their size. S'hyrlus was standing close by.

"How are you feeling?" she asked.

"I am feeling weak, hungry, thirsty, and a little chilled. Otherwise, I seem to be fine. What happened?"

"It has been three days since you were brought here, so your thirst and hunger are expected. What do you remember?"

"I remember lying on the ground, naked, next to Socrates, and you touching us." Suzanne paused, eyes closed to remember. "I remember talking to you in a sunny meadow and you telling me it was all in my mind."

S'hyrlus smiled. "You are becoming, which is a process. You must return here twice more, for the process to continue. For now, though, you can eat and drink and gather your strength." She clapped her hands and several women came forward, seemingly from nowhere. "Prepare food and clothe my new daughter," she said to the women, who scurried to do as commanded.

One young woman returned with a bolt of linen and draped Suzanne in it and tied it on her left shoulder. She helped Suzanne to her feet, and Suzanne leaned on her heavily as they climbed out of the depression. While she climbed, Suzanne could feel her legs shake.

Once out of the depression, the three women walked a short distance to a clearing. Suzanne could see other women rushing about with platters of fruits and vegetables. A few others carried trays of pitchers and tankards.

Her assistant helped her to sit with her back against a younger tree at the edge of the sunlit meadow, and gave her a piece of fruit. When Suzanne raised it to her nose, she could smell a peach fragrance. It took her a moment to realize she was given a fresh plump peach. Since she had never seen a fresh peach, she was uncertain how to eat it. Juice ran down her chin as she bit into the fruit and she relished its sweetness.

"Welcome to the Hamadryad Plane." S'hyrlus smiled.

Suzanne swallowed. "Is this a separate Plane? I was told there were only eight Planes."

S'hyrlus chuckled. "As far as Socrates and the other *Q'estirians* know, there are. However, there are, in fact, more than they know. They pride themselves on what they know, but they don't know as much as they like to think. This is our Plane. Since many of us are *Sh'o Sook J'eid*, they cannot get to this plane, as that would require one of us to bring them here, and that is forbidden. Socrates had mentioned that someone had opened a… portal inside the city. Since there are very few trees of any kind inside the city, and none more than saplings, he was at a loss to explain it. It is possible to open a portal without me or one of my sisters. However, the power entailed is tremendous and not easily accomplished. Hamadryades open portals using the trees and their power, as well as our own, and it is done by the connections between the trees on all Planes. How someone not

Hamadryad would accomplish it is beyond our understanding. Either way, how can you go somewhere that you do not know exists?"

After finishing the peach, Suzanne's assistant gave her a tankard of water and Suzanne gulped it down.

"Are you feeling better?" asked the assistant.

"Much, thank you."

The assistant smiled and bowed away.

"So was I dead?" Suzanne looked to S'hyrlus.

"Mostly, but not completely. I transferred most of your life energy to Socrates. He would not have survived otherwise. But you were not drained completely, and you were brought here before the rest was lost. The Great Oak replenished your life energy and began your transformation—your *becoming*."

The other attendees had all started chatting amongst themselves and were drinking and eating.

"Are all here Hamadryades?" Suzanne said.

"Yes, we are. Some are older and more seasoned. Others are still young and lack knowledge. All here are my daughters. This Plane is divided equally with my seven sisters, and all of us rule our particular area. My sisters have their own daughters, but collectively we are all Hamadryades." S'hyrlus took what looked like a carrot from a passing platter and started munching on it. "Once you are stronger, I will take you to your friends. But I will see Socrates later today to let him know your fate. It should ease his mind."

Suzanne selected a bunch of grapes from a platter. "What changes can I expect from this *becoming*?"

"Physical changes have already begun. By the end of your becoming, you will age backward to about two years after you entered puberty. You will have received the beauty mark of Oxylus."

S'hyrlus turned her head and slipped her hair behind her ear. She lightly stroked her pointed ear with her fingertip.

Suzanne unconsciously copied S'hyrlus's actions and noticed her own pinnae starting to come to a point.

"You will be restricted in your travels," S'hyrlus said, "which should be many, to proximity of the children of the Great Oak." She motioned and another female approached Suzanne and tied a necklace around her throat. "This is the seed of the Great Oak. It is a living thing and should be respected as such. It will allow you to extend your proximity and time away from us and this Plane."

When the necklace was tied, Suzanne touched it and noticed that everyone except S'hyrlus wore an acorn necklace.

"Where will I be allowed to travel?" Suzanne said.

"Anywhere you like. You will see things that you have only dreamed of. There will be times that you will be required to be consort to Q'estirions. It is a high honor for them, and a status symbol, but I do not give my daughters lightly."

I wouldn't mind being consort to Socrates.

"He has earned it several times over," S'hyrlus said.

Jessica awoke, and after showering and dressing, entered the dining area. She kissed Irving on his neck as she passed on her way to the kitchen. It had been four days since Blackwing's battle with Nighthawk.

"Have you heard anything about Suzanne?" Jessica re-entered the dining area with a steaming cup of coffee.

"Nothing yet," Blackwing said. "I have, however, ascertained the identity of my attacker. I'm not absolutely certain, but I believe it to be Phelonius who attacked me after I had Nighthawk in custody."

"Is that allowed by your laws?" Jessica asked.

"No, it isn't. But he feels he is above our… laws, as you call them."

"Do you know what he's doing here?" Irving said.

"From Nighthawk's appearance, I'd say they're here to collect human life force. It's the only reason that makes sense."

"What?" Irving said. "You mean like a vampire?"

Jessica chuckled.

"If I understand your reference, no. Your legends of vampires say that vampires drain people of their blood and those bitten become vampires themselves. That isn't the case with *Q'estirions*. We can drain another living being of its life force to bolster our own, rather than wait for it to build up naturally. How old would you say Nighthawk is, compared to me?"

"He appeared to be thirty years your junior," Jessica said. "No offense."

Blackwing chuckled. "None taken. He is my junior, but only by a year or two. During the battle you saw him take the life force of an Ogre, but he was using it as fast as he could draw it. If he were to draw the life force of a human, several things would happen. First, his own life force would be… refreshed. Second, within days he would appear to be younger, if he didn't use it up. The younger the victim is, the more dramatic the change in appearance. I'm not certain, but I think human life force changes the nature of the magic we use. I think it makes it stronger."

"What happens to the victim?" Irving said.

"If done quickly, they die. If the victim's life force is siphoned off gradually, they would appear to age prematurely." Socrates looked at Jessica. "Being out on the street, you may see people age quite a bit, seemingly overnight.

"Personally, I don't take the life force of sentient beings. If I need to, I prefer trees or small mammals. Trees have a huge amount of life force stored, but I take very little. Also, I think a human's life force is addictive to my kind. There is a rush of vitality that could become… overwhelming."

"What happened after you had Nighthawk in custody?" Jessica said.

"At that point, I barely had enough magic to transport everyone here. If I could have, I would've needed to rest for several days. My grandfather—if it was my grandfather, as I suspect—hit me with an energy orb that drained me, almost to the point of expiring. I don't think that was his intention. I prefer to believe he intended to just render me unconscious, as that was the only way he would be able to take Nighthawk from me."

"So humans are nothing more than a fountain of youth for your kind," Jessica said. "Humans are just a means to remaining youthful, and nothing more?"

"Youth and power, yes."

"Is that how you view us?" Jessica said, anger apparent in her flashing eyes.

"Jess, you need to calm down," Irving said.

"Why? Why do I need to calm down? You heard him. We're nothing more than cattle to them. We're just something to slaughter whenever the whim takes them."

Jessica's tirade was interrupted by a light knock on the back door. When Blackwing opened it, S'hyrlus stood there, in all her magnificence.

"Please come to the Oak," she said to Blackwing.

"What did she say?" Jessica asked.

"We all need to go to the oak grove." Blackwing followed S'hyrlus.

Is this it? Jessica followed Irving and Blackwing out of the house. *Am I going to find out that my friend didn't make it? Am I strong enough to hear it?*

"This is unusual, but I came to give you news," S'hyrlus said to Blackwing, as she touched the bark of the oak tree. "I do not speak their language, but it seemed the others were distressed."

"They are concerned for their friend, as am I," Blackwing said.

When S'hyrlus held out her hand, it was taken by someone inside the tree. Irving and Jessica gasped as Suzanne stepped out of the oak.

"Suzanne!" They rushed to her.

Jessica reached her first and embraced her tearfully. "I thought you were dead," she said into Suzanne's neck.

"I think I was. Or close to it." Suzanne returned the embrace. "But I'm better, now." She moved to Irving and gave him a hug.

"Looking pretty snazzy, Suz." Irving grinned and winked.

Jessica slapped his upper arm. "Nobody uses that term anymore. Most find it offensive."

"I use it all the time," Irving said.

"That's my point. Only a geek like you would still use that term. Lucky for you, you're so lovable I overlook that part of your personality."

"How long can you stay?" Irving said.

"I can't yet. I guess I'm not finished cooking. Or so I'm led to believe. It'll be a while before I can stay longer."

When she was finished with Irving and Jessica, Suzanne turned to S'hyrlus and Blackwing.

Blackwing knelt and bowed his head.

Suzanne bent over to lift his chin. "I do not require you to bow to me. There is no need."

"Yes, there is," Blackwing said. "I would not be here if not for you. I owe you much, and this minor show of respect is not out of line."

"Stand, my son," S'hyrlus whispered.

Blackwing jerked his head towards her. "You have never called me that before, Lady S'hyrlus."

"No, I have not *said* that, but that does not detract from my feeling that way. Suzanne, by her request, is saying that she is uncomfortable with your way of showing respect, and you should honor that, if you honor her." S'hyrlus placed her hand on Blackwing's arm. "You two have a clear mutual respect and a bond. I approve of it. It is a bond that I did not have with your father, and I find myself jealous of it."

"Do you understand what those three are talking about?" Irving whispered, as they turned their back on Blackwing, Suzanne, and S'hyrlus.

"Not a word," Jessica whispered. "I never knew Suzanne could speak their language. You'd think she'd have mentioned it before now."

"Honestly, I don't think she could. She did call Lady S'hyrlus to aid Blackwing, but prior to that she was holding his sphere in close contact for quite some time. Maybe it knew he was injured and who to call and the words to say."

"That seems a little farfetched to me."

"Why? You heard Blackwing say that his sphere helps him to speak our language, at times. To do that, it would have to tap into his brainwaves. To transfer information to Suzanne would be easy if she were holding the sphere, which she was for some time."

Jessica turned toward Irving with a serious look. "You're thinking telepathy, aren't you?"

"With all the other things we've seen, would that be so unbelievable?"

"True. Until one broke my leg, I'd have said there was no such thing as an Ogre. Not in the literal sense, anyway."

"Not to mention twenty-foot demons, gnomes that can grow to be six-feet tall, a vortex that turns people inside out, and a dancing staff. With all that, something as minor as telepathy seems more believable than the rest." Irving tried to stifle a laugh.

"What's so funny?"

"Oh, nothing major. I was just thinking about an old adage. *Be careful what you ask for, you just might get it.* And I wanted to meet a real wizard."

Jessica tried to stifle her own laughter. "And I wanted help with a case."

They both shook their heads.

Blackwing tapped Jessica and Irving's shoulders as he passed them.

"Let's go into the house."

Irving turned and saw the area around the large oak empty.

"Where did Suzanne go?"

"She and S'hyrlus went back."

"Back where?"

"Back to wherever they were before they were here."

Irving looked puzzled. "That explanation told me nothing."

"Suzanne was allowed here just so you two could see that she was okay, but her transformation is in its early stages. She'll be back when she's able."

"What are you going to do about re-acquiring Nighthawk?" Jessica said.

"Unknown. It'll probably require another battle to weaken him, and I don't know if my grandfather will interfere again."

"I have a question about the way you transport us," Irving said, as they entered the house.

"It's called the wizard step." Blackwing sat at the table.

"Whatever you call it, does it require a lot of magic to accomplish?"

"Not too much. The more people I transport, the greater the toll."

"Is there a minimum range?"

"What are you getting at, Irv?" Jessica said. "Just spit it out."

"It may seem trite, but during a fight the best way to avoid getting hit is to not be there."

Blackwing and Jessica looked puzzled.

"For humans, we would dodge and weave, turn sideways to present a smaller target, or spin away from the attack. If his wizard step thing takes less energy than creating a shield, and I'm assuming it would take a lot less than getting hit, he could bounce around using the wizard step to make it harder to hit him."

"Huh…" Blackwing leaned back in his chair. "I hadn't thought of that tactic. For *Q'estirions*, we pride ourselves on being unstoppable. Even after we get hit with weapons, can we take the best someone else gives and keep going. Each hit, however, whittles away at our energy."

Irving leaned in closer to Blackwing. "For humans, if we throw a ball we can move as soon as it's released. The ball would keep going in a somewhat straight line, baring the spin we may transfer to the ball before releasing. Do your energy orbs work the same way?"

"Why do you ask?"

"During your fight with Nighthawk, I noticed that you both left your arms in the position it was in at the time of release. If you could throw an energy orb and then use the wizard step, wouldn't that make it harder to get hit?"

"It would. But it isn't the way we were trained." Blackwing shook his head.

"Look, Socrates, you've already taken all his best shots and wore him down to the point that you had him shackled. Do you really need to go through all that again? Do you really have to be that drained and vulnerable again?"

Blackwing grinned. "You certainly have given me some things to consider. I'd have to use the step within ten or fifteen feet. I wouldn't want to risk a collision during battle. The other thing that concerns me is we are trained not to hit from behind. It's considered… unethical."

"Would it be unethical to lose to someone you've already beaten and shackled before?"

18

PARTNERED

Three weeks after her visit to see Blackwing, Suzanne, having gone through the second stage of her process, was still thinking about her friends as she stumbled out of the depression by the Great Oak. Her experience was less confusing than the first time, and the attendants were still helping her as much as she'd let them.

"We need to have a discussion." S'hyrlus sat in the clearing close to the platters of fruit. "What are your expectations as far as Socrates is concerned?"

"I have no expectations." Suzanne selected an apple from the tray. "I am hoping that the Nighthawk situation is resolved soon so Socrates and I can settle into a more family-centric routine."

"The situation with Nighthawk will be settled soon, one way or the other. My concern is the situation between Socrates and his grandfather. All my years with the *Q'estirions* has shown me that they are not a peaceful people. There is always a war to fight or a conflict somewhere that requires their... special skills."

"Socrates told me a little of his life in his father's home, but I have to ask, what did you get out of it?"

"I do not understand your question."

"Being in a relationship with someone so emotionally… closed off, is there… love?"

S'hyrlus laughed. "You think Neh'Krim and Socrates are closed off, as you put it," she said, after she'd quit laughing so hard. "I can tell you that they are not and never have been. They were trained to be as affectless as possible, to hide their feelings, to not show anger or pain. There are those that would seek advantage over them, so they remove any possible gain from the equation. You have been around Socrates long enough. Has he shown any emotions? If he has not, then you were not paying attention and you need to work on that. You would never see emotion from Socrates if he did not trust you. He trusts you not to remind him of his emotions. He has them, but likes to think he has hidden them. And what do you know of love?" She scoffed. "Is it something that needs to be verbalized every second of every day? I have heard it before and came away wondering who they were trying to convince. What is it to have a partner that lets you be who you really are, no pretenses, no masks that we have and show to outsiders, without judgment? What is it to have someone live and die for a kind word or a simple smile, to say nothing of just being in the same place with you… in silence, because there is nothing that needs to be said, just being present?"

Suzanne saw a few stray tears in S'hyrlus's wistful eyes. A few seconds later, she wiped the tears away hastily.

"You might as well know it now, rather than later," she said. "We are… amorous, from time to time. However, it is said that if one of us dies and is buried, two trees grow from our abdomen."

"Are you saying we are sterile?"

"I do not know what that means. You have been here long enough. Have you noticed any of us coming into season?"

Blackwing had just transported Irving and Jessica to Suzanne's home. The couple, carrying food they'd purchased, began setting out all the little containers on the table, with some additional bowls from the kitchen.

"What's this?" Blackwing said.

Irving talked as he worked. "I finished testing those bits you eat. You were correct in that they were safe for us to eat. It turns out, what you've been eating is a super-duper, vitamin-enriched, dried beef. We both thought it was time to let you try some of our food. So sit and enjoy."

Jessica and Irving sat and snapped two pieces of wood apart and stroked them together briefly.

"What are these?" Blackwing tried to copy his friends' actions.

"Chopsticks," Jessica said. "You hold them this way and use them to pick up the food and put it in your bowl."

Jessica demonstrated. Blackwing frowned as he did his best to copy her example. After several minutes, he was finally able to pick up a piece of meat, and popped it into his mouth. As he chewed, he could taste the moist meat and the hot spices.

"It's a shame you have to drop everything to come get us." Irving popped a piece of vegetable into his mouth. "We can't always get a car to come out, and I feel bad that you have to come get us all the time. I don't like imposing."

Blackwing swallowed another bite. "You can." He reached into a pocket and dropped two more gold coins on the table. "Those can do that, but it's dangerous."

Jessica stopped eating and looked at Blackwing. "You mean, what we wear around our necks can also transport us?"

"Not what I meant." Blackwing chased a vegetable around. "I can make these coins into a means to transport you, like a wizard step. I just have to… enchant them, for lack of a better term." He stabbed the vegetable he had been chasing with the chopsticks. "This tastes good. What's it called?"

Jessica pointed out each container. "Kung Pao chicken, Sichuan beef, Dandan noodles, snow peas, and rice. They have other dishes as well, but we figured you'd most likely enjoy these."

"What did you mean by dangerous?" Irving said.

"Well, once the enchantment is in place, you'd have to be able to picture in your mind where exactly you want to go. If your mind wanders or is impaired, you could end up where you don't intend. It does take practice."

"Somewhere we don't intend?" Jessica said.

"You could re-appear in the middle of the street, between two buildings with no room to get out, inside of a wall, that sort of thing. You could also end up miles away from where you wanted to go."

"That would be bad." Jessica finished eating.

"So we picture were we want to go, and then… what?" Irving was captivated by the thought of doing the wizard step.

"You squeeze the coin with your thumb and next two fingers." Blackwing picked up one of the coins and demonstrated.

"Can we be followed?" Irving said.

"Not once you've initiated the step. There is a range limitation, though. You can't go further than forty miles."

"When *you* do a wizard step," Irving said, "are you limited by distance?"

"Yes. I can't step further than one hundred miles."

"Forty miles would be plenty for us," Jessica said. "What we'd use it for, primarily, is to transport ourselves between work and here."

"Irv, I want to change my name," Jessica whispered, in the dimly lit bedroom of her apartment.

She had been thinking of the training they'd received earlier with the wizard step coins.

"Why?" Irving said.

He, too, had also been processing all the new information, and was close to sleep.

"Part of it is because of how dangerous our lives have become. I've never liked my last name. Who in their right mind would want to be called Jessica Rabbit for the rest of their life?"

Irving rose and turned toward her, resting on his lower arm. "What are you babbling about, Jess?"

"When I was a kid in school, some bright boy looked up my last name. *Sylvilagus* is a genus of the family *Leporidae*, a cottontail rabbit. With a misspelling and a mispronunciation of my last name, I was constantly teased."

"Well, I know I've checked plenty of times and haven't found any cotton on your tail." Irving chuckled. "But I'll be happy to check again."

Jessica smiled. "You're sweet. I don't think I have enough cushion in my tail, but I digress. If something were to happen to me, I'd prefer it if you were the one making the decisions for my care, or final disposition."

"I don't like to think about that. What would you want to change your name to?"

Jessica turned to face him. "I was thinking… I like the sound of *Jessica Strange*."

His serious face changed to one of shock. "That has an implication to it. To me, anyway. Are you sure you'd want that?"

Jessica grinned at him. "I'm well aware of the implications, and I'm comfortable with the idea."

Irving lay back and relished in Jessica cuddling into him.

A couple minutes later, he sat up again. "Wait, are you saying you're willing to enter into a contract with me?"

"That's what I was implying." Jessica chuckled. "You're quick. Nothing gets past you."

Three days after Jessica brought up the subject of a name change, she and Irving were sitting in a lawyer's office.

Jessica looked at the man across the huge desk from the couple. *This lawyer seems to be a self-important, mealy-mouthed little twerp.*

"As you can see, this is the standard matrimonial contract," said the lawyer. "Is either of you pregnant?"

They both laughed heartily.

"I fail to see anything funny. It's a standard question, and by law, has to be asked of both parties. Will there be a name change involved?"

"Yes, I would like to change my name," Jessica replied.

"What will be your new name?"

"Strange."

"Yes, I know the idea of changing your name can be disconcerting, but it isn't required."

"No, my name will be Jessica Jeanine Strange."

"*Ho-ho, he-he, ha-ha-ha.* I see the humor. Your current name?"

"Jessica Jeanine Sylvillagys."

The lawyer looked at her, with a raised brow. "This is a serious matter and shouldn't be taken lightly."

"Believe me, I'm not taking it lightly."

"Are you going to change your name as well?" He looked at Irving.

"Well, to be honest, I thought about changing it to Zeus. No more Irving Melvin Strange. Just plain Zeus. Maybe Thor would be better."

Jessica smacked his upper arm.

"No. No changes for me." He rubbed his arm.

"Since this is the standard contract," said the lawyer, "it assumes the medical power of attorney and rights of inheritance. But it fails to cover the procreation permission needed before any children can be recognized. Do you both understand?"

They both nodded.

"Sorry, I need you both to voice your assent, for the record."

"I understand," Jessica said.

"Same here, I understand," Irving copied.

The lawyer got up to walk around the desk and give the tablet to Jessica.

"Read it carefully, and if you agree, sign with the stylus provided." He removed an ID reader attached to the side of the tablet.

As she signed, he scanned her ID and it was inserted into the document. She then handed the tablet to the lawyer.

He flipped through the pages on the tablet and then handed it to Irving. "Read it carefully and sign with the stylus."

As he signed, his ID was also scanned and inserted.

The lawyer collected the tablet. "As far as the State of Pacific Coast - Washington is concerned, you two are contractually partnered for five years. You should receive a certificate to your phones in a couple days.

A renewal notice will be sent ninety days before expiration. If you fail to renew the contract, it will end on its own."

As the lawyer walked around his desk, Irving and Jessica heard their phones indicate a message. When they opened it, they each saw a billing for five thousand creds. They both cleared the billing for payment.

"Aren't there some sort of vows?" Irving said.

"They aren't necessary. You've already done everything needed, but if you insist..." He sighed and then looked at Jessica. "Do you?"

Jessica was taken aback by the unexpected question and was unsure how to answer.

"Say I do, if you do" the lawyer whispered.

"I do," Jessica said.

The lawyer looked at Irving. "Do you?"

"Well... I suppose," he said, nonchalantly.

Jessica and the lawyer glared at him. "Okay, okay. I do. God, I was just trying to insert a little levity."

"Okay, then. We're done," the lawyer said.

"Feel any different?" Irving said, as they sat at Tony's, toasting each other.

"Not really. And I find it a bit... underwhelming, anti-climactic. I don't know what I expected, but I thought I'd feel... different somehow. It feels like cheap champagne in a plastic glass, if you know what I mean." Her phone indicated a message. "Well, it is official. I'm now Jessica Strange."

"When everyone looks at you funny, please remember that you chose it." Irving finished his drink. "I need to get back to work. I have paperwork to process since I'm newly under contract."

"Same here." Jessica finished her drink, too. "I hope the cap'n isn't still mad at me for declining the promotion."

"You did pass the test, didn't you?" Irving said, as they left.

"Yes. But he's been mad at me for several weeks, now. Hope he's over it."

"Hey, gorgeous, let's go," said Detective Sergeant Michael Taggert, interrupting her submitting the paperwork for her new status.

Jessica glared at him. "That remark is unwanted, inappropriate, and offensive. Do I need to file a complaint?"

"What's the problem?" Taggert said. "I've always called you that and you never said it bothered you."

"Then listen up! From now on, you will refer to me by my name."

"Is there a problem, Sylvillagys?" asked Captain Trooper, from behind her.

"No problem, sir. I was just putting this sexist creep-a-zoid in his place."

She had the name change certificate up on her tablet, and passed it the captain.

Trooped glanced at the tablet. "I see. Detective Taggert and Detective *Strange*, I believe you have a case to investigate. Get to it."

"You changed your name?" Taggert said, as they entered the elevator to the parking garage.

"Yes," Jessica replied, coldly.

"Wait! Strange? You don't mean—"

"Oh, yes, I do mean! You have anything to say?"

Taggert laughing heartily as he got into the self-drive. "You're contracted to that geek?" he said, when his laughter subsided and he could finally speak.

Jessica glared at him. *Tall, handsome—to some, anyway—self-assured, arrogant, and I doubt he has two brain cells to rub together.*

"I'd appreciate it if you'd refrain from discussing my partner while we're on duty."

They sat in silence for the rest of the drive to the crime scene.

Taggert started chuckling as he got out of the self-drive. "I just can't believe it. Someone who looks like you, partnered with someone like that."

As they entered the dilapidated building, they followed other officers to the room in question, where they saw a body hanging from a pipe running across the ceiling. Jessica began looking around, taking pictures, and collecting evidence.

"Looks like a suicide to me," Taggert said.

"Seems to me that you like jumping to conclusions," Jessica replied. "Do we know who he is?" she asked a crime scene tech.

"ID scan identifies him as Joseph Johnson," the tech said.

Jessica's eyes widened. "Last I knew, he was in the rubber room. Why does he look so old? Last time I saw his record, it listed him as a twenty-year-old."

She entered the man's ID and did a search. A second later it came back.

"Yep, that's him. Joseph Johnson aka Crackin. Male, just turned twenty-two, and recent resident of Pacific Northwest Med Center for psychological treatment." She periodically slid through the pages. "Strictly small-time. No known associations with any major criminal organizations. No next-of-kin."

"I still think it's suicide," Taggert said. "Having a birthday can make you do all kinds of crazy shit. Especially if you're already crazy."

Jessica stopped the crime scene tech. "Send me your preliminary findings and make sure I get the autopsy report." She handed him one of her cards.

"Yes, Detective."

"I think we need to go to the hospital and question his doctor," Jessica said to Taggert.

"You handle it. I don't think we need to waste resources on this. An obvious nut-job offing himself in this dump doesn't warrant it."

Taggert left and Jessica followed.

Jessica had just sat at her desk when she got a message to see the captain. When she got to his office door, it opened and she entered.

"Detective, sit please," Trooper said, when she entered, and the door closed.

She sat in one of the chairs that lined the wall opposite his desk.

"What's going on with you?" he said.

"What do you mean?"

"Why would you take Taggert's head off over some comment? It wasn't that bad."

Jessica clenched and unclenched her jaw. "I found his remark offensive. He's my direct supervisor now, and I want things professional. I've always thought he was crude and too full of himself, but now he's going to become insufferable if I don't set him straight."

"I just received the paperwork from Irving. Is this going to become a problem? Can you maintain a business-like relationship while you're on the job?"

"I have no problem keeping things professional here. What I do have a problem with is the constant denigration of Irving by morons who struggle to have more than one brain cell working at the same time."

"You must admit, he is the last person anyone would've thought would be with you… that way."

"What is that supposed to mean? I'm not sure, but I think I've just been insulted."

"I'm sure, and you haven't. How long is the contract?"

"Five years, if it's any of your business. None of you know Irving, other than him being the top technician here. He has another side, you know. We all do."

Trooper held up his hands. "I'm not questioning your judgment, just your timing. How much did Irving have to do with your not accepting the promotion?"

"He left that decision up to me. He didn't influence me one way or the other."

"I had to ask." Trooper shrugged. "You're the best I have, and I guess I see you as the daughter I never had, so I'm overprotective. Does he make you happy?"

"He looks after me and listens to me. He'd never do anything to hurt me. Does that answer your question?"

Trooper looked at his watch and sighed. "It's late. Get out of here. And Jess… congratulations."

19

THE BONDING

"How are you feeling?" S'hyrlus asked Suzanne.

"I am well. Getting stronger daily."

"Good. You will soon be into the third phase of your transformation. The first one took a toll on you, as expected, considering your condition at the time. The second phase was easier. The third phase is by far the hardest, physically and emotionally. At this point, it is unknown if you will survive."

"Why is the third phase so hard?"

"Since you were brought here, the Great Oak has refreshed you, protected you, and tolerated you for our sake. In the third phase, the Great Oak has to bond with you personally, make you one with us, who are one with it. The Great Oak is more than just a tree. It lives and is aware. It has to choose to become one with you, and you have to choose to become one with it. If you succeed, you will know things. You already know things no one has taught you. You speak our language. The Great Oak has imparted that knowledge to you."

"What does failure look like?"

"You will never awaken." S'hyrlus' voice was tinged with sadness.

It had been several days since Blackwing had seen Irving and Jessica. He spent the time training in new techniques, one of which was suggested by Irving, and looked for Nighthawk.

I wonder how Suzanne is doing in her transition. He chuckled at the thought of Irving and Jessica's ever-present banter. How Irving would say something inappropriate, and Jessica's not so gentle corrections.

Then he jerked himself up. *Am I actually missing them? In two hundred fifty years, I've never missed anyone. I've never needed anyone. Now it seems, it pleasures me to be in their company.*

His musings were interrupted by a knock at the back door.

"Enter," Blackwing called.

"Glad your home," Jessica said, as she and Irving entered. "We weren't sure you'd be here. Have you eaten?"

Irving stepped behind Jessica with cartons of food and set them on the table.

"I have. But if that's Sichuan beef, I'd eat some." Blackwing grinned.

It didn't take long to get everything set and for the three of them to sit and start eating.

Irving swallowed. "We have some news. We are contracted."

"Contracted to do what?" Blackwing said.

"I think you'd call it *mated*," Jessica replied. "I am now known as Jessica Strange."

Irving grinned at her.

"Don't you say a thing." She turned her attention to the food.

Irving looked shocked. "I wasn't going to say anything."

"Uh-huh. That *Mr. Innocent* look doesn't work with me. I've known you too long to fall for it." Jessica grinned, with a twinkle in her eye.

Blackwing sat and looked first to one, then the other. "I'm glad you two finally figured out your lives are better together than apart."

"And how long have you known that?" Jessica asked.

"Ever since your injury," Blackwing said, around bites of food. "Maybe a little before that."

Irving laughed. "That's roughly when I figured it out. Thinking of her being injured," he shook his head, "I was so mad I thought I could've whipped my weight in wildcats, and was ready to try."

"Oh, *really*?" Jessica said. "That's the first I've heard of it. Weren't you taking a huge risk? We didn't have a relationship at that time, as I recall. Or were you assuming?"

"Speak for yourself. Let's just say I was hopeful, and call it good."

Blackwing grinned and chuckled.

"What?" Jessica said.

"Oh… nothing," Blackwing replied.

"No, you had something to say, so spit it out."

"Jess, let the poor man eat. You can see how skinny he is. He's starving." Irving continued eating.

"He's always been too skinny, in my opinion, but I want to know what he found so amusing."

"There wasn't anything funny," Blackwing said. "Before you two came, I was just thinking about you both. I appreciate the repartee."

Irving chuckled. "He missed us."

"Oh, that's okay, 'cuz we missed you, too." Jessica smiled. "Have you been looking for Joseph Johnson?"

Blackwing frowned. "No, I haven't been looking for him. I thought he was still in the hospital. Why?"

"He was released a couple weeks ago, but we found him hanging from a pipe in an abandoned building." Jessica picked up her tablet and scanned through the pictures, then stood to hand it Blackwing.

"Do you mind?" Irving said. "I'm trying to eat over here. That couldn't wait until after?" He shivered. "I've already seen them."

Blackwing handed the tablet back to Jessica.

She sat back down. "There was very little petechial hemorrhaging, according to the autopsy. No damage to the cervical vertebrae, and no sign of anything to indicate a drop of the kind associated with hanging. Neither the pipe nor the wire used would've supported a drop, but they were strong enough to support the body post-mortem."

Blackwing frowned. "You suspect Nighthawk or Phelonius of doing this."

"Based on what you've told us about siphoning off life energy... yes."

"How long was he out of the hospital?" Irving leaned back after he'd finished eating.

"According to his doctor, two weeks."

"That would be long enough to cause premature aging," Blackwing said. "The last time was the fatal instance. What are the authorities doing about it?"

"Nothing," Jessica said. "My new detective sergeant has determined that it's a suicide and isn't worth the resources. He's not going to look into it any further. I expect him to close the case in short order."

"Time grows short," S'hyrlus said to Suzanne.

They had been meandering in the woods, toward the Great Oak.

"I have no idea if you are strong enough yet, but it can't be helped. The time has come to complete your transformation."

"I was hoping to see Socrates, Irving, and Jessica once more before the third phase." *I miss them. Probably more than I should.*

"I know, but your emotional tie to them is drawing you away from this Plane. You feel it. If you delay much longer, you will decide to forego the third phase and you will be unable to leave here without one of us taking you for short visits. You will not be able to stay there, and so you will long for them here. You will eventually become bitter, distrustful, contemptuous, and reclusive. Your sisters and I need you to be happy here. We shun those that exhibit negative energies. They will build in you, and they are anathema to this Plane and to the Great Oak."

"Is there anything you can tell me about the third phase that will aid me?"

"All that have experienced the third phase have not passed on what they learned of the process." S'hyrlus frowned. "All they have said is that it is something intensely personal."

As they approached the Great Oak, the ground rumbled and a split developed in the massive trunk.

S'hyrlus stood away. "You must go into the trunk. Trust the Great Oak and be safe in its shelter."

Suzanne looked at S'hyrlus. Concern creased her face as she entered. Once inside the enormous trunk, she heard it closing. She gritted her teeth as the interior became dark, and closed her eyes.

"I hope I have not frightened you," said a rich baritone voice, and Suzanne opened her eyes.

She glanced around and seemed to be in the same meadow she was in with S'hyrlus during her first phase. The only thing missing was the huge oak tree that had shaded the dirt path.

With her, was a man who looked to be in his thirties. Slim, tanned to a golden brown, long, green hair, thin lips, well-muscled, with chiseled facial features.

"This place looks familiar," she said. "Where are we?"

"This?" The man slowly turned around. "This is the place that was uppermost in your mind. I thought you would be more... relaxed here."

"Who are you?"

"I have been called many things in many places and times. Oxylus would work as well as anything else."

"I am Suz—"

"You are Suzanne Rowena Hawks. You are... *ahem*... were a human, recently from the Human Plane. It has been a very long time since I have seen any such as you." He smiled at her shocked look. "You are here to see if I accept you—adopt you, if that is a better term."

"I am not in need of a father or an adoption. *I have no idea what to say, but I felt I had to say something. I hope I haven't offended him.*

"You are correct. That would not be a good thing. Offending me, I mean. Between you and me, I have always hated these meetings. There never seems to be enough time to really get to know someone. S'hyrlus tells me you have a good heart. Do you?"

"I like to think so. I am not sure anyone else would think so."

"Tell me about your father."

The surrounding scene changed to one of flashes of images of Suzanne and her father that filled the sky. She felt small and overwhelmed.

"He seems to have been a good man, with a good heart," Oxylus said.

"I have always felt he did his best."

"And what of his father?"

Again the scene changed to huge images of Suzanne's grandfather, the images changing quickly. They stopped on an image of her grandfather reading to her.

"So both your father and grandfather told you stories?"

"Yes. They were avid readers. My grandfather told the best ones, though."

"Yes… I see. Any stories of me?"

"Not that I remember."

"What kinds of stories?"

"Stories of hobbits, wizards, elves, and ents. Stories of high adventure against tremendous odds."

Oxylus smiled and chuckled. "I have no idea what any of those things are. Come closer." He beckoned her.

When she complied, he grabbed her shoulders and stared at her. As she looked closely at his face, she could see a third-eye appear.

"Will you bare yourself to me?" he said. "Will you show me everything about you? You do know that you stand before me naked."

Suzanne had thought she had a dress on—the toga type she'd worn since coming to the Hamadryad Plane. Now she felt naked.

"I can see into your mind, but you must choose to bare your soul to me."

"I… I do not know how," she whimpered.

Oxylus released her. "I see that. Have you never bore your soul to anyone?"

"Not that I am aware of."

"Will you show me your soul?" He held out his hand. "Just put it in my hand."

Suzanne looked at him. "I do not understand."

"Reach in, grab it, and put in my hand."

"How is that even possible?"

She watched Oxylus put his hand into his chest. When he withdrew it, there was a large, glowing, golden orb in his hand.

"Hold out your hands." He placed the glowing orb into her outstretched hands. "Gently. It is a fragile thing. I am trusting you with mine. Can you not return the favor?"

The orb glowed in Suzanne's hands and she could feel the heat of it on her face. Her expression reflected the awe she felt.

"Inside you there is a spark. That which you call a soul is that spark, that part of you that will continue on after your physical body has run its course. Do you know where it is?"

"Honestly, I have not really looked. I thought it was just a myth. Besides, I was told it was something that cannot be found."

"Here, you can find it, but you have to look for it." Oxylus re-inserted the orb into his chest. "Is it something you would like to find? Finding it may disrupt your firmly established beliefs."

She thought for a few moments. "If I have one, I'd like to find it."

"Would you like my help? If you do, just ask."

"Please, Oxylus, would you help me locate my soul?"

Oxylus smiled at her and chuckled. "I thought you would never ask." He bent over and peered into her chest area with his third-eye. "Found it."

"You did? Where is it?"

"It is roaming around your heart. If you do not want to go in after it, you can always try to coax it out."

"It is okay," she said, doing her best not to frighten the spark within.

"You can come out. No one here will harm you. Come on." *This is taking forever. Is this real, or am I just imagining it?*

"It is as real as you want it to be." Oxylus looked at her.

They were almost nose-to-nose.

After what seemed to be days of coaxing, a little blue spark exited her naval and she cradled it in her palm. She extended her hand to show her success.

"Will you give it to me?" Oxylus said.

Reluctantly, she turned her palm over and watched the tiny spark land on his palm.

"It is such a beautiful little thing," Oxylus looked at it with his third-eye. "Do you trust me?" he said, after some time inspecting the spark.

She nodded.

He reached inside himself again and withdrew the golden globe. He put the spark into the globe and her tears began to flow.

"I have it now." Oxylus put the globe away. "The globe is not just my soul, but all the souls of all my children. I am their protector. Your soul is no longer separate, but is part of the whole and will be kept safe. You are destined to travel far, as all my children do. You will face dangers unimaginable, but you will always know where your soul is.

"Now your time here is almost over. You need to leave very soon."

"How do I do that?"

Everything was suddenly dark and Suzanne was alone. She was feeling claustrophobic. She could feel the sap of the Great Oak running down her face. She opened her eyes and could see nothing, but she knew she was awake and still inside the tree. She started to panic.

"*Calm yourself,*" she heard Oxylus' voice say, inside her mind. "*Listen. When your mind is calm, a word will come to you. When it does, speak it.*"

With resolve, Suzanne slowed her heartbeat and her breathing. She felt a calm come over her. A word came to her mind and she spoke it. She opened her eyes and saw a portal form. Remaining calm, she stepped through.

Suzanne saw S'hyrlus standing a few paces away, and Suzanne grinned at her. She felt different. Tired, thirsty, hungry, and amazing, all at the same time.

"How are you?" S'hyrlus said.

Suzanne inhaled deeply and stretched as high as she could. "I feel absolutely wonderful. How long was I gone?"

"Two days. Although, that means little. As you can now understand, it takes as long as it takes."

Suzanne looked at her queen mother and grinned. "I know."

S'hyrlus hiked Suzanne's toga high on her right thigh, and looked at it. Then she hiked up her own dress, exposing her right thigh. Then she checked Suzanne's ears and grinned.

"It is time for celebration," S'hyrlus said.

As she turned, Suzanne saw her exposed thigh. Just below S'hyrlus' hip was a port wine stain in the shape of an oak leaf. Suzanne quickly looked down at her own thigh and saw the exact same port wine stain. She grinned and walked over to the Great Oak and hugged the ancient tree.

"Bring food and wine. It is a celebration!" S'hyrlus entered the clearing and clapped her hands over her head. "You all have a new sister. Come and welcome her."

Suzanne was a couple paces behind S'hyrlus and was immediately surrounded by what seemed like thousands of her sisters. Each one came over to her, looked at the mark on her thigh, checked her ears, and then stood back and bared their own thigh, displaying their mark. Each one hugged and kissed her before rushing off to gather food and drink.

"We will celebrate for two days," S'hyrlus said. "Then it will be time for you to return to help my son."

"Yes, my Queen." Suzanne bowed and knelt.

"There is no need for you to call me that." S'hyrlus lifted Suzanne to her feet. "I know who I am, and so do you. I do appreciate the honor you just showed, but in all the time you've spent here, have you heard the others refer to me by my title? I'd prefer it if you didn't mention it again."

20

RETURNING

"Opening a portal is relatively simple," S'hyrlus said to Suzanne. They were both standing in a grove of oak trees.

"At the end of your transformation, you were given a word by the Great Oak. That word is for you alone and should not be spoken aloud. A portal is connected throughout the Planes, by other oaks. For us, however, to use one for a portal you first have to check to see if it is connected. Go to that one." She indicated a much smaller tree. "Touch it and focus on it."

Suzanne did as she was directed. "I sense nothing," she said, after a short time.

"Now do the same with this one," S'hyrlus indicated a much larger tree.

Suzanne complied, and could feel other places pulsing through the trunk. Her eyes popped open as she stood away.

"This one is capable of being used for a portal," S'hyrlus said. "To open the portal, fix in your mind the destination you want, by name, or on a person. Think your word, and a portal should open. As an example, if you wanted to go to Q'estiria, fix Q'estiria in your mind and say your word, mentally. The portal would take you to any oak tree located in or around Q'estiria. Just so you know, Q'estiria is the largest city on the Q'estirian Plane. So you may have a few issues until you establish your own references. For me, I happen to know the owner of a leather shop I patronize just outside the city and not far from a grove of oak trees. For you to go to your previous home, concentrate on Socrates and the portal will open and deposit you at the closest point to him. There is quite a bit of trial and error. If you have no questions, open a portal to Socrates."

After taking a few deep breaths to calm herself, Suzanne touched the tree and felt the pulsing. With Socrates fixed in her mind, she said the word to herself and stepped back. Her eyes widened as the portal formed.

"After you, m'lady," she said to S'hyrlus.

She chuckled. "It is always a good practice to go last, as the portal will close shortly after the one who opened it enters."

She stepped through, with Suzanne close behind her.

"I tire of this place," Phelonius said. "It is depressing. Does Helios never shine? What is this place called?"

"The local inhabitants call it See-At-All," Nighthawk said. "Rainfall here is substantial."

"Who in their right mind would want to live here? I long for Q'estiria. Ka-Leif-Ornee-Ah at least has less rain."

"They call the rain liquid sunshine, here. I have no idea why."

"How does the plan progress?" Phelonius said.

"It has... stopped. I spent some time placing wards to warn of Socrates' presence. They have been alerted a number of times, usually when it is the most inconvenient. I have had to stop the importing, as a precaution."

Phelonius glared at Nighthawk. "Maybe I made an error in rescuing you from Socrates. I take it he has not reported any progress?"

"I managed to intercept his last report. The one that names both of us as violating the Council's edicts. No further reports since."

Phelonius slowly turned away from Nighthawk. "That sounded like an attempt at a veiled threat. What will happen if he catches you, or me, and returns us to Q'estiria? Care to guess?"

"No, sir. The mandatory penalty is incarceration and expulsion from our order. However, considering our status, I have no idea how the Council will rule."

"Nor do I," Phelonius growled. "I have half a mind to turn you over to Socrates just to see what will happen."

Nighthawk paled.

S'hyrlus and Suzanne exited the portal and saw Socrates practicing with his sword. She recognized the area as the small grove of oaks close to her house.

It wasn't long before Socrates performed a turn and strike. As he did, he saw them out of the corner of his eye.

"Lady S'hyrlus." Socrates stopped his practice and bowed to the pair.

"Very nice swordplay, my son." S'hyrlus smiled and placed a hand on his shoulder.

"Lady Suzanne." Remaining bowed, Socrates turned toward her.

Suzanne stepped closer to him. "Is that how you greet me after all this time? Please stand."

Once he stood, she rushed to him and threw her arms around his waist and hugged him. Socrates looked at S'hyrlus with a pained look.

She chuckled. "As with all the Hamadryades, this one is… unique unto herself." She cleared her throat and Suzanne sheepishly stepped back. "She is newly transformed, though, and a true Hamadryad. My other daughters have become… more flighty. But this one has more audacity and loyalty than her sisters, and I find that intriguing. It will be interesting to see how you smooth her rough edges. Do you find her acceptable?"

Socrates looked startled. "I do not understand, Mother."

"You have been wanting to establish your own household for some time. Do you accept this one as consort?"

"As you know, Mother, I have neither a manor house nor servants."

"That was not what I asked. As you know, it is the practice of the Hamadryades to choose who they will be a consort for. Prior to her transformation completion, this one had already decided, and that has not changed. So it falls to you. I ask only once more, do you accept her?"

Socrates looked at S'hyrlus with melancholy. "How could I not? If not for her sacrifice, I would not be here. I owe her everything."

"Stand," S'hyrlus said.

Blackwing stood tall, with his left forearm parallel to the ground, palm down.

S'hyrlus looked at Suzanne. "If you agree to be consort to Socrates, take your position."

Suzanne stood beside Socrates and placed her right arm atop his left, palm down.

"May you be content for many years," S'hyrlus said.

She walked to a smaller oak tree and touched it with closed eyes. A sizable limb fell to the ground from it.

"Use this to make for her a staff. Train her in its use."

"I will, Mother. Thank you."

As S'hyrlus turned to leave, Suzanne stepped toward her. "Do you need to leave so soon? Can you stay to meet the others?"

"Not this time. I will come to you again before long." S'hyrlus opened a portal.

Socrates and Suzanne watched her step through the portal, and then it closed.

"Are Jessica and Irving here?" Suzanne turned away from the large oak tree.

"No. They are about their own business, but I expect them later."

In English, Suzanne said, "I'm going to take a shower and change into something more acceptable."

"I will fashion your staff." Socrates walked over to the fallen limb.

Suzanne stood in front of the mirror in her room, having finished her shower. Since this was the first time since her transformation, she stood marveling at the changes to her appearance.

When she met Blackwing, she had kept her hair short, for convenience and ease of care. Now, though, her hair was long and her normal auburn color had flame-red highlights. Her hazel eyes were gone. Bright, deep emerald eyes stared back at her and were more almond-shaped than before. The corners of her eyes seemed to be pulled toward her ear points, which curved upward and towards the back of her neck.

She absentmindedly reached for her makeup, and then stopped. She already looked stunning.

"Can't improve on anything." She chuckled and put the makeup down.

She dug out some clean clothes and tried to get dressed, and found more had changed than she thought. *Are my breasts bigger?* She cupped them and turned sideways. *My hips are narrower and my butt seems smaller.*

"Great. Now I need new clothes!"

After getting dressed, she brushed out her hair. When she looked at her reflection, her hair disappointingly covered her new points on her ears. *Too bad Jess isn't here. A French braid would be a nice look.* She watched as her hair began braiding without her assistance. In short order, she was marveling at her new look while tying the end of her braid. *That's as perfect as you're likely to get.*

"You're still overthinking it," Blackwing said.

They had spent the last couple hours working on Suzanne's defensive staff techniques.

"Don't think about it. The eye sees and the body responds. Relax and let it flow." He started again with another flurry of attacks.

Amid the clacking noises of the staffs making contact, Jessica and Irving arrived.

"Who is this?" Jessica said.

Suzanne became distracted and got bonked on her head. "Ouch!"

"Serves you right," Blackwing said. "Always keep your focus."

Jessica had her service weapon in her hand, and Irving held his sword at the ready. They both glared at the stranger.

"That's a fine how-do-you-do!" Suzanne grinned. "Have I changed so much that I get greeted with drawn weapons?"

"Suzanne?" Irving stored his sword. "Is that you? Wow! You've changed."

Jessica glared at Suzanne. "Put your tongue back in your head, horn-dog," she said to Irving. "That can't be Suzanne. Looks nothing like her and sounds nothing like her."

"Relax, Jessica, it *is* Suzanne," Blackwing said.

Jessica reluctantly put her weapon away. "How do you know?" She kept her stare on Suzanne. "It could be a trick from Nighthawk."

"It isn't a trick," Blackwing replied. "I have it on high authority that it is Suzanne."

Jessica eyed her. "Whose authority?"

"S'hyrlus'. She delivered her herself."

Two hours later, everyone had finished eating.

"It's nice to see that you persuaded Socrates to eat," Suzanne said to the rest.

Irving laughed. "He can definitely put a dent in Sichuan beef."

"Did you open my safe?" Suzanne asked Jessica.

"No, we haven't. It seemed too… permanent. I didn't want to face that my friend had died."

"As far as everyone else is concerned, I am dead. I can't use my tablet, access my accounts, or buy anything. Without a working ID, I don't exist. I find it oddly liberating. Anyway, inside my safe are the instructions you'll need to gain access to my accounts. You do know that I left the house to you and Irving, as well as all my assets?"

"How would I know that?" Jessica said. "You didn't even ask us or mention it? Why would you do that?"

"Mainly, I did it because I have no other family except you and Irv. And then there is the issue with Blackwing. I knew he'd have to be taken care of. Now I'm in the same boat. I need a favor. There've been a number of changes due to my transformation. None of my clothes fit properly."

"I can see a number of the... um... change.," Jessica eyed Suzanne. "Tomorrow I can pick up some of what you need. Did Socrates tell you that Irv and I are contracted?"

"No, he didn't say a word about it." Suzanne gave a big grin. "I'm happy for you. I am Socrates' consort."

Jessica looked at her, mouth agape. "My, you've come up in the world! When did that happen? I thought you've just returned?"

"I have. But before I could even take a shower, I became his consort."

"What does that entail?"

"I have no idea. Socrates has to enlighten me as to the expectations. Do you and Irv sleep here?"

"We have a few times. Our jobs prevent us from moving here permanently. Since we both work for the PD, we have to live in the city, so most of the time we live in my apartment. We haven't yet decided if we're going to live at my apartment, his apartment, or just get a new one. I'm leaning toward my apartment."

Suzanne got up and went to her bedroom. She returned a few minutes later and handed Irving a tablet, then resumed her seat at the table.

"That contains everything you need to claim my estate," she said. "You do have my ID somewhere, don't you?"

"Of course." Irving went through some of the information on the tablet. "It's in my desk at the lab."

"Good. You'll need to take it and the tablet to the lawyer's office.

"Oscar... Dinwittie?" Irving found the name on the tablet.

"That's him. Just take it all to him and he'll do the rest."

"Mind if I ask you something?" Irving said. "What exactly are you?"

He got a stern look from Jessica.

"I mean, I know you were human, but you've... changed. What are you now, Suzanne?"

"Irving! Mind your manners," Jessica barked.

"It's okay, Jess." Suzanne smiled. "I'm what used to be called a Hamadryad."

Irving was silent for a second. He had replaced Suzanne's tablet with his own, and did a search.

"So you're a Greek mythical creature that lives in trees?" he read, from the tablet. "That seems a little odd to me. Ow!" He rubbed his upper arm where Jessica had pinched him.

"That's rude!" Jessica said. "If Suzanne wants to think she is a hama-whatchamacallit, let her."

Suzanne, being a bit peeved, looked at Socrates, who said nothing.

"You have such beautiful hair, Jess," said Suzanne. "Have you ever thought of braiding it?"

"I have, but that would mean Mister Thumbs would have to do it."

"Do you mind if I do it?"

"Not at all." Jessica started to rise.

"No, just remain seated and turn around."

Once Jessica turned her chair and re-seated herself with her back to Suzanne, her hair flared out, like static was pulling it in all directions. Then hair braided itself into a single braid running down the middle of her neck and back. Suzanne pulled out the tie holding her own braid and handed it to Jessica.

"There you go," she said.

As Jessica tied the end of the braid, she looked at Irving, who was staring, mouth agape. She heard Socrates snicker.

"What's the problem?" Jessica said. "We got Snickers over there, and you staring. Haven't you seen someone get their hair braided before?"

"Not like that!" Irving said. "She did it from across the table and without touching your hair. I think I need to look up Hamadryads again and do more research before just passing it off as someone being delusional."

The four sat around the table, three days after Suzanne's return.

"I did some searches," Jessica said, "for unexplained deaths outside the Tacoma area. In the past few days, there has been ten of them and all have been located in either Seattle or Tacoma."

"What was the cause?" Irving's eyes were wide. "Were they all from their life energy being drained, or don't they know yet?"

"There were no pictures attached to the reports, and the few that had IDs didn't match their apparent age with their actual age. All were found just outside of or close to each city's limits, or in abandoned buildings. Autopsy reports were inconclusive as to cause or time of death. The disturbing part is that none are being investigated. They were all designated as addicts, drunks, or homeless, and thus didn't warrant further investigation."

Irving shook his head. "So because they were all throwaways, they don't matter."

A deafening crackling noise punctuated Irving's last statement. It sounded like an arching transformer, but there were no transformers this far outside the city.

Blackwing and Suzanne ran outside as Irving and Jessica looked out a window. They all saw what looked like lightning bolts arching over the house, disclosing a faint dome over the property.

"It's a breach," Blackwing yelled over the noise. "Someone is trying to get through the wards. Over there!" He pointed, after consulting his sphere.

As Blackwing and Suzanne approached the barrier, they saw Nighthawk throw another energy ball toward them, and more arching as the barrier stopped the energy ball. They were flanked by Irving, sword at the ready, and Jessica, service weapon pointed at Nighthawk.

"What do *you* want?" Jessica snarled.

"Blackwing!" said Nighthawk. "My brother. How have you been? All healed, I see. You never call and you never write." He feigned pouting.

"*Brother*?" Blackwing snarled. "My brothers are those that uphold the oath of the *T'et Faqin Q'estirions*. Not some faithless criminal."

"What are they saying?" Jessica whispered to Irving.

"I have no idea," he whispered back. "But look at her hair."

When Jessica glanced at Suzanne, she was taken aback. Suzanne's hair, which had been in a braid a few minutes before, was now a flowing mane of a dark, angry red.

"Criminal?" Nighthawk replied. "Truly your words have cut me—"

"Enough!" Blackwing said. "What is your business here? Have you come to battle once more?"

"I have come to surrender myself to you. I wish to be taken back to Q'estiria."

21

Q'ESTIRIA

Blackwing, followed closely by a bound and gagged Nighthawk, and Suzanne, who was slightly more behind, exited the portal. The sudden change in air pressure caused Suzanne's eardrums to delay in equalizing. As she tried to force a yawn, she noticed the lush purplish-green grass that seemed to go to the horizon, and the sun here was shining bright, even though the sky at home was a dreary overcast that Tacoma residents had gotten used to.

"Looks like we are not in Kansas anymore," she said, more to herself.

"No, this is Q'estiria," Blackwing replied, after inhaling a huge breath. "I do not think I know where this Kansas is. Is it far? Maybe we can go there sometime."

Suzanne, finding it difficult to cover a snicker, decided on a fake cough.

Seeing Blackwing looking off to the horizon in several directions, Suzanne asked, "Are you lost? Which way do we go?"

"This happens sometimes." He tried, with the help of input from his sphere, to get his bearings. "The portal took us to the closest unused oak to where we wanted to go. So we can, and did, end up somewhere other than I was expecting. But I am not lost. We go this way."

He stuck out his left elbow and Suzanne grasped his arm. The trio took a few steps and disappeared. After three wizard steps, they were standing on a small hill. In the shallow valley below was a large town built across an opening formed by a plateau across the valley floor. The cluster of buildings was surrounded by a high wall. Outside the wall, and toward them, were large farms with fenced-off sections for pasture and rows of growing plants. On their side of the center of the valley was a river that cut across their path.

"We can step to this side of the river," Blackwing said, "but the other side is protected. The long walk from the river is intentional, designed to allow the city to prepare for attacks."

"Is there a possibility of attack?" Suzanne said.

"Not that I am aware of, but things are always changing and they like to be prepared for most possibilities."

"They are paranoid," Nighthawk said.

Blackwing had ungagged him so he could drink.

"Why not let me go, and then you can show your *Lady* the wonders of Q'estiria? I think you are in for a rude awakening before you get me to the Council."

"The humans have a saying—business before pleasure. For me, this will give me no end of pleasure to see you confined." Blackwing replaced his gag.

As the trio walked the dusty road to the main gate of Q'estiria, Suzanne noticed many people staring after them.

"Why are all these people staring at us?" she whispered. "It's making me feel self-conscious."

"While they see *T'et Faqin Q'estirions* often," Blackwing whispered back, "they seldom see one of the *Sh'o Sook J'eid*. To be honest, it is the way you are dressed, to a smaller degree. I am used to seeing you in jeans, a button-up shirt, and hiking shoes. They have not seen clothes like you are wearing.

"Lady S'hyrlus mentioned a leather crafter when she was instructing me on portals."

"I know the one. His shop is just ahead on the left. If you wish to stop there, you are free to do so."

"I can wait. You need to see to Nighthawk first."

As they approached the gate, the trio was met by several youngsters of the *T'et Faqin Q'estirions*, all of whom snapped to attention.

"Commander Blackwing," said the obvious leader of the group. "To what do we owe this pleasure?"

"Prisoner," Blackwing replied. "Escort him to confinement." He pushed the bound and gagged Nighthawk toward the group, who held him. "I will follow and remove the bindings once he is safely incarcerated."

"Charges?" the leader said.

"Multiple violations of the Council's edicts, to start."

The leader frowned.

"There are other charges, but I need to talk to the Indicter General to be accurate."

"But Commander, this is Chief Commander Nighthawk."

"I know who it is! Do as I have instructed, or you could join him."

"This is all highly irregular," the youngster grumbled, but complied.

Blackwing and Suzanne followed the small procession of guards to a large building just inside the gate. As they walked, Suzanne tried to see everything. The narrow streets seemed to be packed dirt or clay, and wound in all directions. The buildings seemed to be well-constructed brick and wood.

"No unauthorized persons beyond this point," the young leader said to Suzanne, after they had entered a stout building.

"Wait here," Blackwing whispered. "I'll be back shortly."

Suzanne nodded and looked around for a bench to sit on as Blackwing, Nighthawk, and all the guards disappeared through a thick wooden door.

"That was an unexpected development," Irving said, shortly after the portal closed. "I'd have thought that Blackwing was going to have to hunt him down."

"I thought so, too," Jessica said. "After all my years in the PD, it's still hard to understand the criminal mind. Do you feel like Tony's for dinner?"

"Tony's sounds good to me. Let's lock up the house and go. How long do you think Blackwing will be gone?"

"I have no idea," Jessica said, as they both walked around locking the house. "He gave me no indication of how long they would be."

Seconds after locking the house, Jessica and Irving were seating themselves at Tony's. Shortly after placing their order, Jessica received a text from Captain Trooper.

"Great," Jessica said, irritated.

"What is it?"

"I'm to report to City Hall tomorrow morning," Jessica read the text, "for honor guard duty, in full uniform. I don't know the last time I wore it and I don't know if it is presentable."

"Is it at home or at the precinct?"

"It's at home. I don't wear it often and I have no place to store it at the precinct."

"Well, that tells me what we're doing after dinner."

The next morning, Jessica, along with nine other officers, was lined up in the hallway leading to Mayor Worth's office. Each officer was dressed just as she was. Polished black riot helmet with its visor down, hiding their faces. Black armored arm and leg guards. Polished black Plexi-shields with the police emblem on them, and tonfa-style riot sticks.

Jessica looked at the rest of the officers. *We all look like damn stormtroopers.*

The heads-up display showed each officer's position and allowed a darkened view of the surroundings.

Captain Trooper called them all to attention as the elevator doors parted, and everyone hit their shields with their tonfas, making a resounding bang.

Jessica's mouth hung agape as she saw who exited the metal car. There was Mayor Worth talking to a much younger version of Blackwing.

Blackwing and Nighthawk are off somewhere. He looks just like Blackwing, only maybe approaching thirty. That has to be his grandfather, Phelonius Blackwing! Maybe if I try to make myself small, he won't notice me. After all, I've never met him or him me, and all of us standing here look alike. What is he doing here? Surely he isn't the VIP.

She breathed a little easier as Phelonius stood away from her, with the mayor between them. But she followed the pair with her eyes and concentrated on not drawing attention to herself.

Mayor Worth and Phelonius ceased talking as they passed between the double line of officers. Jessica's heart, which had been pounding since the pair exited the elevator, skipped a beat when Phelonius stopped and Mayor Worth took a few more steps. Phelonius turned slowly toward her, a snide grin on his face.

Jessica didn't think, just responded. Before anyone could stop her, she launched at Phelonius, turning the long arm of the tonfa to run down her ulna. When she hit Phelonius with her shield, her arm, tonfa first, struck him below the chin and forced the pair to the opposite wall. The two officers that were standing there broke the impact of Jessica and Phelonius.

It was then that Jessica felt a pressure against her shield. She braced herself to pin Phelonius more tightly, but she was forced backward into the wall she was previously standing in front of. Before she could recover and launch again, she felt hands holding her, forcing her down to the floor. She felt the pressure of her fellow officers sitting on top of her, preventing her from moving at all. She felt the needle puncture her neck, near her clavicle, and the hallway went black.

Nighthawk entered the small cell after the bindings and gag were removed, without the guards forcing him.

"This looks familiar." He smirked as he looked around. "I do not believe I have seen it from this perspective, though."

"The assistant indicter general will be in shortly to take your statement, sir," said the head of the guards. "Is there anything you require?"

"No, I require nothing." Nighthawk slowly lowered himself to the pallet near the back wall.

It took no time for Suzanne and Blackwing to retrace their steps in the maze of hallways, to the heavy door they'd passed through only minutes before.

"Sir, please wait in here." The head guard opened a door to a small room just before they could exit the larger heavy door. "Someone in authority will come to debrief you. Who is your strangely dressed visitor?"

"She is not a visitor," Blackwing said. "She is the Lady Suzanne, *Sh'o Sook J'eid*. She is my consort and witness. I would be grateful if you saw to her needs."

"Her needs will be tended."

Blackwing entered the small room and sat in a chair opposite the door, at the wooden table. He retrieved his sphere and placed it into the depression on the table, and settled himself to wait.

Just as the head guard exited the heavy door, the Lady S'hyrlus entered from the opposite door and walked over to the young guard.

"Do you require this one?" She indicated Suzanne.

"At some point she will have to give her statement to the assistant indicter general, but he has not arrived yet."

"Who is the assistant indicter general these days?"

"We have several, m'lady, but Timoroose Hornsdoodle will be the assistant indicter general that obtains her statement."

"She will be coming with me. I have a room at the Cloven Hoof. If Socrates Blackwing is released before I return, please inform him. I will return her here in two hours, more properly attired I hope."

"As you wish, m'lady."

"Follow me and say nothing," S'hyrlus said to Suzanne, in her own language.

Several minutes later, S'hyrlus and Suzanne arrived at the Cloven Hoof

Inn and entered S'hyrlus's room. When she entered, S'hyrlus reclined on the bed.

"I am surprised at my son," she said, from her reclined position. "He knew you would not be taken seriously dressed like that."

"He did mention your leather crafter when we were walking toward the city. It was my choice to deal with Nighthawk first."

"Luckily, I thought you would be here sooner than later. I arrived here after leaving you." S'hyrlus motioned to a bundle of leather on the foot of the bed. "Those were delivered a couple hours ago. They are yours and are acceptable here. Appearances are important, especially here, and must be maintained."

Suzanne stripped down to her underwear and began unfolding the leather. First out was her leather britches. When she held them up, they appeared to be too small.

"Try them on," S'hyrlus said. "They will stretch to fit you properly."

As Suzanne pushed her leg into the britches, she could feel the leather expand to accept her. Once she had them on, she fastened the button that held the waist and felt the leather adjusting to her frame. She bent at the knees and the britches expanded to accommodate her movements.

"Feels like they're painted on." Suzanne ran her hand over her hips, gluteus maximus, and legs.

It was then that she felt the seam of her underwear around her thighs and decided to remove them.

"Better?" She finished with the leather britches.

"Much!" S'hyrlus said. "You will not need that either." She indicated Suzanne's bra.

Suzanne removed her bra and proceeded to the next item—a vest that laced up the front, with no shoulder straps. When it was half-laced, she bent over and shook her breasts into the provided cups. As she straightened, the vest finished lacing by itself. She tried to pull the vest down to cover her navel, which was clearly visible.

"Those fit you nicely." S'hyrlus smiled. "They are made of the same materials and processes as Socrates'."

"So they are armored?"

"I do not know what that is, but they will resist fire, as well as swords and other projectiles. The boots and cloak are the same materials as well. Here, and other places, bare feet are acceptable, and I prefer it. However, in some of the places you are likely to go with Socrates, you are going to need them."

As Suzanne slipped her feet into the boots, they laced and tied themselves. She could feel them contouring to her feet. Once they were on, she raised her feet and noticed that she could feel the protection the boots provided, but they were light and extremely comfortable. Far more comfortable than her own hiking shoes.

The cloak was made of the same material as her boots, vest, and britches. She put it over her shoulders and found a silver clasp fashioned into the shape of an acorn.

"The cloak has a deep hood, in case you get caught in the rain. Like everything else, it repels rain, and you will stay warm and dry in the worst of downpours. It also has pockets on the inside to store your other clothes, or anything else."

When Suzanne had finished dressing, she looked to S'hyrlus and saw the broad smile on her face.

"Now you are properly adorned. The only other advice I can give is whenever you walk anywhere, do it like you belong there. Own wherever you are. You belong everywhere you happen to be. When you can do that, you will command the respect we are due. Can you return to where I found you, or do you need me to show you? You and Socrates can stay here for as long as you are here. I will be leaving soon, but I wanted to give you your new clothes."

"I can find it. You have my deep appreciation for the clothes and the advice. I have no idea why they are holding Socrates for so long, but I think we will keep the room until we leave."

Shortly after Suzanne left, AIG Hornsdoodle entered the small room that held Blackwing. He spent the next hours questioning Blackwing, making copies of the pertinent parts of Blackwing's sphere, and inspecting the original orders.

"Have I answered your questions to your satisfaction?" Blackwing drank from his tankard.

Hornsdoodle sat with his fingertips pressed together for a few seconds.

"I am… unsure," he said.

"Unsure? What is there to be unsure about?"

"I think we have… um… a situation."

"What kind of a *situation*?"

"By the strict interpretation of the edicts, you have violated them, as well as Nighthawk. I have yet to question Nighthawk, and I have no doubt as to the veracity of your account or the circumstances. However, someone from the Council will have to talk to you and determine if you violated the edicts and their intent. That will happen after I submit my completed report to the Council. So for the time being, you are not to leave the city."

"What happens to Nighthawk?"

"His disposition is, as yet, undetermined. He is guilty of attacking one of his subordinates, trafficking in *Brui K'sha U'ien* and *P'koosh*, and probably others, and for transporting a subordinate unwillingly to a forbidden Plane."

"What about all the humans he murdered?"

"These... *humans* are not recognized by the Council as a sentient species. At this point, they are nothing more than farm animals. Extinguishing them is not against Council edicts. Nighthawk will remain incarcerated until the Council rules. Your witness is also restricted. Should you not honor these restrictions, you will be assumed to be guilty, and thus, be hunted and apprehended. I have thousands of new *T'et Faqin* anxious for their first bounty."

When Jessica regained consciousness, she found that she was cuffed to a metal table in an interrogation room. Someone had removed her armor, and after looking around the room, she found that it was nowhere in sight. She was still groggy from the narcotic used to render her manageable.

Her attention snapped to the door when she heard it unlock, and scowled at Michael Taggert as he entered.

"Glad to see you're awake." He crossed the room and sat in a chair opposite her, the metal table she was cuffed to, between them. "I was wondering if you were going to OD, you were out so long." He flipped through pages on a tablet. "The first obvious question is why?"

"Why what?" Jessica said.

"Why would you attack a visiting dignitary?"

"I wasn't attacking him. I was trying to restrain him. Besides, he's no dignitary."

"Why would you want to restrain him? Do you know him? Have you ever seen him before? What makes you think he is other than presented?"

Jessica ground her teeth. *How much do I reveal. If I say too much, they're going to lock me away in some deep dark hole.*

"Phelonius Blackwing is no dignitary," she spat.

Taggert stared at her, mouth partially open.

"How do you know his name?" he said. "We took great care to keep his name secret, and yet you know. Care to explain?"

"I didn't know his name until this moment." Jessica grinned.

"Then how *did* you know? A name like that just doesn't roll trippingly off the lips."

"You told me. All I had was a suspicion. When I threw the name out, your expression told me all I needed to know. You really aren't very good at this."

22

POLITICIANS

"That woman is so damned stubborn!" Taggert had spent the last several hours trying to get all the information Jessica was keeping to herself.

"Is it that, or are you incapable of getting the information from her?" said Captain Trooper.

Taggert had entered his office some time ago and was just starting to make some sense rather than just ranting.

Trooper was losing patience with him. "Maybe you're going about it the wrong way. Or hasn't that entered your feeble brain?" He got up and stormed to the interrogation room. "Isolation mode! All recordings off." He looked around and saw the lights turn off on the multiple cameras, then sat across from Jessica and stared at her. "Jess, I really need you to talk to me."

"Why should I? You gave the keyword to empty the observation room and turn off all recording devices, but how do I know that it was accomplished? You've drugged me and cuffed me in here like a common criminal."

"We had no choice, Jess. You appeared to have gone berserk outside

Mayor Worthless's office. To protect you, and us, we had to get control of you as best we could."

Jessica glared at Trooper. "I can understand some of that, but why am I still cuffed in here? Am I under arrest?"

Trooper pulled a key from his pocket and unlocked her cuffs. "You've done nothing illegal." He put the cuffs and key in his pocket. "You have, however, embarrassed Mayor Worthless. He's the one that wants you removed from the force. Not me."

"I've not heard you refer to him that way before." Jessica massaged her wrists.

"Mayor Lester Worth is a typical politician—ergo worthless. The citizenry may've voted him in, but that doesn't mean they know him. Not the way I do."

The chair screeched as Jessica slid it back to stand. "If I'm not under arrest, then I am free to go?"

"You can… but I would feel better if you answered a few questions first. You know there are lots of questions others are going to want answers to. Help me, Jess. Help me to understand."

Jessica paced behind her chair. "How can I trust that there's no surveillance in here?"

After a couple minutes, she sat but didn't slide the chair toward the table.

"Ask," she said. "But I reserve the right not to answer."

"Fair enough." Trooper reached into his pocket and dropped a gold coin on a chain, onto the table. "We found this around your neck." He dug into another pocket and tossed another gold coin onto the table. "We found this one in your pocket." He again dug into another pocket and tossed yet another gold coin onto the table, away from the other two. "And this one I was given by the mayor's new best friend. I don't need Irving to do a comparison to know that they're all the same. Can you explain it?"

Jessica scooped up the two coins that belonged to her. She placed the one with a chain around her neck and it disappeared down the front of her unitard.

She looked at Trooper and frowned. "I would keep that one away from your skin, if I were you. You may be better off to not carry it at all."

"You obviously know something about this." Trooper indicated the gold coin that remained on the metal table. "Care to enlighten me?"

"It's not that I don't trust you, but... I don't trust you. I know where I got mine, but I wouldn't trust the source of yours. Remember my last qualifications? How you doubted I actually shot what I did?" She tapped the point on her unitard where the coin hung underneath.

Trooper's mouth flopped open and he leaned forward. "You're serious?"

She nodded, with a serious expression.

"And this one?" He indicated the single coin on the table.

She shrugged.

Trooper leaned back. "What about the other one?"

"I could show you, but you wouldn't believe it." She frowned.

"I started the same way you did. So I have a certain amount of... curiosity. I'll try to keep an open mind."

"Is my phone handy?"

Trooper opened the drawer on his side of the table and handed over her cell phone. She placed a call.

"Tony's, after work." She hung up, then stood and motioned Trooper over to her. "Put that somewhere safe."

He got to his feet and put the coin inside the drawer.

"Take my arm," she said.

When he had a grasp on her arm, she squeezed the coin and they both disappeared.

Seconds after leaving the interrogation room, Trooper and Jessica reappeared outside her apartment building. He headed to some bushes and expelled the contents of his stomach.

"Sorry about that," he said.

"Don't worry about it. It's a side effect. Know where we are?"

"It looks like your apartment building over there."

"It is. If you've recovered, take my arm."

When Trooper took her arm again, they both disappeared.

When they both reappeared, they were once again inside the interrogation room. Trooper looked a little green around the gills.

"You okay, Cap'n?"

Trooper checked his phone for the time. "We went to your neighborhood and back in only a couple minutes?"

Jessica nodded. "Most of the delay was you retching."

Trooper plopped into a chair. He tapped the table above the drawer that held the gold coin.

"Recommendations?" he said.

Jessica looked grave. "I'd have Irving seal it up in something until my source gets back. Then, if you'd like, I could have him give me a read on it to see if it's safe to touch. But that's just my opinion. Take it for what it's worth."

"Sounds like a reasonable precaution." Trooper nodded. "I need to ask why. Was it to protect the mayor?"

"Honestly, I don't give a shit about the mayor. I was protecting my city."

"I can respect that, but how did you know?"

"Do you remember the Joe Johnson case?"

"The suicide?"

"It wasn't suicide."

"Phelonius?"

"Either him or his minion."

"Proof?"

"If I had proof, I don't think I'd be in here. To say Joe Johnson was a suicide is just too incredulous for words. I've seen lots of suicides and so have you. Take a good look at the pictures taken at the scene and draw your own conclusions."

Trooper sat thinking for some time. "Call Irving. I want," he tapped the table a couple times, "put into a small lockbox and delivered to my office."

Suzanne and Socrates had been in Q'estiria for a full three days and were sitting in the Inn's dining area, enjoying a meal. Many of the patrons would glance in their direction and then whisper to their companions.

"Why is everyone staring at us?" Suzanne whispered. "It's making me wonder if my face is on straight."

Socrates chuckled. "I am certain that it is on straight. People will do whatever they will. Try to ignore it."

As she returned her attention to the rough loaf of bread and bowl of stew, an older *T'et Faqin Q'estirion,* by the look of him, approached them.

"Remain seated." His voice had the same penetrating quality as Socrates'. "Do I have the honor of addressing the hero of the *Ha'Jakta Ha'Dreen B'kota* War?"

"I am Socrates Blackwing."

"All honors be to you. I am—"

"Cornelius Blackwing."

The much older wizard bowed. "Might I join you?"

Socrates nodded and motioned to a chair across the table. Cornelius sat.

"Who is this *lovely* creature?" he said, in a flirtatious tone.

"This is the Lady Suzanne, *Sh'o Sook J'eid,* and my consort. Suzanne, this is Cornelius Blackwing, member of the *Sh'tuk Q'estiria Faqin,* and grandfather of my grandfather." Socrates placed one of his pewter tankards in front of Cornelius.

Cornelius picked up the tankard and nodded to them both. "I have come to task you, Socrates. I have become aware of the confusion surrounding you, your lovely consort," he smiled flirtatiously at Suzanne, "and Malthuvius Nighthawk."

"To which *confusion* are you referring?"

"As you know, Malthuvius handed you orders at your meeting after the capture of Pontifar Grimstar."

Socrates nodded.

"The orders given to you were not sanctioned by the Council and we had no knowledge of them being issued. Another event that happened at the same time was your promotion. That, too, was not sanctioned by the Council."

Socrates sat motionless for a few seconds. "You are saying that since my field promotion was not sanctioned or recorded, my consort is not recognized?"

"Essentially. Who performed the ritual, if I may ask?"

"The Lady S'hyrlus."

"Herself? Impressive!"

Socrates shrugged.

"That, of course, supersedes any sanctioning required by the Council," Cornelius said, nervously.

"I thought it might."

Cornelius frowned. "I am expecting this matter to be resolved quickly, so you are hereby commanded to present yourself to the Council chambers in the morning."

"Cornelius," Socrates halted him from leaving, "I do not mean to offend you or the Council. A lack of a relationship between you and I is necessary, but I find it obtrusive."

"In what way?"

"I would have preferred to know my elders more intimately, but that is not our way."

Cornelius smiled. "I would prefer the same," he whispered, "but as you say, it is not our way, nor has it been for thousands of years." Cornelius smiled as he rose to leave, and patted Socrates' shoulder. "Feel free to bring your Lady tomorrow."

The next morning, Socrates was standing at a table facing the full Council. Cornelius Blackwing sat in the leadership position, center of the Council's dais. To his right were Thaddius Crowfoot and H'Difa Thunderclap. To his left were D'Tomia Nighthawk and Syn'Chin

Hornsdoodle. Blackwing had never seen the Council and knew their names only with the help of his sphere. All of them looked forebodingly grim.

Cornelius banged a heavy rock, smooth and shiny from much use, and all became quiet.

"Commander, sit, please," he said, once silence was attained.

Socrates seated himself.

"Having reviewed your statements and examined the available facts, we have but a few questions. Were you aware of the edict concerning the Eighth Plane?"

"I was," Socrates replied.

"And yet you were on the Eighth Plane, in violation of the edict. Why?"

"I was given orders that at the time I assumed to be valid, directing me to the Eighth Plane for the purpose of investigating and apprehending violators of the edict, and to gather intelligence on the residents there."

"Were there others from the Known Planes there?"

"Not at first. However, I did find evidence to indicate that at some earlier time, others from the Known Planes had been there. The... humans keep their records in written form and bind them into what they call books. Some of these books contain many myths and legends, many of which describe those from the Seven Planes. They may call them by different names than we do, but they bare extraordinary similarities."

"Are these *humans* a threat to us?" Thunderclap said.

"They could be, if antagonized. Currently, they are not."

"Do they show any signs of being civilized?" Crowfoot said.

"They have edicts—what they call laws. Their laws can be intrusive, but generally show a high degree of civilization. They are not the mindless brutes we are led to believe from our education."

"Who is the Lady sitting behind you?" said D'Tomia Nighthawk.

Socrates motioned that Suzanne should stand, and she did.

"This is Lady Suzanne. She is Hamadryad, *Sh'o Sook J'eid*, and my consort, by ritual performed by the Lady S'hyrlus."

"Is it true that she was once a human?" D'Tomia said.

"It is."

"Lady Suzanne, in your opinion," D'Tomia said, "are humans sufficiently mature to be joined with the rest of the Seven Known Planes, or should we just eradicate them?"

Everyone began grumbling and talking loudly amongst each other, to the point that Cornelius had to bang the dais several times with the rock to regain order. Suzanne shifted from one foot to the other.

"That question is out of line," Cornelius shouted.

"It may be," D'Tomia said, "but it is a question that needs answering."

"In my opinion," Suzanne said, after the room was silent, "humans are too immature to join with the rest of the Planes. Attacking them, however, would be a colossal mistake. You may win most of the battles, but they would destroy everyone and everything on the planet. They would reduce it to nothing more than a burned-out cinder."

Everyone stared at Suzanne, mouths agape.

"Such a thing is possible?" Cornelius asked quietly, being the first to recover.

"It is," Suzanne replied. "And they would not hesitate to use it. They have had that capability for over one hundred years."

"How is it possible?" D'Tomia said. "By what means can this be accomplished? Force her to answer," he shouted to the rest of the Council.

"Having been human, and now Hamadryad, I bear loyalty to both, and to peace and life. The how is not important. The fact that it is possible, *is*. I have nothing more to say on that subject." Suzanne sat.

"I would like to add," Socrates said, over the renewed din of arguments, "the human technology is behind our own, in most areas. However, in a few areas, theirs exceeds ours."

Amongst the noise of the Council members renewed arguing, Cornelius banged for order.

Failing to get it," he shouted, "Council is in recess. We will call you when we reconvene."

After the Council Members left the main chambers, Blackwing left. Suzanne, sensing some disquiet, followed and both sat in the hallway.

"You certainly know how to stir things up," Blackwing said, in English, chuckling.

"You helped." Suzanne also chuckled. "If you wanted someone to just sit there and say nothing, then you should've said something, given me a heads-up. I'm sensing that there's something else going on with you, though. You can tell me, you know."

Socrates became fidgety. "Last night you were wondering why everyone was staring. You thought they were staring at you, but they weren't. They were staring at me."

"Why would they be staring at you? Aren't you what humans would call a war hero?"

"It's true that the instructors at the academy have built me up for my performance during the war, but that isn't how this so-called civilized society views me. I was angry when my father was killed, and that anger made me foolish, which is how I became disfigured. From this society's viewpoint, they just want me to go away. They don't like being reminded of the horrors of war."

"That's terrible."

Socrates shrugged. "I refuse to hide, partly to remind them of it, and partly to make them feel guilty because they didn't do enough. Because of that, the Council could very well incarcerate me. Lock me away so they don't have to be reminded. It's part of the reason I was assigned duties that kept me away from Q'estiria for so many years."

"If someone else had defeated Nighthawk and brought him in—someone without your disfigurement—what should happen?"

"They would be promoted to the same rank as Nighthawk, at the least. However, that won't happen here because then I would be around them a lot more, being stationed here. What is it you humans say? No good deed goes unpunished?"

A young *T'et Faqin Q'estirion* came over to the couple. "They are returning. Please re-enter the Council Chambers."

"Quiet!" Cornelius said, after the Council members were in their conferencing anteroom.

"This is unconscionable," D'Tomia Nighthawk boomed. "When I agreed to the apparent facts that Malthuvius has betrayed the Council, I had no idea that these humans were anything but a minor nuisance. Now to find out that they may be capable of destroying themselves and taking the Seven Known Planes with them is unacceptable. What a bunch of savages."

"There has to be a way to mitigate that possibility," H'Difa Thunderclap said, nervously.

"For me, I want Socrates Blackwing to… to go away." Syn'Chin Hornsdoodle frowned. "That horrendous scar is offensive."

Several of the others nodded and grumbled their agreement.

"We are all better served if he never returns," said Hornsdoodle.

"You are being uncharacteristically quiet, Thaddius Crowfoot," said Cornelius. "Do you have an opinion on the situation?"

Crowfoot frowned. "Malthuvius Nighthawk has been a problem since he became associated with Phelonius Blackwing and the *Ha'Jakta Ha'Dreen B'kota* War. Now I think we are facing an insurgency. Socrates, on the other hand, has been exemplary. To many of the *T'et Faqin Q'estirions*, he is a hero."

Cornelius exhaled loudly. "I feel Socrates' violation of the edict concerning the Eighth Plane is the Council's fault. He had no way of verifying the false orders and no way to return from there, mainly because of his scar and the unreasonableness of the *Sh'o Sook J'eid*. A scar he received distinguishing himself in the war. That being said, I may have an idea."

"Order!" Cornelius banged the rock on the dais. "The Council is now reconvened." He picked up a paper from a small stack and read from it. "To the reason the Council was convened this morning, all our questions have been answered. Therefore, it is the Council's opinion that Commander Socrates Blackwing has been found faultless in his violation of this Council's edict concerning the Eighth Plane, as he had initially refused the false order that sent him there and was transported while unconscious."

The paper was passed from one Council member to another, each signing it.

"Further," Cornelius picked another page from the small stack, "we also recognize his field promotion to commander, and thus his bonding to his consort is valid and recognized."

The paper was passed around and Cornelius picked up another.

"In addition, Commander Blackwing has demonstrated his loyalty to this Council, his valor, on numerous occasions, and those qualities that exemplify the best of the *T'et Faqin Q'estirions*, which is lacking in most of the younger members. He is hereby promoted to Chief Commander."

The paper was passed around and Cornelius picked up another.

"It is the opinion of the Council that entry to the Eighth Plane remains banned for any residents of the Seven Known Planes, except those having business with the ambassador to the Eighth Plane. Chief Commander Blackwing will act as that ambassador on the Eighth Plane and will be under the direct authority of this Council. We also recognize humans as sentient beings."

Another paper was passed around and Cornelius picked up another.

"In the case of Malthuvius Nighthawk, he has been found guilty of violating the edict and willfully causing a fellow member of the *T'et Faqin Q'estirions* to violate it as well. His penalty will be determined later, and Chief Commander Blackwing will be apprised. By his admission, the defense of following orders given by Phelonius Blackwing, a warrant has been issued for his immediate apprehension and the suspension of his rank and privileges."

Two papers were passed around.

When all the papers were signed, a clerk collected them and presented the documents to Socrates.

"Before we adjourn, I would like to make an observation," Cornelius said. "Chief Commander Blackwing, you are out of uniform." He paused for a few seconds. "If I may be permitted?"

Socrates nodded and Cornelius passed his hand in Socrates' direction, though several feet away. A three-inch wide band of platinum replaced the three quarter-inch-wide gold bands that held Socrates' hair.

"*That* is more appropriate. Council adjourned."

Once in the hallway, outside the Council chambers, Suzanne and Socrates breathed a little easier.

"What the hell just happened?" Suzanne said, in English.

"What didn't you understand?"

"It sounded like you went from being a possible prisoner, to a couple promotions."

Socrates shrugged. "Some of those promotions were overdue. So it's not... how you say... a big deal?"

"But an ambassadorship on top of it?"

"That was your doing." Socrates chuckled. "What you said about humans being willing and able to destroy their own planet. I'm sure they figured they needed an ambassador to prevent that, and since I'm familiar with humans, I was the logical choice."

"And Phelonius?"

"He is what you'd call... a wanted man. He has no rank now and can be apprehended and transported back here."

"For whatever reason, I was under the impression that your rank had something to do with your wizarding powers. Since he has no rank, does that mean he is no longer a threat?"

"On the contrary, he is more of a threat now. He has nothing to constrain him and he still has his followers in the *T'et Faqin Q'estirions*."

A small group of *T'et Faqin Q'estirions* came over to Socrates.

"Chief Commander Blackwing," the young officer-in-charge said, in *Q'estirian*. "Council member Cornelius Blackwing sends his respects and asks that you and your Lady speak privately in his office."

23

THE AMBASSADOR ARRIVES

Socrates stood with his left arm level and Suzanne rested her right arm on his.

"Lead on."

A pair of *T'et Faqin Q'estirions* formed up on either side of the couple and the young leader escorted them through many twisting hallways. They finally stopped at a massive ornate oaken door. The leader knocked, using the huge golden knocker. He opened the door after a few seconds. Blackwing and Suzanne entered, and he closed the door behind them.

"Socrates! Come in, come in," Cornelius beckoned. "And, of course, the lovely Lady Suzanne." He leered at her. "Come and sit. Talk to me for a few minutes. I know you are anxious to return to the Eighth Plane, but I wanted to clarify a few things first. There is one question I simply must ask. What you said about the humans destroying their world, was that an exaggeration?"

Suzanne sat in one of the plush chairs while Socrates stood close to her.

"No, it was not an exaggeration," she said. "I spoke as truthfully as I could."

"Hmmm…" Cornelius paced around the plush room a few times. "I was afraid of that. I was hoping you were trying to scare that *P'koosh Z'airka* Nighthawk." He took a deep breath and exhaled slowly. "It worked out for the best, then. The reason I asked you here was to explain. You are to report to me regularly."

Socrates started to complain and Cornelius raised a hand and looked away.

"I know you have an issue with reporting, but it is critical. We have to know what is going on over there on the Eighth Plane. The last thing we need is a misunderstanding with the humans. You understand what it would mean if the Eighth Plane was destroyed."

Socrates nodded. "On my sphere was a section that showed an outline of a portal. Did you see it?"

Cornelius frowned. "Yes, I saw it. Disturbing, that. Where did the portal come from?"

"I have no idea. At the time I thought the figure inside the portal was Malthuvius Nighthawk, but upon scrutinizing the area where the portal formed, there were no trees. That led me to believe either Malthuvius or Phelonius, or both, had that ability without using the *Sh'o Sook J'eid*. If Malthuvius has that ability, then he requires being watched closely."

"He is under constant heavy guard. In addition, he is being held apart from the Source."

"Then there is Phelonius's followers. You are aware he has many?"

Cornelius chuckled. "You are thinking like a politician. There may be hope for you yet. Yes, I am well aware of Phelonius's followers. Before today, if something were to befall me, he would be promoted onto the Council. As of the signing of the warrant, that is no longer true. We are watching his followers, the ones we know, but we are aware that there may be more that are hidden. That returns us to your reports. You will be accompanied by two squads of five of our brothers. Train them in all the things you feel are necessary. You may have sympathizers for either Malthuvius or Phelonius. If you find any, you are to send them back here and report it. If any refuse to learn or follow orders, report it and return them. Your appointment is an important posting, and any stationed there should be proud."

"What about Phelonius?" said Blackwing.

"What about him? The Council has put up with his usurpations for many decades. You are *T'et Faqin Q'estirion*. You know your duty."

Jessica was walking in the grove when the portal opened behind her. Immediately, ten *Q'estirians* surrounded her, staffs brandished, and babbling something. She could tell they were shouting orders, but since she didn't understand the language she just stood still.

"Hold!" Blackwing said, in *Q'estirian*, as he exited the portal. "She is *K'obi Sha Shin J'oi Faqin*."

Suzanne, upon her exit from the portal, ran to Jessica. "Stand away!" She put herself between Jessica and the wizards.

The wizards all looked skeptically at Blackwing. Then they finally stood away from Jessica and relaxed their posture.

"Sorry," Suzanne said to Jessica. "They're new here. They were just doing their job."

"I can appreciate that. They scared me, though. Who are they?"

"Think of them as security."

Jessica frowned. "Security? For who and from who?"

"The *new* Ambassador—"

"Hello, Jess." Blackwing walked to her. "Sorry about all this. I didn't mean to startle you."

"Will one of you make sense?" Jessica said. "What the hell is going on?"

"Meet the new Ambassador," Suzanne said.

"Ambassador? Ambassador to who?"

Blackwing took a deep breath. "I'm now the *Q'estirian* High Council Ambassador to the humans on this Plane."

Jessica laughed. "What happened? Nobody else wanted the job?" Then she became serious. "You're a little late. That title has been filled."

"Is Irving around?" Blackwing said. "What are you doing here at this time of day?"

"I was temporarily suspended. Irv is at work. I came out here to think and plan. Phelonius showed himself a few days ago and is declaring himself ambassador."

"I want to hear more about this. But first I need to get my brothers settled." Blackwing walked in the direction of the barn, all ten of the new wizards following him.

"That is quite the outfit," Jessica said to Suzanne. "It should get you arrested."

Suzanne chuckled. "It's a present from Lady S'hyrlus. It's what's acceptable in *Q'estirian* society. What I was wearing when we left was drawing too much attention."

Jessica turned Suzanne around. "And this outfit doesn't draw attention? What are they, dead?"

"Far from it. I got to meet Cornelius Blackwing."

"Who's he?"

"Grandfather of Phelonius and head of the High Council."

"What was he like?"

"He was an older version of Socrates and a typical politician. More… substantial than Socrates, mostly gray hair, affable, and flirtatious."

"I have a hard time visualizing someone like Socrates being both affable and flirtatious."

Blackwing led the younger wizards toward the barn. Two of them had broken off and stood by the doors to the house.

"There is plenty of room in the barn for you and your brothers," Blackwing said to the young leader. "This is a strange place and you will need to learn the language. They call it English." He produced his sphere and the leader did the same. "I am sending you the language. Use it when you enter *T'gorn E'fal*. There is one other human that is also *K'obi Sha Shin J'oi Faqin*. He is not to be hindered in any way. His name is Irving Strange. I will also send you an image of him so you and your brothers will recognize him. Since this place is far outside your normal experience, if you do not understand, ask me or Lady Suzanne. She is also here to help. I placed wards around the perimeter of the property, but send a couple brothers to check and re-enforce them, if required. I do not expect them to stop Phelonius, but they should alert us. Questions?"

"None at this time, Ambassador."

"Might I know your name?"

"B'runix Hornsdoodle, Ambassador."

"Carry on." Blackwing strolled to the house.

As Blackwing approached the back door of the house, the youngster posted there snapped to attention, and Blackwing entered. Jessica and Suzanne were already inside, sitting at the table, talking. As he passed them, he set a tankard in front of each.

"Tell me why you're suspended." He got out a tankard for himself and sat in his usual place.

Jessica took a sip from her tankard. "I had to do an Honor Guard outside the mayor's office. Phelonius walked in with the mayor, and for whatever reason, I slammed him against a wall with my riot shield and tonfa. They had to drug me, cuff me, and lock me in an interrogation room for several hours."

"Was he in any kind of a disguise?" Blackwing said.

"Nope. He just walked in like he owned the place."

"So how did you explain it?"

"I gave my captain a few clues as to why I perceived a threat. He bought it, for now, and released me. I took him to my apartment using the jump coin."

Blackwing sat silently for a few seconds. "I trust that you only did what you had to do, but attacking Phelonius was foolish and dangerous. So Phelonius has set himself as Ambassador?"

"That's the rumor, from Irving and others. Phelonius gave out several gold coins while he was at it. My captain has one, and I suggested strongly that he avoid touching it or handling it. He found my jump coin and my necklace while I was unconscious, and compared them to the one he'd gotten from Phelonius. It didn't take a genius to see that they were all the same."

"Smart," Blackwing said. "If Phelonius gives anything to anyone, it's prudent to question his motives. It could be something as simple as appealing to their greed—"

"Or it could be something more nefarious. That was my thinking, and that's why I warned him about the coin. I did mention that I'd have you inspect it, just in case."

"You mentioned me?"

"Of course not. I referred to you as *my source*. I did call Irving and told him to bring some Sichuan, enough for fourteen. Being the bright boy he is, he'll figure we have guests."

"They're not guests. They are tasked with keeping me and Suzanne safe. I'm unfamiliar with being in this position, so it's something I have to grow into."

After dinner, which was entertaining for Suzanne, Irving, and Jessica to watch the newcomer *Q'estirians* try to figure out chopsticks, Irving was tasked with creating an algorithm for translating the *Q'estirian* documents into something humans could read. He and Jessica marveled at the drawn runes that covered the pages of parchment.

When Suzanne looked at the formal Diplomatic Introduction, it took her a few seconds before she could read and understand the runes.

"When did you learn to read these runes?" Irving said.

"I don't know. This is the first time I've seen writing like this. It must be imparted knowledge from my transformation, which would explain how I can speak *Q'estirian* and *Hamadryad*."

"Any other imparted knowledge?" Jessica said.

"I have no idea. I had to hear *Q'estirian* spoken to be able to speak it. It's like something just clicked inside my brain. I didn't know I could read it either, until I saw these pages."

"So how did you manage to wangle an ambassadorship?" Jessica asked Blackwing.

"That was Suzanne's doing. She scared the Council into it."

"I did no such thing."

"How did she manage that?" Jessica asked Blackwing.

"She mentioned that the humans could, and would, destroy this planet if they were attacked."

"Well, that's a given." Jessica shrugged. "It is fairly common knowledge. We've been close to doing it to ourselves several times. Why would that scare them so much?"

"In the Seven Planes, there are two predominant theories pertaining to the different Planes. One theory is that the Planes are isolated with tenuous and fragile connections. Should one Plane be destroyed, all of its connections would be broken, which could possibly isolate other Planes. The other theory is that all the Planes are so interconnected that if one were to be destroyed, a cascading effect would eventually destroy all the Planes. As I stated, they're just theories, but the testing of them is a fearful thing. There are other theories as well, but the two I described are the predominant ones. Nobody wants to… push their luck, as you say. So in an effort to avoid something like that from happening, I was appointed ambassador to the humans."

Irving handed the original ambassadorial document to Blackwing. "What's your plan for dropping that little tidbit of information on the powers-that-be? Most humans won't believe you even exist. Others, the ones that know better, will resist you."

"Why would they resist me?"

"Not just you," Irving said. "Your kind. Some would see your presence here as an invasion, which the politicos will run with at every turn. As it pertains to Mayor Worth and Phelonius, I'm sure Phelonius offered something of value to our illustrious mayor, who would sell his grandmother for the price of a cup of coffee. They're not going to like you showing up and usurping their little deal, whatever it is. They won't believe the documents you present are real and binding."

"Phelonius would know as soon as he saw the originals. So what's the solution?"

"Let me think on it. Maybe with what we know of our system, Jess and I can come up with one."

While Irving and Blackwing talked, Jessica bent close to Suzanne.

"Not much diversity," she whispered, glancing at the new arrivals. "They all look like Blackwing."

"I know," Suzanne whispered back. "Q'estiria was worse. The only ways you can tell them apart are rank and the amount of grey hair. Even the tonal qualities of their voices are similar."

"Can you come out to the alley, Cap'n?" Jessica said into her phone. "Walk toward Tony's. Bring the coin with you. I'll meet you."

"Well?" Blackwing said, as she hung up.

"He'll be out soon. I'll step down and then step him up here." She looked around to the two *Q'estirions* that flanked Socrates. "Have they learned the language yet?"

Socrates chuckled. "Not completely. They need to practice, though. You do know if it's a trap, you could be captured."

"I know it's a possibility, but I trust my gut with the cap'n."

"It's your call, Jess."

One of the other *Q'estirions* whistled. Jessica barely heard the predefined signal. She rushed to the edge of the roof and looked over the edge. She saw a figure that she assumed was Captain Trooper, exit the precinct and walk toward her favorite eatery. It was then that a strange feeling of *déjà vu* came over her and left quickly. Once she was comfortable with the situation, she disappeared from the edge and reappeared in the alley. When she gripped the walking person's arm, she disappeared from the alley and reappeared on the roof.

The rooftop was darker than the alley, but not so dark Trooper couldn't see outlines. All three *Q'estirians* surrounded her and her passenger, staffs at the ready. Captain Trooper started to activate his service weapon.

"Don't, Cap'n. It would only complicate things further." Jessica stopped the motion of his gun arm.

"Okay, Jess, I trust you. But who are these," he looked around at the other three on the roof, "individuals."

Blackwing stepped forward, towering over the smaller man. "Captain Trooper, I am Socrates Blackwing, *Q'estirian* Ambassador from our High Council." He bowed, then reached into his inner breast pocket to pull a folded printed page, and handed it to the captain.

"Blackwing? Any relation to Phelonius?"

Trooper took the paper, then set a locked box on the roof as he produced his phone and activated the light. He snapped the page open and read it.

"Very fancy. High-quality paper, too. Am I to believe your kind speak and write in English?"

"We don't, but I do. My… security aren't quite, how you say… up to speed. I do have a copy of the original, but you wouldn't be able to read it. Is that the coin?" Blackwing indicated the locked box.

Trooper bent to pick it up.

"No need."

Trooper saw the barely outlined shadow make some hand motions, and the box popped open and the coin inside floated out and was raised to Blackwing's eye level. It spun slowly and flipped a few times before it floated back into the box, and the box closed.

"How many of these coins were handed out?" Blackwing said.

"I'm not sure. Things were kind of…" Trooper looked at Jessica, "crazy. I got one, and I think the officers who restrained Jess each received one."

"Did he say anything when he gave them to you?"

Trooper shook his head. "Nothing."

"My assessment is that the coins are dangerous," Blackwing said. "I'd recommend that you seal them in lead and bury them in rock. I detect nothing, but that doesn't mean there isn't something waiting to be activated at a later time."

"I'll take that under advisement." Trooper picked up the box.

"One more piece of business." Blackwing handed him two more pages.

"What's this?"

"It's a warrant for Phelonius'... arrest. One is in English so you can read it. The other is a copy of the original document."

Trooper put the documents in his pocket. "I'll look at them later. Is there anything else?"

"I have nothing else. Do you?"

"I'm assuming that should I need to, I contact you through Jessica?"

"Yes. Be warned. Things have just gotten more dangerous for you and all humans. Phelonius is not one you should underestimate. By now, he surely knows that the warrant exists. He has others that keep him informed."

"I do have a suggestion. If you're amenable, I'd like to assign Jessica to you as a special diplomatic liaison." Trooper picked up the box.

Blackwing nodded. "I would agree with that."

"Good." Trooper stuck out his hand.

The other two *Q'estirians* said something that neither Trooper nor Jessica understood.

"What is it?" Jessica looked around for possible threats.

"My security is a bit nervous." Blackwing gave a slight smile. "Nothing you need to worry about. Jessica will return you." He shook the offered hand. "Until we see each other again, be well."

Trooper grinned. "You, too."

Trooper took Jessica's arm and the two of them left.

Blackwing and the two *Q'estirians* left as soon as Jessica and Trooper did.

There remained no sign that anyone had ever been there.

24

DRAINING THE SWAMP

The full Council had been meeting for some time on the disposition of Malthuvius Nighthawk.

"What are we going to do with Malthuvius?" said Cornelius Blackwing. "Is there any doubt of his guilt?"

No one said anything.

"So it comes to degree."

"I think the blame should fall on Phelonius Blackwing," said D'Tomia Nighthawk. "He tainted a talented young *T'et Faqin Q'estirion* with promises of power."

"Of course he did," H'Difa Thunderclap said. "However, Malthuvius was not under any kind of coercion when he tried to take the life of Socrates Blackwing. He did that of his own volition."

"True." D'Tomia Nighthawk bowed his head.

"Since the conception of the High Council," said Syn'Chin Hornsdoodle, "it has always been difficult to pass judgment on those of our own bloodlines. The Council realized, ages ago, that since we are made up of the five major bloodlines, we would be called upon to pass judgment on one of our own. But if we will not, then who will?"

"Have you all gotten a good look at Malthuvius?" said Thaddius Crowfoot. "I, for one, would like to know how he has managed to look younger than our youngest graduates. I have asked him, but he refuses to divulge it."

Cornelius strolled around the room. "Our kind, of all the creatures of the Seven Known Planes, are the only ones that do not maintain familial relationships." He stopped behind D'Tomia and patted his shoulder. "And I sympathize for my brother Council members. However, as Syn'Chin said, if not us, then who?" He continued his stroll. "Malthuvius, as well as others, think we are a group of out-of-touch oldsters, too weak to do anything else or to be taken seriously. What this comes to, for me, is either we mean what we say or we do not. If I do not mean what I say, I will step aside. That day is not today. Malthuvius and Socrates grew to maturity together. They knew each other intimately. That did not stay Malthuvius' hand when he tried to strike down Socrates, but I will adhere to our custom of not ending a life unless absolutely necessary. I do not find that the facts warrant going to that extreme, but I am but one vote."

"Do you know Jessica Strange?" Captain Trooper asked John Smith.

He didn't think that was his real name, but it was the only name he had.

"No, I don't believe I've had the pleasure." Smith smiled flirtatiously at Jessica. "Aren't you a detective sergeant?"

"No, she is currently on special assignment," Trooper said.

Jessica stared at Smith. *I don't like this guy. Tall? I suppose he is. Handsome? Some would say so. Arrogant? Oh, you betcha. There is an air of superiority about him that screams Fed.*

"Doesn't this VIP own a watch?" Smith had been checking his every few seconds. "Who is this... *individual*?"

"Sorry, if I'm late," said a deep penetrating voice, from behind Smith. "I thought the appointment was for 10:00 a.m. Oh, look at that. It's exactly 10:00 a.m."

Smith nearly jumped out of his chair. "Where did you come from?"

"Mr. Smith, this is our VIP, Ambassador Socrates Blackwing." Trooper looked as if he was enjoying Smith's discomfiture and tried to stifle his own grin.

"Ambassador? From where?" Smith sneered.

"Captain?" Jessica said.

"Yes, I know," Trooper said. "No cams, no mics, no motorcars. And more importantly, no interruptions."

Blackwing stepped forward and handed Smith two sets of two pages.

"The first document, as you can see, is my ambassadorial introduction. The top page is the English version."

"And the second set?" Smith said, without reading it.

"An arrest warrant."

"What are these Seven Known Planes? I've never heard of it, whatever, or wherever, it is."

Blackwing took a deep breath and exhaled loudly. "It is too complex to go into detail. Suffice it to say that the Seven Known Planes are more than seven times the size of your planet."

"The whole planet? Wow, that's pretty big," Smith said, with a condescending tone. "And you're the ambassador?"

Blackwing took out a coin and released it. It floated, turning slightly.

"I didn't come here to be insulted by this condescending cretin," he said to Trooper.

Smith was having trouble taking his eyes off the slowly spinning coin that defied gravity. But when he heard *cretin*, he decided to speak up.

"Hey! That was—"

The coin had slammed into his chest, knocking him back into the chair, and pressed him. He puffed hard, trying to breathe.

"Socrates, please?" Trooper said. "I'm sure his doubt can be removed, somehow." He looked at Smith. "Can't it?"

Smith nodded but said nothing.

"In my role as Ambassador, I've come to try to ensure that humans don't destroy your world. That is something, I believe, your leaders could appreciate. I would like you to take my introduction letter to your leaders. My government is not looking to invade or dominate your kind. Our only concern is in your capability to destroy this planet. Your other affairs do not interest us at all. The arrest warrant is for one of my kind. His crimes are listed. We would like some assistance in tracking him nationally, if it comes to that. We don't need your help in the apprehension. Your kind wouldn't last long against him anyway."

Blackwing crooked a finger and the coin returned to floating.

"The individual we seek has handed out several coins like this, so get a good look. These coins are potentially dangerous. We've found some in Tacoma, but have no idea where he's been or if we have them all. You have access to files regarding gold sales. That's information we would like to have, as it pertains to the coins."

Smith reached with his left hand to touch the coin.

"Don't touch," Blackwing said.

Smith touched the coin anyway. It gave him a small shock, then flattened and attached to his left wrist.

"Hey! What is this?"

Blackwing grinned. "I told you not to touch. From what I've observed, you like intimidating others. I am *not* intimidated by you or anyone else."

Smith leveled his Desert Eagle at Blackwing.

He smirked. "Pull the trigger if it will make you feel better."

Smith pulled the trigger and… nothing happened. He pulled the trigger several more times and then looked at the hand cannon, surprised he hadn't gotten the expected loud report.

"My turn?" Socrates said.

"Now, Ambassador, let's not be too hasty," Trooper said. "I'm sure we can come to some sort of understanding."

Suddenly, Smith was suspended in the air, by his left arm.

"Relax, Captain, I won't hurt him too bad… yet." Blackwing turned his attention to Smith. "As you can see, you are powerless against me." He held out his hand. "Now surrender your weapon."

Smith thought about it, and pulled the trigger several more times. Finally, he surrendered and gave up his weapon.

"Jessica, take charge of this?" Blackwing handed the weapon to her, behind him.

As Jessica took the weapon, Smith was gently lowered into his chair. After he was re-seated, Blackwing went over and touched the gold band. It released Smith and returned to its original shape, in Blackwing's palm.

"Are you understanding all this?" he said.

Smith nodded and exhaled.

"I guess you were right, Captain Trooper," said Blackwing. "Now, then." He shifted to Smith. "To explain. These coins can be useful tools, or they can be devastating weapons. The ones we seek have the potential for causing no end of trouble and pain. I am trying to prevent that."

"So what do you want from me?" Smith said.

"I want you to function as a delivery boy, in regards to my papers. Other than that, I would like your help, as I stated before, and if you don't want to give it..." Blackwing paused, "stay out of the way. Captain Trooper will send a copy of those documents to your supervisors, letting them know you have them and that we have explained everything to you, just in case you decide to try to keep all this information to yourself."

Smith looked at the captain with a concerned look, and Trooper smiled back.

Blackwing, Irving, and Jessica had spent the last three days waiting for an audience with Mayor Worth. They spent those days getting the ten other *Q'estirians* comfortable with the new tactics and with the English language. Now, they were waiting outside the mayor's office.

"Captain Trooper, how nice to see you again." Mayor Worth opened his office door.

As he looked around the room, a brief recognition passed over his face when his vision locked on Blackwing. He averted his gaze and looked at Jessica.

"What's *she* doing here?" he squawked to Trooper.

"Mayor, this is Ambassador Socrates Blackwing and our liaison to his office, Jessica Strange."

At the mention of his name, Blackwing saw recognition flash over the mayor's face again. Blackwing glanced around with his left eye to see the outlines of five of his guards, and smirked.

"Is she safe?" Worth whispered to Trooper.

Trooper chuckled. "Of course not. She's the most effective officer I have. There's nothing safe about her. She has, however, assured me that she won't do something... untoward, unless ordered to."

"You keep a short leash on her," the mayor whispered to Trooper. "And who is this?" he said to the room, an ambassador, you say?"

As Worth sat behind his desk, Blackwing handed him papers and then sat across from the mayor.

"What's this?" Worth glanced at them.

"Papers of introduction, and a warrant," Trooper replied.

Worth looked through the papers. "What's wrong? Can't he speak for himself?"

Blackwing tossed a coin onto the mayor's desk.

"What's this?" Worth picked it up and studied it.

"Have you ever seen anything like that?" Blackwing said, his voice deep and foreboding.

The mayor turned it over in his hand several times. "Can't say I have."

The object went from coin to golden handcuffs.

"Hey!" the mayor squawked.

"Shouldn't have lied to me." In *Q'estirian*, Blackwing said, "The coins are over there, behind a hidden panel."

Worth watched as several things seemed to move by themselves and a panel opened.

Jessica went to the opened panel and found a metal briefcase. "Heavy." She set the case on the mayor's desk. "Open it."

"And if I refuse?" he snarled.

"Never mind, Jessica." Blackwing spoke to the case in a foreign language and the latches sprung open.

Jessica opened the case and everyone there could see the intoxicating shine of polished gold coins.

Captain Trooper pulled Worth to his feet. "Lester Worth, you are under arrest for aligning yourself with a multi-planal criminal and jeopardizing the city and its residents, for accepting bribes from said criminal, and because you're a scumbag and I don't like you."

"Aren't you going to Mirandize me?"

Trooper laughed. "We haven't Mirandized anyone for fifty years. Too bad you're too incompetent to know that."

"One of you stay behind and hidden," Blackwing said, in *Q'estirian*. "The rest of you alternate to provide relief. Do not try to apprehend Phelonius alone. But if you can follow him safely, then by all means, do so."

"Captain, place your cuffs on Worth, and I'll remove mine."

Trooper placed his cuffs on the mayor. Once they were on and secure, Blackwing removed the golden cuffs.

"Take my arm," he said to Trooper, "and keep a good grip on your prisoner." He looked at Jessica carrying the case, and nodded. She took his other arm and all four disappeared.

"Where is he," Trooper screamed at Worth, who was cuffed to the metal table, for the tenth time.

"I have no idea who you're asking about. I want a lawyer," Worth said, also for the tenth time.

"Care to explain where you got the coins?" Trooper said, his voice betraying his frustration.

"No, I don't feel the need to unburden myself to you. And again, I want a lawyer."

"Terrorists don't get lawyers. They get a one-way trip to Camp McMurdo."

"Where?"

"Antarctica. There, you get to freeze your ass off and that's about it. No calls, no visitors, and no escape. You think about that for a while."

Trooper left the interrogation room and entered the observation room, where Blackwing and Jessica had been watching and listening.

"I can't deal with that... that twit one more time!" Trooper said. "I want to wring his neck."

"You want me to take another run at him, Cap'n?" Jessica said.

"Why? You've tried a dozen times yourself and we're no closer than we were six hours ago."

"You've been using, how do you say... legal means, to get information," Blackwing said. "How about trying something... less conventional?"

Trooper looked at Socrates. "What did you have in mind?"

When the door to the interrogation room opened, Lester Worth saw Blackwing, Jessica, and Trooper enter. Blackwing sat directly opposite Worth, and Jessica and Trooper sat on either side of him. He produced a crystalline sphere and Worth's gaze was drawn to it.

"Touch it," Blackwing said.

Worth gingerly touched the glowing globe with a finger, as did Jessica and Trooper.

"Don't think about your gold coins," Blackwing said, his voice low and penetrating.

Worth's mind went to the gold coins he'd been given, all six cases. His memories went to the locations of all the cases.

When Worth understood what was happening, he tried to remove his finger from the surface of the glowing globe, but couldn't. There was something compelling about it and he didn't want to remove his finger from its warm surface.

"Contacting Phelonius," Blackwing said.

Worth's memories ran to a view of him texting in his office.

"Where is Phelonius?"

Worth suddenly became aware and removed his finger from the sphere's surface. Jessica and Trooper did the same.

"So you think you three will get anything out of me by ganging up on me? I'm stronger than that!" Worth smirked. "I still want a lawyer!"

Trooper, Jessica, and Blackwing got up and left the room.

Irving, Jessica, Trooper, and Blackwing were sitting in Trooper's office.

"Did he know what was going on?" Jessica asked Blackwing.

"No. From the time I said not to think about gold coins, a part of his mind closed off. The part that would stop him from telling us something he had knowledge of, and his memories told us what we wanted to know. When asked about Phelonius's location, he knew nothing and his mind re-established control."

"What have you found out, Irving?" said Trooper.

"First of all, you all understand Troy ounces—"

"I don't," Jessica said.

"Well, to keep it simple, Troy ounces are used for precious metals. What we usually use is the avoirdupois ounce, of which it takes sixteen to make an avoirdupois pound. One avoirdupois pound equals 14.566 Troy ounces. Each of the coins that Blackwing and his kind use is precisely 1.1 Troy ounces per coin. That comes to a shade over thirteen coins to the pound. The case we found wasn't quite full. There was room for 133 coins, or ten pounds."

"So either he's distributing," Trooper said, "or he's used some, or he's collecting and the case wasn't quite filled. What's the potential danger, Blackwing?"

"Unknowable. If the mayor has sixty pounds, or close to it, the potential is great. My question is, who else has that many?"

"Why is it unknowable?" Trooper frowned.

"Each coin can be… imbued with special properties. No one knows what properties they've been imbued with. With my most potent, for the lack of a better term, *spell*, I could use fifty and eliminate every human inside the city limits."

"Fifty cases?"

"Fifty coins."

Over the next seven days, Blackwing and his small band of *T'et Faqin Q'estirions* searched the offices and residences of the entire City Council. All of them were jailed. Captain Trooper managed to hold them all incommunicado.

When the offices of Police Commissioner Michael Behrnson were searched, they found twelve filled cases of the gold coins, and City Attorney Diego Hernandez had fourteen. In all, forty cases of coins were confiscated.

The entirety of Tacoma was searched for any sign of Phelonius, without result.

Blackwing, Jessica, and Trooper gathered in Trooper's office.

"Any sign of Phelonius?" said the captain.

His eyes were baggy and bloodshot after he'd spent many a night in his office.

"None." Jessica rubbed her aching head and neck. "We've all been searching everywhere we can think of, using every tactic available, and still nothing. I wouldn't have thought it possible that someone could completely disappear."

"Where are you storing the coins?" Blackwing asked Trooper, who looked more ashen than usual.

"We have them in a vault in the sixth sub-basement," he said, the exhaustion apparent in his voice.

"Will they be safe?" Blackwing said.

"How the hell would I know? They're behind a twelve-inch thick armored door with several types of locks, and sealed with one-inch lead sheets. There are checkpoints along the way, with armed guards who have no idea how to get to the vault. The cases are as safe as we can make them. Will it be enough?" Trooper shrugged. "Who knows. I'm hoping it will be."

25

THE OTHER SHOE

Phelonius Blackwing was in Los Angeles, continuing his corruption of political leaders—not that they needed any persuasion in that arena—when the notification came from his contacts on Q'estiria.

Malthuvius Nighthawk incarcerated for fifty years, his sphere showed.

These humans do not understand integrity. Phelonius shook his head. *They will knowingly elect thieves and liars to rule over them.* He smirked. *San Diego yesterday, Los Angeles today, and San Francisco tomorrow. Then the Land of Port, See-At-All, and Tacooma. Strange names for even stranger places.* He flashed a wry grin. *Malthuvius was always a good soldier. He knew how to follow orders, even the ones that would disadvantage him. But my plan proceeds.*

The time is almost here. Phelonius had just concluded his business in Seattle. His associates had informed him that the Tacoma City Council had mysteriously disappeared. *The stage is set. All the cases are in place.*

The animals will all go away, but you cannot build without first clearing the land.

"Are you and your charges taking advantage of this brief respite?" Blackwing entered a small room in the barn that had been established for them, away from the others.

"Yes, Ambassador, they are all becoming quite fluent in English," said B'runix Hornsdoodle.

"Are any of them sympathizers of Phelonius or his cause?"

"His *cause*? What is his cause?"

"Who knows? The only cause I can discern is the fracturing of the High Council."

The two leaders frowned and pursed their lips.

"There are a couple of them that I wouldn't trust to arrest Phelonius," said B'runix, "should that opportunity arise."

"I believe we've found all the cases we're going to find. No matter what happens, I want those that have shown any sympathies for Phelonius to be kept away from Irving, Jessica, and the Lady Suzanne."

"Lady Suzanne is surely in no danger. If she becomes injured in any way, the Lady S'hyrlus will cut off all ties for the Seven Known Planes. No one would be so—"

"Reckless? Foolhardy?" Blackwing said. "That might be true, but I won't risk it. I feel there are events in motion, and I'm unable to discern the greater plan."

"The Big Picture, as the humans say?" asked B'runix.

"Yes, the Big Picture. From now on, Jessica and Suzanne are to stay at the residence. Irving is needed elsewhere from time to time, so he has to be free to travel. I have discussed the dangers with him and he understands."

"We'll see to it, Ambassador."

"Good. I want everyone to be well-rested. You are free to make your own assignments."

Blackwing left the barn.

"I need to get back to work," Irving said, after eating with Blackwing, Suzanne, Jessica, and the two leaders of Blackwing's guard.

"Pack up some of the leftovers for Cap'n Trooper and take them with you," Jessica said. "He's been spending all his time at the precinct, and I doubt he's eaten well, if at all."

"I will," Irving said. "But I doubt he'll eat. He can be quite stubborn."

"So can I. You tell him that if he doesn't eat, I'll come down and nag him until he does."

"Why are you so—"

"Overprotective?"

"I was going to say fussy over him, but yeah."

"He's like the father I wish I had. He watches over the rest of us and does what he can to help, but he refrains from being too sheltering. He allows us to be who we are, and he tries to understand."

Irving chuckled as he packed some of the leftovers. Once he finished, he kissed Jessica goodbye and vanished.

Shortly after Irving left, Blackwing received a personal message to his sphere.

It is time we had a discussion. I am waiting.

Blackwing stood. "Gather your men. "Disperse them as we discussed, and add one for Captain Trooper. I need five to come with me."

"What is it?" Suzanne said.

"I don't know for certain but this could be our chance to end this. I received a message from Phelonius."

Jessica and Suzanne paled.

"You two stay here. There are guards to see to it that you do."

"I need to go to the precinct," Jessica said.

"No, you don't. I have a guard on Irving and one on Trooper, so there is nothing you can do there. I need you here to… keep Suzanne company."

"I thought you were going to ask me to help protect her."

"That, too."

As Blackwing and the five guards materialized atop one of the shorter building roofs, he scanned the sky with his left eye. He could see a few delicate strands of the Source focus into a funnel shape directly above one of the taller rooftops.

"He's over there." Blackwing pointed toward the building. "I want you five to follow me. Make yourselves invisible. I don't know if he'll be able to sense you, but I want it to be a surprise, if possible. Stay alert and aware."

"Is this wise, Ambassador?" asked B'runix Hornsdoodle. "This seems like a trap, and you are putting yourself at risk unnecessarily."

"I'm expecting it to be a trap, but I am, and have always been, *T'et Faqin Q'estirion*. It's what we do."

All of the guards nodded.

"Greetings, Socrates," said Phelonius, without turning around.

He was standing close to the edge of the roof, looking out over the city, his unfastened duster flapping in the light breeze.

"Phelonius. I have a warrant—"

"For my arrest and return to Q'estiria. Yes, I know." Phelonius exhaled loudly. "You do not get to be my age without preparing for such things. I hear you are Ambassador now, and Chief Commander. Well done!" He paused. "Nothing to say? I witnessed the battle between you and Malthuvius, you know. You have become quite a formidable warrior."

"Is that what this is about? Is it to be battle between us?"

Phelonius turned slowly to face Socrates. He was mostly in shadow. What light there was came from the upper floors of this building's taller neighbors.

Phelonius shrugged. "We are who we are. There are those on the Council that would like you to terminate me, or me you. Did you know that?"

"Those are not my orders."

"You used to mock my... what did you call them... tantrums, from when I was younger. But did you know that you have your own legend? In the *Seven Known Planes*, you are referred to as the wild wizard—uncompromising, and the one who singlehandedly defeated eight *Ha'Jakta Ha'Dreen B'kota*, in the war. Are you still that wild wizard, or have you been tamed and purchased by rank and status? Are you a puppet of the Council?"

"I am no one's puppet."

"That is something still to be determined." Phelonius took a deep breath. "Well, *T'et Faqin Q'estirion*—if you still are one—do your duty. I hope you do not mind if I defend myself."

Phelonius moved his hand, a quick and deceptive movement, and a ball of energy flew from it toward Socrates. But Socrates had disappeared and reappeared behind Phelonius. Socrates hit him with two of his own energy balls. For the next minute, a flurry of energy balls were released in every direction. Socrates wasn't hit, but all his shots hit their mark. Two of the five guards were hit by stray energy balls and terminated. More than once, Socrates had re-emerged close enough to touch Phelonius.

"Stand still," Phelonius yelled. "I only need to hit you once and this will end!"

During another melee of energy balls, one of the guards had stepped close enough that he managed to slap a coin on Phelonius's wrist. This caused more confusion for Phelonius and allowed Socrates' energy balls to hit his adversary several times. While Phelonius was reeling from the flurry, another guard got close enough to slap a coin on his other wrist, binding his hands in front of his body, and he fell backward.

As he was being stood up, Phelonius screamed and fought against his bonds. Then he quit struggling and started laughing maniacally.

Socrates looked at him. "What is so funny?"

"Well, Ambassador," Phelonius spat, "that was nicely played, nicely played. I have not seen that tactic before, and I thought I had seen it all. But now we come to your decision. If you terminate me, or if I cross the barrier between Planes, death and destruction will rain down."

"What would you have me do?"

"Release me. You can afford to be magnanimous. You go your way and I go mine. Our paths need never cross again."

"That would be a violation of my orders."

"You dare not violate your orders. Do not question your masters. Be the dutiful puppet of the High Council!" His maniacal laughter took over again.

B'runix Hornsdoodle reported to Blackwing as he was ordered, at the dining room table.

"I want all content that the guards have on their spheres, as it pertains to this operation, forwarded to me," Blackwing said, without looking up. "I need them for my report to the High Council. Make sure to add the names of our fallen brothers. How is the prisoner?"

B'runix looked at Jessica and Suzanne. "He is… uncomfortable being bound and gagged. The two coins are intact and functioning. We can transport him anytime."

"Why two coins?" Jessica asked Blackwing.

"The first coin is primarily the handcuffs. The second adds thickness to the first and is acting to transfer Phelonius' accrued powers to the cuffs. They are keeping him powerless." To B'runix, he said, "I want to transport him within the hour. You are dismissed."

"I looked in on Phelonius before he was gagged," Jessica said, after B'runix had left. "He was saying something I didn't understand, gibberish. But that laugh… he's definitely looney tunes."

"Send a message to Trooper and Irving," Blackwing said. "Tell them we've got him and he'll be gone soon. Also, tell Irving thank you for the tactics. We couldn't have done it without his help."

"So is it really over, then?" Suzanne said.

"For now. But I can't be sure." Blackwing frowned.

"Then what's wrong?"

"I don't know. It all seemed… too easy. I feel like I'm missing something. The idiom *waiting for the other shoe to drop* seems appropriate."

Blackwing, Suzanne, B'runix, with the other two surviving members of the team, and two others controlling Phelonius, gathered at the large Oak tree. Jessica had come to see them off.

Suzanne opened a portal and watched as everyone going to Q'estiria walked through, and then she followed, leaving Jessica behind.

"Remove his gag," Blackwing said, once on the *Q'estirian* side of the portal. "Give him something to drink."

Phelonius accepted the tankard of water.

He took a sip. "Boom!" Took another sip. "Boom!" He took yet another sip. "Boom!" He repeated this mantra until the tankard was empty.

Jessica returned to the dining room table to wait for Irving to come home, or for Blackwing and company to return. She knew both events should happen soon, as Blackwing was only crossing to hand over Phelonius to other guards in *Q'estiria*. There would be a prisoner transfer and replenishment of those lost.

She picked up her tablet and was scrolling through some local news items, when a red banner popped up on the screen.

Urgent! Pacific Coast Attacked. The expected death toll could be in the tens of millions.

Her heart pounded as she clicked the story to get more information.

We have just received thousands of reports of an attack on the Pacific Coast. Witnesses reported people inside the affected zones aging and dropping dead in seconds. As far as we know, there were no explosions and the affected area runs from Bellingham, Washington, to as far south as San Diego, Pacific Coast-California. At this time, the CDC is sending teams to assess the affected areas.

When Blackwing and Suzanne entered the house, they saw Jessica sitting at the table, staring at her tablet. She didn't even acknowledge them.

"Jess, are you okay?" Suzanne moved around to look over her shoulder.

"They're all gone," Jessica said, tears streaming. "Everyone I've ever known or cared for is gone. Irving, Trooper, all gone."

"What's wrong?" Blackwing said. "We were gone for only twenty minutes. What's happened?"

Suzanne motioned for him to come beside Jessica and look at her tablet. He scowled as he read the story. Then he received a message on his sphere.

Malthuvius Nighthawk and Phelonius Blackwing have escaped custody.

He played us. Anger swelled within him. *He played all of us and we fell right into it.*

Blackwing slammed his fist onto the table and everything on it jumped.

Dear reader,

We hope you enjoyed reading *Blackwing*. Please take a moment to leave a review, even if it's a short one. Your opinion is important to us.

Discover more books by Stephen Drake at https://www.nextchapter.pub/authors/stephen-drake

Want to know when one of our books is free or discounted for Kindle? Join the newsletter at http://eepurl.com/bqqB3H

Best regards,

Stephen Drake and the Next Chapter Team

You might also like:

Desa Kincaid – Bounty Hunter by R.S. Penney

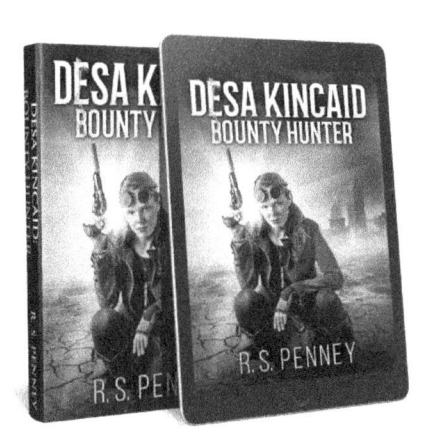

To read the first chapter for free, head to:
https://www.nextchapter.pub/books/desa-kincaid-bounty-hunter

GLOSSARY

Brui K'sha U'ien: Brown gnome.

Faewyld: In the wild parts of the land; away from the more civilized towns.

Grum K'sha U'ien: Green gnome.

Ha'Jakta Ha'Dreen B'kota: Loosely translated as 'Dragon Herders' or 'Dragon Riders'.

K'obi Sha Shin J'oi Faqin: Loosely translated as 'trusted friend to Wizards'.

L'Tuin Auld F'allie: A ritual challenge; loosely translated as 'I challenge your authority'.

N'tia K'ojin Shaq: A command; loosely translated as 'release from me' or 'loose from me'.

GLOSSARY

P'koosh F'aeul: Derogatory term; loosely translated as 'fodder for Ogres'.

P'koosh Z'airka: Loosely translated as 'Ogre dung'.
Sha Shin: Friend

Sh'o Sook J'eid: Loosely translated as 'Gatekeepers' or 'Portal Guards' – Usually wood nymphs.

Sh'tuk Q'estiria Faqin: Ruling council of Q'estiria

Sh'tuksa Q'estiria Faqin: The court of the Ruling Council of Q'estiria

T'et Faqin Q'estirions: Loosely translated as 'Wizard Warrior of Q'estiria' or 'the Called of Q'estiria'

T'gorn E'fal: A meditative, trance-like state.

T'orqute: Amulet or indicator.

ABOUT THE AUTHOR

Stephen Drake, a retired computer programmer of twenty-plus years, is an American fantasy/sci-fi author. He is an avid Harley-Davidson Motorcycle enthusiast, and versed in many survival skills such as martial arts and bow hunting. He is also an avid reader of sci-fi, especially that by R.A. Heinlein and John Scalzi.

Although he has been a long-time resident of Washington State, he was born in Iowa and has lived in Wisconsin, Nebraska, Iowa, Montana, and Virginia. He draws on his experiences to create gripping and believable stories.

OTHER BOOKS BY THIS AUTHOR:

The Displaced series:

Displaced (book one)

Civilization (book two)

Resolutions (book three)

The Blackwing saga:

Blackwing (book 1)

Jessica Strange (book 2) (WIP)

CPSIA information can be obtained
at www.ICGtesting.com
Printed in the USA
BVHW031736190421
605301BV00009B/321/J